BELFAST NOIR

BELFAST NOIR

EDITED BY
ADRIAN McKINTY & STUART NEVILLE

Published by Akashic Books
©2014 Akashic Books

Series concept by Tim McLoughlin and Johnny Temple
Belfast map by Aaron Petrovich

Cover photograph by Alexander R. Hogg, April 20, 1915, from the archive collection of the Belfast Corporation, courtesy of the Deputy Keeper of Records, Public Record Office of Northern Ireland, PRONI reference number LA/7/8/HF/4 (no. 225).

ISBN-13: 978-1-61775-291-9
Library of Congress Control Number: 2014938691

Akashic Books
Twitter: @AkashicBooks
Facebook: AkashicBooks
E-mail: info@akashicbooks.com
Website: www.akashicbooks.com

ALSO IN THE AKASHIC NOIR SERIES

BALTIMORE NOIR, edited by LAURA LIPPMAN

BARCELONA NOIR (SPAIN), edited by ADRIANA V. LÓPEZ & CARMEN OSPINA

BOSTON NOIR, edited by DENNIS LEHANE

BOSTON NOIR 2: THE CLASSICS, edited by DENNIS LEHANE, JAIME CLARKE & MARY COTTON

BRONX NOIR, edited by S.J. ROZAN

BROOKLYN NOIR, edited by TIM McLOUGHLIN

BROOKLYN NOIR 2: THE CLASSICS, edited by TIM McLOUGHLIN

BROOKLYN NOIR 3: NOTHING BUT THE TRUTH, edited by TIM McLOUGHLIN & THOMAS ADCOCK

CAPE COD NOIR, edited by DAVID L. ULIN

CHICAGO NOIR, edited by NEAL POLLACK

COPENHAGEN NOIR (DENMARK), edited by BO TAO MICHAËLIS

DALLAS NOIR, edited by DAVID HALE SMITH

D.C. NOIR, edited by GEORGE PELECANOS

D.C. NOIR 2: THE CLASSICS, edited by GEORGE PELECANOS

DELHI NOIR (INDIA), edited by HIRSH SAWHNEY

DETROIT NOIR, edited by E.J. OLSEN & JOHN C. HOCKING

DUBLIN NOIR (IRELAND), edited by KEN BRUEN

HAITI NOIR, edited by EDWIDGE DANTICAT

HAITI NOIR 2: THE CLASSICS, edited by EDWIDGE DANTICAT

HAVANA NOIR (CUBA), edited by ACHY OBEJAS

HELSINKI NOIR (FINLAND), edited by JAMES THOMPSON

INDIAN COUNTRY NOIR, edited by SARAH CORTEZ & LIZ MARTÍNEZ

ISTANBUL NOIR (TURKEY), edited by MUSTAFA ZIYALAN & AMY SPANGLER

KANSAS CITY NOIR, edited by STEVE PAUL

KINGSTON NOIR (JAMAICA), edited by COLIN CHANNER

LAS VEGAS NOIR, edited by JARRET KEENE & TODD JAMES PIERCE

LONDON NOIR (ENGLAND), edited by CATHI UNSWORTH

LONE STAR NOIR, edited by BOBBY BYRD & JOHNNY BYRD

LONG ISLAND NOIR, edited by KAYLIE JONES

LOS ANGELES NOIR, edited by DENISE HAMILTON

LOS ANGELES NOIR 2: THE CLASSICS, edited by DENISE HAMILTON

MANHATTAN NOIR, edited by LAWRENCE BLOCK

MANHATTAN NOIR 2: THE CLASSICS, edited by LAWRENCE BLOCK

MANILA NOIR (PHILIPPINES), edited by JESSICA HAGEDORN

MEXICO CITY NOIR (MEXICO), edited by PACO IGNACIO TAIBO II

MIAMI NOIR, edited by LES STANDIFORD

MOSCOW NOIR (RUSSIA), edited by NATALIA SMIRNOVA & JULIA GOUMEN

MUMBAI NOIR (INDIA), edited by ALTAF TYREWALA

NEW JERSEY NOIR, edited by JOYCE CAROL OATES

NEW ORLEANS NOIR, edited by JULIE SMITH

ORANGE COUNTY NOIR, edited by GARY PHILLIPS

PARIS NOIR (FRANCE), edited by AURÉLIEN MASSON

PHILADELPHIA NOIR, edited by CARLIN ROMANO

PHOENIX NOIR, edited by PATRICK MILLIKIN
PITTSBURGH NOIR, edited by KATHLEEN GEORGE
PORTLAND NOIR, edited by KEVIN SAMPSELL
PRISON NOIR, edited by JOYCE CAROL OATES
QUEENS NOIR, edited by ROBERT KNIGHTLY
RICHMOND NOIR, edited by ANDREW BLOSSOM, BRIAN CASTLEBERRY & TOM DE HAVEN
ROME NOIR (ITALY), edited by CHIARA STANGALINO & MAXIM JAKUBOWSKI
SAN DIEGO NOIR, edited by MARYELIZABETH HART
SAN FRANCISCO NOIR, edited by PETER MARAVELIS
SAN FRANCISCO NOIR 2: THE CLASSICS, edited by PETER MARAVELIS
SEATTLE NOIR, edited by CURT COLBERT
SINGAPORE NOIR, edited by CHERYL LU-LIEN TAN
STATEN ISLAND NOIR, edited by PATRICIA SMITH
ST. PETERSBURG NOIR (RUSSIA), edited by NATALIA SMIRNOVA & JULIA GOUMEN
TEHRAN NOIR (IRAN), edited by SALAR ABDOH
TEL AVIV NOIR (ISRAEL), edited by ETGAR KERET & ASSAF GAVRON
TORONTO NOIR (CANADA), edited by JANINE ARMIN & NATHANIEL G. MOORE
TRINIDAD NOIR (TRINIDAD & TOBAGO), edited by LISA ALLEN-AGOSTINI & JEANNE MASON
TWIN CITIES NOIR, edited by JULIE SCHAPER & STEVEN HORWITZ
USA NOIR: BEST OF THE AKASHIC NOIR SERIES, edited by JOHNNY TEMPLE
VENICE NOIR (ITALY), edited by MAXIM JAKUBOWSKI
WALL STREET NOIR, edited by PETER SPIEGELMAN

FORTHCOMING

ADDIS ABABA NOIR (ETHIOPIA), edited by MAAZA MENGISTE
BAGHDAD NOIR (IRAQ), edited by SAMUEL SHIMON
BEIRUT NOIR (LEBANON), edited by IMAN HUMAYDAN
BOGOTÁ NOIR (COLOMBIA), edited by ANDREA MONTEJO
CHICAGO NOIR 2: THE CLASSICS, edited by JOE MENO
JERUSALEM NOIR, edited by DROR MISHANI
LAGOS NOIR (NIGERIA), edited by CHRIS ABANI
MARSEILLE NOIR (FRANCE), edited by CÉDRIC FABRE
MEMPHIS NOIR, edited by LAUREEN P. CANTWELL & LEONARD GILL
MISSISSIPPI NOIR, edited by TOM FRANKLIN
MONTREAL NOIR (CANADA), edited by JOHN McFETRIDGE & JACQUES FILIPPI
NEW ORLEANS NOIR 2: THE CLASSICS, edited by JULIE SMITH
PROVIDENCE NOIR, edited by ANN HOOD
RIO NOIR (BRAZIL), edited by TONY BELLOTTO
SAN JUAN NOIR (PUERTO RICO), edited by MAYRA SANTOS-FEBRES
SEOUL NOIR (SOUTH KOREA), edited by BS PUBLISHING CO.
ST. LOUIS NOIR, edited by SCOTT PHILLIPS
STOCKHOLM NOIR (SWEDEN), edited by CARL-MICHAEL EDENBORG & NATHAN LARSON
TRINIDAD NOIR 2: THE CLASSICS, edited by EARL LOVELACE & ROBERT ANTONI
ZAGREB NOIR (CROATIA), edited by IVAN SRŠEN

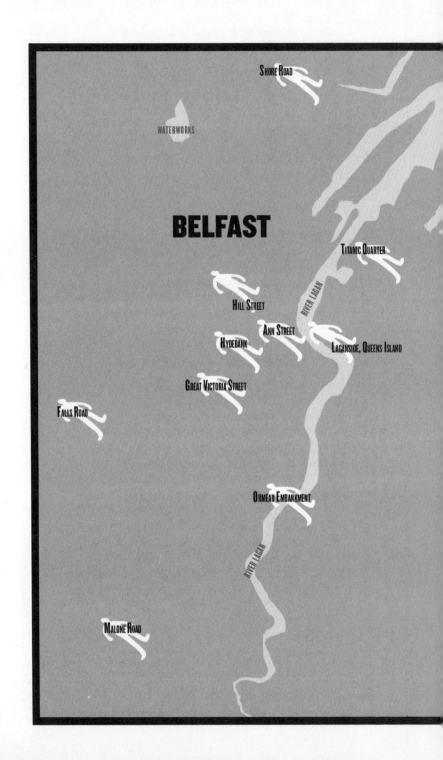

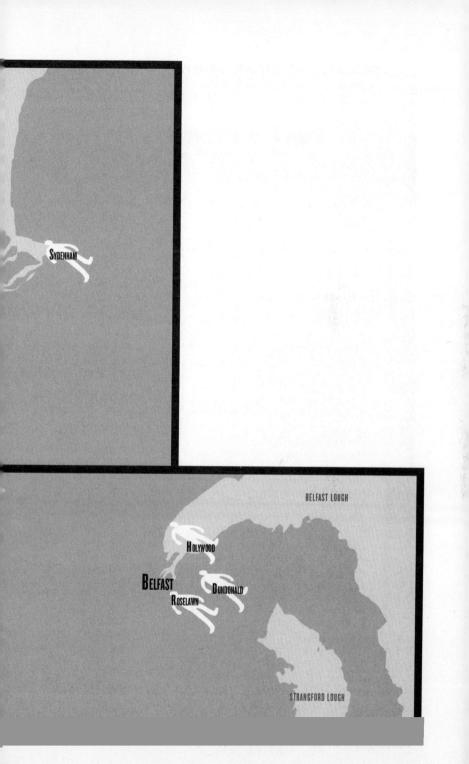

SYDENHAM

BELFAST LOUGH

HOLYWOOD

BELFAST DUNDONALD

ROSELAWN

STRANGFORD LOUGH

TABLE OF CONTENTS

13   *Introduction by Adrian McKinty & Stuart Neville*

21   *Foreword by David Torrans*

PART I: CITY OF GHOSTS

25   **BRIAN MCGILLOWAY**   Roselawn
The Undertaking

45   **LUCY CALDWELL**   Dundonald
Poison

68   **LEE CHILD**   Great Victoria Street
Wet with Rain

83   **RUTH DUDLEY EDWARDS**   Falls Road
Taking It Serious

PART II: CITY OF WALLS

99   **GERARD BRENNAN**   Hydebank
Ligature

111   **GLENN PATTERSON**   Ann Street
Belfast Punk REP

120   **IAN MCDONALD**   Holywood
The Reservoir

PART III: CITY OF COMMERCE

133   **STEVE CAVANAGH**   Laganside, Queens Island
The Grey

153   **CLAIRE MCGOWAN**   Titanic Quarter
Rosie Grant's Finger

174   **SAM MILLAR**   Hill Street
Out of Time

200   **GARBHAN DOWNEY**   Malone Road
Die Like a Rat

PART IV: BRAVE NEW CITY

219   **EOIN MCNAMEE**   Ormeau Embankment
Corpse Flowers

231   **ARLENE HUNT**   Sydenham
Pure Game

245   **ALEX BARCLAY**   Shore Road
The Reveller

252   **About the Contributors**

INTRODUCTION
The Noirest City on Earth

F ew European cities have had as disturbed and violent a
history as Belfast over the last half-century. For much of
that time the Troubles (1968–1998) dominated life in Ireland's second-biggest population centre, and during the darkest
days of the conflict—in the 1970s and 1980s—riots, bombings,
and indiscriminate shootings were tragically commonplace. The
British army patrolled the streets in armoured vehicles and civilians were searched for guns and explosives before they were allowed entry into the shopping district of the city centre.

A peace process that began in 1998 with the signing of the
Good Friday Agreement has brought a measure of calm to Belfast, but during the summer "Marching Season" rioting between
Catholic and Protestant working-class districts often flares up to
this day.

Belfast is still a city divided. East Belfast is a largely Protestant working-class district. South Belfast is a prosperous middle-
class enclave centred around Queens University. West and North
Belfast, where Catholic and Protestant working-class districts jut
up against one another is the area of greatest conflict and where
the fracture lines are at their most raw. So-called "peace walls"
have been built to separate adjacent streets of Protestant and
Catholic families, with more having been added since the peace
agreement of '98.

The north of Ireland has always been a slightly different place
than the south. For centuries Ulstermen and -women have been

blessed with a unique accent, a mordant sense of humour, and a taciturnity unshared by most of their countrymen in the rest of the island. Attempts have been made to explain the province of Ulster's singularity by laying the blame at the door of thousands of dour Scottish planters who began arriving in the northeast of Ireland in the early 1600s. Of course the Ulster plantation changed the religious complexion of the north, but well before then "the land beyond the Mournes" revelled in its exceptionalism. Ulster was the most Gaelic and least English province of Ireland in the early seventeenth century, and further back into the mists of prehistory the story of the Táin Bó Cúailnge was that of Cuchulain, champion of Ulster, battling the forces of Erin.

Belfast was little more than a village for much of this time. The name probably derives from the Irish, *béal feirste*, which means river-mouth, and for centuries it was an uninteresting settlement on the mudflats where the River Lagan joined Belfast Lough.

In the nineteenth century shipbuilding, heavy engineering, and linen manufacture led to Belfast's exponential growth, and by 1914 a tenth of all the ships and a third of all the linen clothes made in the British Empire were coming from the city. Belfast was Ireland's boom town and Dublin the mere administrative capital.

But World War I, the 1916 Easter Rising, and the Irish War of Independence (1919–1921) led to the creation of a border that separated the six counties of Northern Ireland from the twenty-six counties of the Irish Free State. Post-partition Northern Ireland suffered from an inferiority complex. Cut off from cultural developments in Dublin and London, Belfast became something of a provincial backwater. Belfast was heavily bombed by the Luftwaffe in World War II and postwar reconstruction was piecemeal at best.

International literary trends tended to pass Ulster by, and Northern Irish fiction itself went through a lean period until well after the end of World War II. A rare cultural highlight was F.L. Green's *Odd Man Out*, which led to Carol Reed's extraordinary film noir adaptation starring James Mason.

But the decline of engineering, shipbuilding, and linen manufacture had a devastating impact on Belfast and it was a gloomy, depressed, unfashionable Victorian city that encountered the years of conflict and low-level civil war known euphemistically as the Troubles.

What began as a series of peaceful marches for civil rights for Northern Ireland's Catholic minority in the late '60s quickly morphed into street violence and random sectarian attacks. As the crisis in the north intensified, the British government deployed the army and suspended Northern Ireland's parliament. Direct rule from London did not allay the fears of the Catholic minority and the Provisional Irish Republican Army began to recruit volunteers for their campaign to violently overthrow the British. In reaction to the IRA bombings and shootings, successive British governments panicked: interring IRA suspects without trial, flooding Northern Ireland with yet more soldiers, and strengthening the local police—the Royal Ulster Constabulary. And of course violence spiralled into more violence. The Ulster Volunteer Force (UVF) reformed to counter the Provisional IRA, and the Ulster Defence Association (UDA) became an umbrella group for various Protestant factions. Of course the majority of those killed were innocent civilians on both sides.

A depressing three decade–long cycle of atrocities and massacres had begun.

By this time much of Northern Ireland's writing talent—intellectuals such as Brian Moore, C.S. Lewis, and Louis Mac-Neice—had left the province to ply their trade under brighter lights, and Belfast languished culturally until the early 1970s when in the midst of the Troubles the city became the focus of an extraordinary group of poets who went on to attain world renown: Seamus Heaney, Paul Muldoon, Derek Mahon, Ciaran Carson, Michael Longley, Tom Paulin, among others. Based loosely around Queens University, these young poets produced the greatest body of Irish literary work since the Gaelic revival. As the violence worsened, ironically, Belfast grew in cultural confidence, kick-started by this incendiary poetry, which in turn provided the kerosene for the other arts. By the late-1970s Northern Ireland saw a boom in playwriting, screenwriting, song-writing, and finally in novel writing.

Bernard MacLaverty's *Cal* (1983) was one of the first and best crime novels to address the complexities of life during the Troubles, and the Belfast-set *Lies of Silence* (1990) by Brian Moore established the city as a labyrinth of twisting allegiances and blind alleys. Eoin McNamee's *Resurrection Man* (1994) is a portrait of Belfast as a city of the abyss in which sociopathic Protestant serial killers stalk the streets looking for random Catholic victims. *Resurrection Man* was based on the true story of the Shankill Butchers.

Also in this period, a series of "Troubles Trash" airport thrillers were published by British and American authors seeking to cash in on Belfast's infamy, some becoming best sellers and Hollywood films that were largely derided in Northern Ireland for their didacticism and unsophisticated analysis of the situation.

In the 1990s a native series of Belfast police procedurals appeared, written by the witty Eugene McEldowney, and home-grown satirist Colin Bateman began his long run of novels that mined the rich vein of dark humour that has always been one of the city's defining characteristics.

Finally in 1998 a peace deal was reached between Protestant

and Catholic factions and a new legislative assembly set up at Stormont. The uneasy truce established on Good Friday 1998 has held, for the most part, for a decade and a half.

Walking through Belfast city centre today, you'll see the same range of chain stores and restaurants that can be found in just about any part of the British Isles. Some might argue that the evidence of Northern Ireland's economic growth—the peace dividend, as it's known—has robbed the centre of Belfast of its character, but few citizens miss the security turnstiles, the bag searches, the nightly death of the city as it emptied out. Most feel the homogenisation of Belfast is a price worth paying for the luxuries other places take for granted. It might seem a cynical observation, but the truth is, those comforts—the restaurants, the theatres, the cinemas, the shopping malls—are the things that probably guarantee that the peace will hold. Only the most hardened individuals would feel a return to the grey desolation of the '70s and '80s is a sacrifice worth making for whatever political ideals they're too embittered to let go of.

The most visible sign of Belfast's transformation is the Victoria Square shopping centre, a glittering network of walkways, escalators, and staircases that traverse enclosed streets, a temple of much that is crass and shallow in the modern world, yet a strangely beautiful image of rebirth. Had anyone tried to build such a place in the Belfast of the '80s or early '90s, it would have been irresistible to the men of violence. If such an architectural bauble had ever been completed, it would have been bombed within days of opening. The people who planted the bomb would have claimed it as an economic target, a blow against capitalism, a crippling of Belfast's business life. Or perhaps it would have just been nihilism: at the time many felt that when the bombers destroyed the Grand Opera House, the ABC Cinema, the Europa Hotel, and other landmarks, it was simply because they couldn't bear the thought of Belfast's citizens having anything good, anything decent, anything shiny to brighten the drudgery of their lives.

For all the shimmer and shine of the new Belfast, you can still walk a mile or two in almost any direction and find some of the worst deprivation in Western Europe. Those parts of the city have not moved on. While the middle class has enjoyed the spoils of the peace dividend, working-class areas have seen little improvement. The sectarian and paramilitary murals are still there: crude memorials to the fallen "soldiers" of the conflict, to heroes and martyrs still revered. For a small outlay, you can tour these murals in a black taxi with a knowledgeable guide at the wheel, ready to tell you who died where. You can see Belfast's bloodstains up close and personal. This is the city that gave the world its worst ever maritime disaster, and turned it into a tourist attraction; similarly, we are perversely proud of our thousands of murders, our wounds constantly on display. You want noir? How about a painting the size of a house, a portrait of a man known to have murdered at least a dozen human beings in cold blood? Or a similar house-sized gable painting of a zombie marching across a postapocalyptic wasteland with an AK-47 over the legend UVF: *Prepared for Peace—Ready for War.* As Lee Child has said, Belfast is still "the most noir place on earth."

Despite its relative newness as a city, Belfast has a rich psychogeography: on virtually every street corner and in nearly every pub and shop something terrible happened within living memory. Belfast is a place where the denizens have trained themselves not to see these scars of the past, rather like the citizens of Besźel in China Miéville's novel *The City & the City.*

This volume contains fourteen brand-new stories from some of Belfast's most accomplished crime and literary novelists and from writers further afield who have a strong connection to the city. The stories take place in all of Belfast's four quarters and in a diverse number of styles within the rubric of "noir."

We have divided the book into four sections—City of Ghosts, City of Walls, City of Commerce, and Brave New City—which we think capture the legacy of Belfast's recent past, its continuing challenges, and a guess or two at where the city might go in the future.

We believe that *Belfast Noir* is an important snapshot of the city's crime-writing community and indeed represents some of the finest and most important short fiction ever collected on contemporary Northern Ireland. We hope that this book will serve as a record of a Belfast transitioning to normalcy, or perhaps as a warning that underneath the fragile peace darker forces still lurk.

Adrian McKinty & Stuart Neville
July 2014

FOREWORD

BY DAVID TORRANS

S o, *you want to open a specialist crime-fiction bookshop in Belfast? Are you mad?!*
This was the general response here in 1997.

Those who cared about my personal and financial well-being were supportive and terrified in about equal measures. At that time the vast majority of our stock originated from the other side of the Atlantic—the attraction of the "other" is always present—along with the more obscure British, European, and Asian crime fiction in print at that time. As is the way with change, the more obscure at one time can become the mainstream somewhere down the line: Mankell, Rankin, McDermid, et al. were all "new" authors at one point, bringing a fresh and exciting approach to the genre.

Searching for new authors is probably the most satisfying part of our work, and as each year passed by the arena within which to choose increased.

Yet, something was missing . . .

The local scene regarding the crime-fiction genre was somewhat lacking. I would find myself filtering onto the shelves books by fine literary novelists who combine style and narrative with a sense of dark foreboding in much of their work, all important elements in the best of crime fiction. Thankfully, from this point on, things were brewing within the genre in this part of the world, and new names started to appear on the shelves.

That is not to say that all fiction within the genre is Belfastcentric. Much of the best writing from this part of the world combines the urban with the rural; we are, after all, a place filled with contradictions—social, political, and environmental—and this provides the perfect material for the genre to flourish.

Now, almost twenty years on, I can happily say that our focus within the shop veers much more strongly toward the "local." Procedural, satirical, thriller, and of course noir elements of the genre are all present, and whilst from a gender perspective it is slightly skewed toward the male, this too is starting to change.

That an anthology such as *Belfast Noir* is even possible is a sign of how far both the genre and the city have come. When authors better known for literary or even science fiction are ready to tackle crime stories set in a city once torn apart by sectarian strife, you know both Belfast and Northern Irish noir have come of age.

David Torrans has been a figurehead in the Belfast, Northern Irish, and wider Irish crime-fiction scenes for two decades. His bookstore, No Alibis, has been featured in media around the globe.

PART I

CITY OF GHOSTS

THE UNDERTAKING

BY Brian McGilloway

Roselawn

I t's the one thing they'll never stop," Brogan said. "A hearse. Think about it. Not only will they not stop you, they'll probably halt the traffic to let you past."

Healy nodded, unconvinced. The room was sharp with chemicals; the new embalmer, Mark Kearney, was learning the ropes and was still too heavy-handed with the fluid. Not that Healy had had any choice with that particular apprenticeship.

To their left, two women whispered in a hushed sibilance next to the coffin, one with her hand laid proprietarily on the satin-covered edge of the wood. Occasionally, Healy noticed, one finger would extend slightly, just touching the ends of the dead man's hair. It wasn't his wife; she'd been in twice to straighten the flag that was draped over the lower half, drooping in the middle under the weight of sympathy cards being laid there.

"You'd have nothing to do," Brogan said. "Pick it up from an address in Dundalk, bring it to the pub. We've the back room hired for the day for the 'wake.' Bring it in, leave it a few hours, then take the coffin back to your own place. You get to keep the box, and you'll make a few pounds."

"I don't know, Brogan. What's in it anyway?"

Brogan stared at him, his mouth a tight white line. "You know better than to ask."

"I'll be the one driving it," Healy said. "It's my business we're talking about."

He felt Brogan grip his arm, just at the crook of his elbow. "*Your* business? How much has your fucking business earned from all the burials we've brought you? Like fucking state funerals, some of them."

Not to mention all the other burials they'd caused, Healy thought, but said nothing, nodding lightly. "I know," he managed finally. "And I appreciate the trade."

"Your fucking business could burn to the ground some night, if you're not careful."

"I know," Healy said, raising a placatory hand.

"Or, God forbid, that cute blondie you're shifting could fall down the stairs and damage her skull. Not that there'd be much to damage in there, judging by what Mark tells me."

"Leave Laura out of it!"

"I hope to," Brogan said. "That'll be your choice."

Just then, a heavy man lumbered through the doorway, chest wheezing from the exertion of climbing the stairs. When he saw the two men standing, he raised his chin briefly in greeting, then limped his way across to the coffin. He offered a perfunctory blessing, laid his hand, not on the dead man's, but on the flag beneath him, then raised the fingers that had caressed the material to his mouth, kissing them lightly.

Healy could feel the floorboards beneath them bounce as the man approached, extending one stocky hand.

"Bad day, men," he said.

"It is, John," Brogan offered.

"The last of the old guard," John said gravely, glancing toward the coffin as if to reassure himself that the man in question was still there.

"Fucking stand-up guy," Brogan agreed.

"He never turned. Not once. Even was dead against decommissioning, back in the day."

"They don't make them like him anymore."

"Fucking watery sell-outs sitting on the hill now wouldn't understand the meaning of country."

Brogan nodded his head. "Country," he repeated, snorting.

"So, how's my boy doing?" John asked. "I appreciate you giving him a start."

"Mark?" Healy asked. A bit too fond of the embalming fluid, personally and professionally, he wanted to say. "Great," he did say. "A natural."

"At handling the dead? He's a chip off the old block!" Brogan said, slapping John lightly on the bicep. John reciprocated with a bark of laughter, causing the two women at the coffin to turn and stare at them, like incensed librarians.

"So, are you in?" John asked, quickly regaining his solemnity, regarding Healy through two narrowed eyes, the pupils pinpoints. *Like piss holes in snow*, his father used to call them. John clasped his hands in front of him, his nostrils flaring.

Healy glanced at Brogan. Brogan might threaten to burn down your business or hurt your girl, but Big John Kearney—well, everyone knew he wouldn't threaten, he'd just turn up someday with the petrol can and matches and make you do it yourself. And stiff you for half the insurance claim as compensation for the inconvenience you'd caused him in making him come to your house.

"I'll help out any way I can," Healy said. "I don't want anyone getting hurt with whatever it is I'm driving."

John laughed, the ripples spreading across the shirt taut on his belly. "Hurt? Since when did undertakers become so fucking squeamish?"

Brogan joined in the laugh, though mirthlessly, his grip on Healy's arm tightening. "He's only taking the piss. Isn't that right, Healy? He's in. Aren't you? *Aren't you?*" The repeated question squeezed through gritted teeth.

Healy saw it now. They all had their jobs to do to keep Big John happy. He'd have to collect the coffin and bring it up to Belfast. Brogan's job had been to convince him to do it.

"I'm in," Healy said, already feeling his stomach sicken, even as the grip on his arm relaxed and his sense of shame in himself ballooned.

"Good man," John said, slapping him on the shoulder. "We knew we could count on you. Don't worry. It'll be nothing that could hurt you. So, no panicking."

Flu season was always busy, but this one was no joke. Three bodies were lying downstairs. Healy had had to ask Laura, his girlfriend, to come in and do makeup on the ones that weren't too badly damaged. He'd had to promise her a shopping weekend in Dublin as a thank you, despite the fact she'd made her first attempt, an eighty-five-year-old woman with heart failure, look like she was on the game.

"That's the modern style," Laura had protested when Healy told her to thin down the thick black eyebrows she'd drawn on.

"For whores maybe," Healy had snapped. "She's not going out for the fucking night, Lar, she's being buried. I'm sure God won't mind if her eyebrows aren't the most fashionable when she reaches the big gates."

"She doesn't *have* any fucking eyebrows!" Laura had screamed. "That's why I needed to give her some. Imagine your eyebrows falling out. I hope I don't live to be old aged."

Healy stopped himself from warning her that old age might be too optimistic a target if she didn't shut up and get working on the bodies. Mark Kearney, the son of Big John, sat beside a particularly badly mashed-up guy who'd fallen off a roof, trying to shift his Sky satellite dish, a book on cosmetics in one hand, a lump of skin-coloured putty in the other. To his left was an older man, most of his face missing from a self-inflicted shotgun wound.

"This one will be a bastard to make look like he's still alive," Mark said. "Can we just put a Halloween mask or something on him? Who would he like to look like?"

"He's being cremated anyway," Healy said. "Just get him embalmed and shut up the coffin. There's no wake."

"That's sad," Laura opined from across the room. "No wake?"

"He must have been a sad bastard," Mark said. "Shooting himself in the face."

"He was Jack Hamill, actually. He taught me," Healy explained. "I started out working for him. He owned the undertakers on the Ormeau Road. He worked some of the worst shit of the Troubles. Reconstructing people who'd had parts of their heads blown off, limbs missing, multiple shootings. He gave it up, couldn't take it anymore. All the dead bodies."

"Jesus," Laura said, whistling softly, sitting back now, regarding the corpse with a little more respect.

"Which is probably why he shot himself in the face. Having to carry all that shit around with him ever since."

"And he doesn't want a wake?"

Healy shook his head. "He wanted to be prepped and cremated. That was it. *I want none of the shit,* he said."

"I understand that," Mark said. "Once you know the tricks of the trade, it takes away the magic."

"You don't know the tricks of the trade yet; you used far too much fluid on the last one," Healy said. "In five hundred years' time, if they dig him up, he'll still look like he did last night."

"Like Lenin," Mark offered. "Except without the ear falling off."

"Did John Lennon's ear fall off?" Laura asked, pausing mid-lipstick application. "That's sad too, considering he wrote such beautiful songs."

Healy shook his head as Mark, behind his book again, struggled to hide the shaking of his shoulders as he laughed.

"I don't think Scarlet Passion was Mrs. Owens's colour, Lar," Healy said. "Not since the 1940s, anyway."

The following morning, just before dawn, Healy was back at the office, getting the hearse ready for the drive south. Laura had made him a packed lunch, as if he was going on a school outing. She'd filled a Tupperware box with the remains of the previous evening's lasagne. Healy hadn't had the heart to point out that, while the hearse contained many things, a microwave oven was not one of them.

The drive down the M1 was uneventful. The road was busy, lorries and buses spraying the ground water in their wake in iridescent arcs. The address that Mark Kearney had handed him the previous day listed the coffin as being at a house on the outskirts of town. When Healy finally found it, after being sent to the same field twice by his sat nav, a small man, greying brown hair, glasses, came to the door.

"I'm Healy."

"Congratulations. What do you want?"

"Big John sent me to collect remains."

"Did he now?" The man straightened up, pulling himself to his full height. "Leave me the keys. You can go and sit in the living room. We'll be half an hour."

Healy handed over the keys as instructed, then turned back to the car. "You wouldn't have a microwave in there, by any chance, would you?"

Twenty-five minutes, and one lukewarm lasagne later, he was back on the road. The coffin, polished pine, had already been loaded into the back of the car. A wreath, saying *Granda*, had been laid alongside it, showing through the rear windows. Healy noticed the dirt on the plastic flowers, figured they'd lifted it off someone's grave to make their ruse look more realistic.

As he got into the car, something struck him. He sat in silence, afraid to turn on the ignition, absurdly, he realised, listening for ticking.

"What's wrong?" the small man asked, blinking furiously behind his glasses.

"It's not going to explode, is it?" Healy asked. "If my girlfriend phones me? It's not going to kill me?"

"That'll not be a problem," the man said.

"What is in there?" Healy asked conspiratorially.

"You can use your phone," the man replied. "Except to phone the cops. That call *will* kill you. Eventually."

The first stretch of the journey, he thought he was going to be sick. He found that, as he drove, his gaze flicked repeatedly to the rearview mirror, to see if he was being followed, either by the cops or by the people who'd loaded the coffin into the hearse. Every pothole in the road seemed to shake the car violently, every sharp bend brought back memories of stories he'd heard in school about mercury tilt switches. He remembered Tommy Hasson stealing thermometers from the school's chemistry lab, saying he would sell them for the mercury. Tommy ended up blowing the fingers off his right hand in an accident involving fireworks and a hammer. He was thirteen at the time. Tommy Five Fingers they called him after that. Though never to his face, of course.

Healy was back on the easy bit of the M1 within twenty minutes. This return leg was quieter than the journey down, little traffic heading north in the middle of the morning. As a result, when the marked garda car pulled out from the lay-by and merged into the traffic behind him, Healy noticed it almost instantly. He told himself that they'd picked someone up speeding, but they seemed in no hurry to catch up with anyone. He knew it wasn't him; if anything, he was going too slowly, keeping on the inside lane, overtaking only when absolutely necessary. His concern was twofold: not only did he not want to be stopped for a traffic violation, but he was also still not convinced by the small man's assertion that whatever cargo he was carrying wasn't going to blow up.

The garda car maintained its distance behind him. He wasn't sure if he was being followed or not. He reckoned if they were actually tailing him, they'd have been more surreptitious about it, maybe used an unmarked car. Instead, they had quite literally announced their presence, sitting in the *Garda Only* bay along the side of the road, driving behind him now in a white car with fluorescent yellow stripes up the side.

For a few moments, he toyed with the idea of deliberately speeding, hoping they'd pull him over and search the coffin. Whatever he was carrying wouldn't make it to the streets of Belfast and he'd be able to say it'd not been his fault. But he realised that he didn't even know the name of the people who had given him the coffin, only the name of the supposed remains inside, Martin Logue. Plus, if they asked who'd told him to collect it, he'd have to grass on John Kearney. He'd never survive that. His best bet would be to get clear of the cops and abandon the hearse in a field somewhere. Claim he ran out of petrol. Except, if they were following him, they'd be able to check. He thought he'd been clever, filling up the tank the previous day in preparation for the run; now he cursed his foresight for having deprived him of an excuse to dump whatever it was he was bringing north.

He ran through the alternatives in his mind. Explosives, obviously, but the glasses man seemed to have discounted that. Drugs? Big John did sell some to supplement his income. Guns?

Again, a possibility. Maybe there actually was a dead person in the coffin. Or a living one? A kidnap victim?

"Hello!" Healy shouted over his shoulder. "Is there anyone in there?"

Silence.

Maybe they were gagged.

"Tap on the wood if you can hear me," Healy said, then waited, aware that if someone actually did tap on the wood, he'd probably shit himself with fear.

Silence.

The car was still behind him. In fact, it stayed behind him for almost the entire way to the border, before finally overtaking all of the traffic and speeding ahead of him, cutting off the motorway at the next junction.

He allowed himself to relax a little, turning on the radio, hesitating briefly as he did so, lest the radio waves detonate whatever was in the coffin. If, of course, whatever was in the coffin was detonable.

He crossed the border just south of Newry, instantly on the lookout for any PSNI vehicles that might have been waiting for him, perhaps alerted by the gardai. In the end, it was not until he was passing the sign for Cloughogue Cemetery that he spotted them.

The car was a silver Vauxhall, unmarked in contrast with the garda car, but unmistakable nonetheless due, mostly, to the dark green tint of the bulletproof glass on the windows of the vehicle. He'd no idea how long they'd been behind him. He'd checked at the border, but hadn't spotted them.

Despite Big John's warning, panic got the better of him as he neared Banbridge. Seeing the turnoff for the Outlet shopping complex, he indicated and pulled in, watching the PSNI car continue on along the Belfast Road. Aware that a parked hearse with a coffin in the back—especially one festooned with a floral arrangement to *Granda*—might attract some attention, he parked up at Burger King and went in for fries and a burger to make it appear that lunch had been his primary reason for stopping, rather than an attempt to lose a police tail.

"Should you leave that out there unattended?" the pimpled teen who had taken his order asked, nodding out to where the hearse sat. "With a dead person in it?"

"He's not going anywhere," Healy managed, blushing at having used the line.

"True that," the teen offered, then turned to fetch his food.

Despite having already eaten lukewarm lasagne barely an hour earlier, Healy managed the food until he went back out to the hearse and spotted, at the far end of the car park, the same silver Vauxhall, parked, its occupants seemingly having gone to Starbucks for their lunch.

He turned and went back into the fast-food restaurant, heading straight for the toilet. He pulled out his phone and called Mark.

"This thing of your dad's? I've company following me up the road. Can you check what he wants me to do? Should I still go to the pub with it?"

Kearney grunted and hung up. Healy forced himself to pee, lest someone come into the toilet and wonder what he was doing in there.

He was zipping up when Mark called back.

"He said bring it here. Wait until it calms, then take it to the pub."

"Take it there?" Healy protested. "My own premises?"

"Aye. We're flat out here, by the way, so get a move on. And we've that cremation at two for the saddo you knew, so someone needs to take him across. Tony said he'd do it. You should be back by then, anyway."

Healy bit his lip, annoyed at being ordered about by Mark Kearney, a youth with such a startling sense of entitlement that he'd deliberately failed every GCSE he'd been entered for, telling his teachers that he didn't need GCSEs for what he'd be doing. Healy suspected reconstructing dead people's faces had not featured on his list of future careers.

He strolled out to the car park again, feigning nonchalance, scanning the parking bays for the silver car, which had vanished once again. He began to wonder if indeed it had been the same one at all. Perhaps it had been a different police car. Or just some dick with really heavily tinted glass on his windscreen.

He was fairly certain it was the same one though, when it picked up his tail again just outside Lisburn. This time it held steady, three cars behind him, all the way onto the Westlink and into Belfast.

He pulled into the parking bay of his premises, shouting for Kearney to close the shutters behind him as quickly as possible and to get the coffin out of the hearse.

He ran to the toilet and brought up both his lunches in four heaving gasps. He was sitting on the ground, his face pressed against the cool ceramic, when he heard someone tapping at the door.

"I'm in here!" he snapped.

"I know," Laura called back. "That's why I'm knocking! The cops are here to see you. They're upstairs."

A fifth heave, bringing up nothing but yellow spittle.

There were two officers waiting for him when he went up. Both were in uniform, right down to the peaked caps.

"Officers," Healy said, his mouth acrid with the taste of bile. "Everything all right?"

"Are *you* all right?" one, the elder of the two, asked. "You look like death warmed up."

"I'm fine."

"Better hope they don't mistake you for someone should be in one of your own coffins," the other offered, laughing good-naturedly, like they were old friends.

"So, what can I do for you?"

"You collected a coffin this morning, in Dundalk?"

"Is that a question?"

The officer nodded. "It is."

"I did. That's right. I've only arrived back with it."

"Do you know the person in the coffin?"

Healy shook his head. "No. The order came in over the phone. Someone called Martin Logue."

The officer nodded his head, as if this was as he'd expected all along. "Was he the person who ordered the collection or the person in the box?"

"He was the deceased. Sorry, who are you, exactly?"

"I'm Inspector Hume," the man said. "This is Sergeant Fisher. We've reason to believe that you've been transporting illegal cargo across the border."

"Why?" Healy asked.

"That's what we hoped you'd tell us," Fisher said.

"No, why do you think I was bringing across something illegal?"

"You recently employed Mark Kearney as an apprentice here, is that right?" Hume asked.

"Again, why?"

"We know you did. I'm sure you know who Mark's father is? You were speaking to him the other night at a wake house."

"I know of him," Healy said.

"Is Mark here at the moment?"

Healy swallowed back a sudden rush of sour water that filled his throat and went across to the top of the stairs.

"Mark? Can you come up here?"

A moment later, Kearney appeared at the top of the stairs, wiping his hands on a cloth, as if he were a mechanic completing a job.

"Yes?"

"Officers Hume and Fisher would like a word." Healy widened his eyes meaningfully in a way he hoped Kearney would understand, though the message of which he was himself not entirely sure.

"What?"

"Martin Logue? The deceased remains which just arrived here. It was your father who arranged their transport, is that right?"

Kearney raised his chin defiantly. "What of it?"

Hume smiled. "So that's a yes," he said. "What's your father's interest?"

"Martin was my uncle," Kearney replied. "Whatever the fuck it's got to do with you. Dad wanted him brought home. Offered to handle the wake and burial."

Healy tried not to look at Kearney lest his respect for the alacrity with which the boy was lying was apparent. Instead he nodded, his hands clasped in front of him, head lightly bowed. From below, he heard the thud of the metal shutters closing and wondered whether Hume and Fisher had been a distraction upstairs so that a second PSNI team could enter the workroom unseen below and search the coffin without their knowledge.

However, Hume had clearly heard it too, for he looked beyond Healy to the staircase with concern. "Where is Logue at the moment?" he asked.

"Where I left him. Downstairs," Healy said, glancing at Kearney who nodded.

"We'd like to see the coffin." Hume opened the fold up top of the reception desk and stepped behind it to where Healy and Kearney stood.

"You'll need a warrant," Kearney said. "That's my uncle's coffin you're desecrating."

This time Healy couldn't stop himself staring at Kearney, both for his unexpected audacity and his vocabulary. Thankfully, whether he realised it or not, he was taking responsibility for the coffin. Whatever they found in there, Kearney and his father would have to answer for it, not Healy.

"Lucky we have one, then," Hume said, handing a copy of the document to Healy, still the man nominally in charge of the place, and passing on out through the doorway that led to the staircase.

Healy followed, handing the sheet to Mark Kearney, assuming he'd have a better working knowledge of what it should contain. He felt sick again, felt the ground lurch to one side as he walked. The stairs seemed to shift under him, so much so that he needed to hold the rail with both hands to keep himself steady.

Hume and Fisher were already standing at the coffin when he reached the ground floor, twisting the locking screws, one by one, to open it. Healy stopped at the foot of the stairs, wondering if he'd have time to make a run for it once they opened the lid. If he allowed some distance between them, he'd at least have a head start.

They removed the last of the screws and hefted up the lid, raising it in such an angle that the contents were hidden from Healy. He could, however, see the look of revulsion on both their faces as they surveyed the contents. Intrigued, he felt himself moving forward, compelled toward the box against his own better judgement. As he approached, he saw, for the first time clearly, the view that had elicited such a reaction from the two policemen. The man in the coffin, dressed in a suit, had no face. It took him less than a second to recognise the ring he wore on his finger and realise that the corpse was not Martin Logue at all, but his old mentor, Jack Hamill.

Healy took the lid from Fisher. "Happy now?" he asked, quickly checking the nameplate on top. It did say, *Martin Logue*. Kearney, the sneaky little bastard, must have switched the lids of Logue and Hamill's in anticipation of just this scenario.

Sure enough, the insouciance of Mark's swagger as he came down the stairs confirmed as much.

"Jesus, I hope it's a closed wake," Fisher commented, glancing again at the dead man. "You've not done a great job of the reconstruction."

"We've not started yet," Healy said. "On account of dealing with you."

"Do you still want to search him?" Kearney asked.

Hume, leaning into the coffin, yet turning his head slightly away from it, patted the corpse quickly, feeling in around the few spaces between the sides of the box and the body.

"I'm sorry for your trouble," Hume offered when he was done. "We'll leave you to it, men."

Healy had to stop himself from hugging Kearney as they watched the silver Vauxhall drive away from the front street. Dealing with the police had momentarily distracted him from his other concerns.

But only momentarily.

"Right, we'll give it half an hour to make sure they're gone and we'll get Martin Logue across to the pub and out of my fucking business," Healy said. He glanced at Kearney, hoping that something in the young man's expression would reveal what exactly the contents of the coffin marked *Martin Logue* had been. "And thanks for that."

Kearney accepted the words with a nod.

Laura appeared in the doorway. "Mrs. Owens is done now. She looks good, if I do say so myself. Better than she did when she was alive, anyway. Being dead suits her."

Healy nodded. "You're a star, Lar. Thanks."

"I know," she beamed. "Tony was in already too. He said the traffic's bad so he wanted to start on his way to Roselawn for the two o'clock."

"What?" Healy managed, sweat popping on his forehead. He glanced at the clock on the wall. It was two fifteen.

"The two o'clock. He took the old guy who blew his face off. Hamill? Tony took him on over to Roselawn for the cremation."

Healy sat in his office, staring at the phone. By the time someone in Roselawn had answered his call, the cremation had already begun. There was nothing left to do, no way to prevent it or turn it back. There was also no way he could show up at Kearney's pub with Hamill's corpse. And now Hamill would have to be buried in some way. And Big John Kearney would have to be told. And Roselawn would no doubt be in touch whenever whatever was in that coffin started to burn. He guessed that it wasn't explosives the moment someone answered the phone. The heat, he figured, would already have set them off if that had been what was inside the box.

Brogan met him outside City Hall. A small group of flag protestors were gathered, holding aloft Union Jacks of their own to compensate for the absence of one fluttering over the council building.

"So, how the fuck did this happen? Just so I can tell Big John."

"His son swapped the lids when the cops arrived. They came

down to search the coffin and opened the one they thought I'd brought up, but it was actually Jack Hamill."

"That was a good move. And I thought that young fella was thick."

Healy nodded. "The cops had him and me upstairs, answering questions. For ages," he said, exaggerating in spite of the fact that Mark Kearney would undoubtedly be asked for his own version of events by his father too. "Tony, my driver, landed and lifted the coffin marked *Jack Hamill*, which actually contained . . ." He looked to Brogan, hoping he'd finished the sentence for him.

"Shit. So Mark kind of caused it?"

"Kind of," Healy said quickly, spotting a get-out. "He thought he was helping."

"He did," Brogan admitted. "At least the cops didn't get the stuff and link it to Big John."

"Look, speaking of the stuff? If it's explosives in there, Rose-lawn will know. When they explode, like."

Brogan shook his head. "That's not going to be a problem."

"Or drugs? Every bird in Greater Belfast will be flying around stoned if they're burning a coffin full of dope. They'll find out."

Brogan smiled. "Jesus, calm yourself, Healy. It's guns! Don't worry."

"Guns?" Healy's stomach lurched. "The bullets will be firing everywhere."

Brogan shook his head, laughing. "It's all right. Just pistols."

"*All right?* Crematoriums use fucking magnets to pull out the metal bits of the body that aren't burned," Healy explained. "When the burning finishes, they'll find a load of guns stuck to the magnet. They'll come back to me about it."

Brogan grimaced, laid a hand on Healy's shoulder. "Just say nothing. You know nothing. Someone in Dundalk arranged it; you don't know their names or where they live. That's your story and you stick to it. But you can't name Big John, or me obviously. Or we'll kill you."

"I'll go to jail," Healy said, the weight of the hand seeming to put him off balance.

"Then we'll do that girl of yours instead."

"I can't go to jail," Healy responded, aware that his eyes were filling.

"You'll not get long if you say you knew nothing about it. You could be out in less than a year. And we'll see you right. You'll be looked after."

"It's not fucking fair!" Healy snapped, loud enough for a blonde woman in a Union Jack hat-and-scarf set to look across at them.

"Them's the breaks, Healy. Remember, you can't name us. Whatever happens, Big John will see you're looked after. And you'll not owe any more favours. We're all square now. I'll even get that halfwit of a son of his out of your hair."

Healy felt his phone vibrate in his pocket, recognised the number as Roselawn. "That's them now," he said, dread running like lead through his veins, settling in the nest of nerves that seemed to be twisting around his stomach.

"Good luck, buddy," Brogan offered, patting his shoulder and walking off, nodding to the blonde woman. "You're a stand-up guy too."

There was no sign of the police car at Roselawn when Healy arrived. The woman who had called simply said that he was required over an issue regarding the cremation of Jack Hamill. He attempted, for a moment, to feign surprise, but didn't see the point. "I'm on my way," he'd said, resignedly.

He recognised Lorcan Kirk, one of the staff, when he went in. Kirk was speaking with a young couple about the various services that they could supply for the young woman's father. Healy stood in the waiting room, unable to sit and flick through the *Ulster Tatler,* refusing the offer of tea from the receptionist, feeling fairly sure that he'd not be able to keep it down.

"Mr. Healy," Kirk said when he finally entered the room, "thanks for coming in. Mr. Hamill's cremation is finished and, well, it was a little odd. There was a lot of ash, but no bone. And we found some unusual things on the magnet when we were done."

Healy nodded. "I know."

"Was Mr. Hamill the Bionic Man?" Kirk asked, handing Healy a small brown cardboard box.

"What?"

"You expect the odd metal plate. Implants and that. But I don't think we've ever seen quite so many on one body. One of the staff thought we'd cremated RoboCop." He chuckled softly, as if aware that too raucous a laugh would be inappropriate under the circumstances.

Healy opened the lid of the box. It was three-quarters full of black pieces of metal of various shapes and sizes, including springs and pins. But there was nothing traditionally gun-shaped.

"So, what are they?"

Healy swallowed dryly. "Surgical implants," he said. "Mr. Hamill was a base jumper in his spare time. A lot of broken bones and joints, apparently."

"So broken there were none left after the cremation?"

Healy shrugged. "I couldn't tell you."

Kirk nodded. "I see. He mustn't have been very good."

"What?"

"As a base jumper. His ashes are here, if you want to take those too. Though the urn is only half full."

Healy peered down at the scraps of metal. He couldn't understand how the guns had ended up in pieces, the confusion countered by the relief he felt that they could no longer be used for their original purpose.

Kirk came into the room with a small plastic box of ashes that, absurdly, reminded Healy of the Tupperware container Laura had used for his lunch.

"Thanks," Healy said, heading for the door.

"I didn't know they did surgical implants," Kirk said, as he passed.

"Who?" Healy turned, stared at him, desperate to get away.

"Glock. The company that make the plastic pistols."

"Apparently so," Healy replied, his mouth dry.

"It's the strangest cremation we've done in some time, I have to tell you," Kirk said, openly irritated now at Healy's circumspection.

"I wouldn't think of it as a cremation so much as a . . . decommissioning . . . And an undertaking remarkably well done at that," Healy added, then pushed out through the door into the weakening winter sun.

POISON

by Lucy Caldwell

Dundonald

I saw him last night. He was with a girl half his age, more than half, a *third* his age. It was in the bar of the Merchant Hotel on Skipper Street. They were together on the crushed-velvet raspberry banquette. Her arm was flung around his shoulder, and he had an arm around her too, an easy hand on her waist. She was laughing, her face turned right up to his, enthralled, delighted. They kept clinking glasses: practically every time they took a sip of their cocktails they clinked glasses. I was alone, on a stool at the bar, waiting for my friends—friends I hadn't seen in years, but who, even years ago, were always late. I'd ordered a glass of white wine while I waited; I picked it up with shaking hands. It was *him*. There was no doubt about it. His face had got pouchy, and his hair, though still black—dyed, surely—was limp and thinning. When he stood up, he was shorter than I remembered.

But it was him.

I hadn't seen him in years. I scrambled to work out the numbers in my head. Sixteen—seventeen—almost eighteen. All those years later and there he was, entwined with a girl a fraction of his age. He must be nearly sixty now.

I bent my head over the cocktail list as he walked toward me, letting my hair fall partly over my face, but I couldn't take my eyes off him. His eyes slid over the women he passed, thin, fake-tanned bare backs and sequinned dresses, stripper shoes. He didn't look once at me. I'd lived away too long, and I'd forgotten how dressed-up people got on a Saturday night: I was in skinny jeans and a blazer, and not enough makeup. I watched him walk along the striped carpet and out toward the toilets, and then I turned to look at his companion. She had her head bowed over her phone and she was jiggling one leg and rapidly texting. She suddenly looked very young indeed. I'd put her in her midtwenties but it was less than that. I felt a strange tightness in my chest. She put her phone away and uncrossed her legs, recrossed them, tugged at the hem of her little black dress. She picked up her empty glass and tilted her head right back and drained the dregs, coughed a little, set the glass back down, and slung her hair over the other shoulder. She had too much makeup on: huge swipes of blusher, exaggerated cat eyes. She glanced around the bar, then took out her phone again, flicked and tapped at it. She wasn't used to being alone in a bar like this. It was an older crowd and she felt self-conscious, you could tell. The men in the chairs opposite her were in their forties at least, heavy-jowled, sweating in their suits, tipping back their whiskey sours. I watched the relief on her face when he appeared again, how she wriggled into him and kissed him on the cheek. As they studied the menu together, giggling, their heads bent confidentially together, I suddenly realised she wasn't his lover.

She was his daughter.

She was Melissa. Seventeen years. She'd be eighteen now. Perhaps they were out tonight celebrating her eighteenth birthday.

With a surge of nausea I realised, then, that what I'd been feeling wasn't outrage that she was too young for him, or contempt, or disgust. It was simpler, and much more complicated than that.

I don't remember whose idea it was to go to Mr. Knox's house.

One minute we were giggling over him, nudging elbows and sugar-breath and damp heads bent together, and the next minute someone was saying they knew where he lived, something about a neighbour and church and his wife, and suddenly, almost without the decision being made at all, it was decided that we were going there.

Was it Tanya?

There were four of us: Donna, Tanya, Lisa, and me. We were fourteen, and bored. It was a Baker day, which meant no school, and we had nothing else to do. It was April, and chilly; rain coming in gusty, intermittent bursts. The Easter holidays had only just ended, and none of us had any pocket money left. We'd met in Cairnburn Park just after nine, but at that time on a wet Monday morning it was deserted. We'd wandered down to the kiddie playground but the swings were soaking and after a half-hearted couple of turns on the roundabout we'd given up. The four of us had trailed down Sydenham Avenue and past our school—it was strange to see the lights on in the main building, and the teachers' cars all lined up as usual. Then, more out of habit than anything else, we crossed the road to the mini-market. We pooled our spare change to buy packets of strawberry bonbons and bags of Midget Gems and Donna nicked a handful of fizzy cola bottles. We ate them as we trudged on down toward Ballyhackamore. The rain was getting heavier and none of us had umbrellas, so we'd ended up in KFC, huddled over the melamine table, slurping a shared Pepsi. We were the only ones in there. The sugar and the rain and the boredom made us restless, and snide. We'd started telling stories, in deliberately too-loud voices, about people we knew who'd ordered plain chicken burgers and complained when they came with mayo. There's no mayo in it, the person behind the counter would say. Oh yes there is. Oh no there isn't. And it would turn out that the mayo was actually a burst sac of pus from a cyst growing on the chicken breast. The girl behind the counter was giving us increasingly dirty looks and we realised that if she chucked us out we really had nowhere to go; so we changed tack then and started slagging each other, boys we'd fancied, boys we'd "seen," or wanted to "see," as the expression went.

And then the conversation, almost inevitably, turned to Mr. Knox.

We all fancied Mr. Knox. No one even bothered to deny it. The whole school fancied him. He was the French and Spanish teacher, and he was part French himself, or so the rumours went. He was part-something, anyway, he had to be: he was so different from the other teachers. He had dark hair that he wore long and floppy over one eye, and permanent morning-after stubble, and he smoked Camel cigarettes. Teachers couldn't smoke anywhere in the school grounds, not even in the staffroom, but he smoked anyway, in the staff toilets in the art block or in the caretaker's shed, girls said, and if you had him immediately after break or lunch you smelled it off him. He drove an Alfa Romeo, bright red, and where the other male teachers were rumpled in browns and greys he wore coloured silk shirts and loafers. On "Own Clothes Day" at the end of term he'd wear tapered jeans and polo necks and Chelsea boots and, even in winter, mirrored aviator sunglasses, like an off-duty film star. He had posters on his classroom walls of Emmanuelle Béart and a young Catherine Deneuve and Soledad Miranda, and he lent his sixth-formers videos of Pedro Almodóvar films.

But that wasn't all. A large part of his charge came from the fact that he'd had an affair with a former pupil, Davina Calvert. It had been eight years ago, and they were married now: he'd left his wife for her, and it was a real scandal, he'd almost lost his job over it, except in the end they couldn't dismiss him because he'd done nothing strictly, legally wrong. It had happened long before we joined the school, but we knew all the details. Everyone did. It was almost a rite of passage to cluster as first- or second-years in a corner of the library poring over old school magazines in search of her, hunting down grainy black-and-white photographs of year groups, foreign exchange trips, prize days, tracking her as she grew up to become his lover.

Davina Calvert, Davina Knox. She was as near and as far from our lives as it was possible to get.

Davina, the story went, was her year's star pupil. She got the top mark in Spanish A-level in the whole of Northern Ireland, and came third in French. Davina Calvert, Davina Knox. Nothing happened between them while she was still at school—or nothing anyone could pin on him, at least—but when she left she went on a gap year, teaching English in Granada, and he went out to visit her. We knew this for sure because Lisa's older sister had been two years below Davina Calvert, and at the time was in Mr. Knox's Spanish A-level class. After Halloween half-term he turned up with a load of current Spanish magazines, *Hola!* and *Diez Minutos* and *Vogue España*. They asked him if he'd been away, and where he'd been, and he answered them in a teasing torrent of Spanish that none of them could quite follow. But it went around the school like wildfire that he'd been in Granada, visiting Davina Calvert, and sure enough, when she was back for Christmas at least two people saw them in his Alfa Romeo, parked up a side street, kissing, and by the end of the school year he and his wife were separated, getting divorced. The following year he didn't even pretend to hide it from his classes: when they talked about what they'd done over the weekend he'd grin and say, in French or Spanish, that he'd been visiting a special friend in Edinburgh. Everyone knew it was Davina.

We used to picture what it must have been like, when he

first visited her in Granada. The winding streets and white medieval buildings. The blue and orange and purple sky. They would have walked together to Lorca's house and the Alhambra and afterward clinked glasses of sherry in some cobbled square with fountains and gypsy musicians. Perhaps he would have reached under the table to stroke her thigh, slipping a hand under her skirt and tracing its curve, and when he withdrew it she would have crossed and uncrossed her legs, squeezing and releasing her thighs, the tingling pressure unbearable.

I imagined it countless times: but I could never quite settle on what would have happened next. What would you do, in Granada with Mr. Knox? Would you lead him back to your little rented room, in the sweltering eaves of a homestay or a shared apartment? No: you'd go with him instead to the hotel that he'd booked, a sumptuous four-poster bed in a grand and faded parador in the Albaicín—or more likely an anonymous room in the new district where the staff wouldn't ask questions, a room where the bed had white sheets with clinical corners, a room with a bathroom you could hear every noise from. The shame of it—the excitement.

And back in the KFC on the Upper Newtownards Road, on that rainy Monday Baker Day in April, we knew where Mr. Knox and Davina lived. It was out towards the Ice Bowl, near the golf club, in Dundonald. It was a forty-, forty-five minute walk. We had nothing else to do. We linked arms and set off.

It was an anticlimax when we got there. We'd walked down the King's Road, passing such posh houses on the way; somehow, with the sports car and the sunglasses and the designer suits, we'd expected his house to be special too. But most of the houses on his street were just like ours: bungalows, or small redbrick semis, with hedges and lawns and rhododendron bushes. We walked up one side, and down the other. There was nothing to tell us where he lived: no sign of him. We were starting to bicker by then. The rain was teeming down and Tanya was getting worried that someone might see us, and report us to the school. We slagged her—how would anyone know we were doing anything wrong, and how would they know which school we went to, anyway, we weren't in uniform—but all of us were slightly on edge. It was only midmorning, but what if he left school for some reason, or came home for an early lunch? All four of us were in his French class, and Lisa and I had him for Spanish too: he'd recognise us. We should go: we knew we should go.

The long walk back in the rain stretched ahead of us. We sat on a low wall to empty our pockets and purses and work out if we had enough to pay for a bus ticket each. When it turned out there was only enough for three, we started squabbling: Tanya had no money left, but she'd paid for the bon-bons, and almost half of the Pepsi, so it wasn't fair if she had to walk. Well, it wasn't fair for everyone to have to walk just because of her. Besides, she lived nearest: there was least distance for her to go. But it wasn't fair! Back and forth it went, and it might have turned nasty—Donna had just threatened to slap Tanya if she didn't quit whinging.

Then we saw Davina.

It was Lisa who recognised her, at the wheel of a metallic-blue Peugeot. The car swept past us and round the curve of the road, but Lisa swore it had been her at the wheel. We leapt up, galvanised, and looked at each other.

"Well come on," Donna said.

"Donna!" Tanya said.

"What, are you scared?" Donna said. She had thick glasses that made her eyes look small and mean, and she'd pushed her sister through a patio door in a fight. We were all a little scared of Donna.

"Come on," Lisa said.

Tanya seemed like she was about to cry.

"We're just going to look," I said. "We're just going to walk past and look at the house. There's no law against that." Then I added, "For fuck's sake, Tanya." I didn't mind Tanya, if it was just the two of us, but it didn't do to be too friendly with her in front of the others.

"Yeah, Tanya, for fuck's sake," Lisa said.

Tanya sat back down on the wall. "I'm not going anywhere. We'll be in such big trouble."

"Fine," Donna said. "Fuck off home then, what are you waiting for?" She turned and linked arms with Lisa, and they started walking down the street.

"Come on, Tan," I said.

"I have a bad feeling," she said. "I just don't think we should."

But when I turned to go after the others, she pushed herself from the wall and followed.

We found the house where the Peugeot was parked: right at the bottom of the street. It was the left-hand side of a semi, and it had an unkempt hedge and a stunted palm tree in the middle of the little front lawn. You somehow didn't picture Mr. Knox with a miniature palm tree in his garden. We clustered on the opposite side of the road, half-hidden behind a white van, giggling at it; and then we realised that Davina was still in the car.

"What's she at?" Donna said. "Stupid bitch."

We stood and watched awhile longer, but nothing happened. You could see the dark blur of her head and the back of her shoulders, just sitting there.

"Well, fuck this for a game of soldiers," Donna said. "I'm not standing here like a big lemon all day." She turned and walked a few steps down the road and waited for the rest of us to follow.

"Yeah," Tanya said, "I'm going too. I said I'd be home for lunch."

Neither Lisa nor I moved.

"What do you think she's *doing*?" Lisa asked.

"Listening to the radio?" I said. "Mum does that sometimes if it's *The Archers*. She doesn't want to leave the car until it's over."

"I suppose," Lisa said, looking disappointed.

"Come on," Tanya said. "We've seen where he lives, now let's just go."

Donna was standing with her hands on her hips, annoyed that we were ignoring her. "Seriously," she shouted, "I'm away on!"

They were expecting me and Lisa to follow, but we didn't. As soon as they were out of earshot, Lisa said, "God, Donna's doing my fucking head in today."

She glanced at me sideways as she said it.

"Hah," I said, vaguely. It didn't do to be too committal: Lisa and Donna were thick as thieves these days. Lisa's mum and mine had gone to school together and the two of us had been friends since we were babies: there were photographs of us in the bath together, covered in bubbles, bashing each other with bottles of Matey. We'd been inseparable through primary school, and into secondary. Recently, though, Lisa had started hanging out more with Donna, smoking Silk Cuts nicked from Donna's mum and drinking White Lightning in the park at weekends. Both of them had gone pretty far with boys. Not full-on sex, but close, or so they both claimed. I'd kissed a boy once. It was better than Tanya—but still, it made me weird and awkward around Lisa when it was just the two of us. I'd always imagined we'd do everything together, like we always had done. I could feel Lisa still looking at me. I scuffed the ground with the heel of one of my gutties.

"I mean, seriously doing my head in," she said, and she pulled a face that was recognisably an impression of Donna, and I let myself start giggling. Lisa looked pleased. "Here," she said, and she slipped her arm through mine. "What do you think Davina's *like*? I mean, d'you know what I mean?"

I knew exactly what she meant.

"Well, she's got to be gorgeous," I said.

"You big lesbo," Lisa said, digging me in the ribs.

I dug her back. "No, being serious. She's got to be—he left his wife for her. She's got to be gorgeous."

"What else?"

"She doesn't care what people think. I mean, think of all the gossip. Think of what you'd say to your parents."

"My dad would go *nuts*."

"Yeah," I said.

We were silent for a moment then, watching the blurred figure in the Peugeot.

"D'you think anything did happen while they were at school?" Lisa suddenly said. "I mean it must have, mustn't it? Otherwise why would you bother going all that way to visit her? I mean like, lying to your wife and flying all the way to Granada?"

"I know. I don't know."

I'd wondered about it before: we all had. But it was especially strange, standing right outside his house, his and Davina's. Did she linger at his desk after class? Did he stop and give her a lift somewhere? Did she hang around where he lived and bump into him, as if by chance, or pretend she was having problems with her Spanish grammar? Who started it, and how exactly did it start, and did either of them ever imagine it would end up here?

"She might have been our age," Lisa said.

"I know."

"Or only, like, two or three years older."

"I know."

We must have been standing there for ten minutes by now.

A minute longer and we might have turned to go. But all of a sudden the door of the Peugeot swung open and Davina got out: there she was, Davina Calvert, Davina Knox.

Except that the Davina in our heads had been glamorous, like the movie sirens on Mr. Knox's classroom walls, but this Davina had messy hair in a ponytail and bags under her eyes, and she was wearing scruffy jeans and a raincoat. And she was crying: her face was puffy and she was weeping openly, tears just running down her face.

I felt Lisa take my hand and squeeze it. "Oh my God," she breathed.

We watched Davina walk around to the other side of the car and unstrap a toddler from the backseat. She lifted him to his feet and then hauled a baby car-seat out.

We had forgotten—if we'd ever known—that Mr. Knox had babies. He never mentioned them or had photos on his desk like some of the other teachers. You somehow didn't think of Mr. Knox with babies.

"Oh my God," Lisa said again.

The toddler was wailing: we watched Davina wrestle him up the drive and onto the porch, the baby car-seat over the crook of her arm. She had to put it down while she found her keys, and we watched as she scrabbled in her bag and then her coat pockets before locating them, unlocking the door, and going inside. The door swung shut behind her.

We stood there for a moment longer. Then: "Come on," I found myself saying. "Let's knock on her door." I have no idea where the impulse came from, but as soon as I said it, I knew I was going to do it.

Lisa turned to face me. "Are you insane?"

"Come on," I said.

"But what will we say?"

"We'll say we're lost—we'll say we're after a glass of water—I don't know. We'll think of something. Come on."

Lisa stared at me. "Oh my God, you're mad." But she giggled. And then we were crossing the road and walking up the driveway and there we were standing on Mr. Knox's porch.

"You're not seriously going to do this," Lisa said.

"Watch me," I said, and I fisted my hand and knocked on the door.

I can still picture every moment of what happens next. Davina opens the door (Davina Calvert, Davina Knox) with the baby in one arm and the toddler hanging off one of her legs. We blurt out—it comes to me, inspired—that we live just round the corner and we're going door-to-door to see if anyone needs a babysitter. All at once, we're like a team again, me and Leese. I start a sentence, she finishes it. She says something, I elaborate. We sound calm, and totally plausible. Davina says, Thank you, but the baby's too young to be left. Lisa says can we leave our details anyway, for maybe in a few months' time. Davina blinks and says okay, sure, and the two of us inch our way into her hallway while she gets a pen and paper. Lisa calls me Judith and I call her Carol. We write down, *Judith and Carol*, and give a made-up number. We are invincible. We are on fire. Davina asks what school do we go to, and Lisa says, not missing a beat, Dundonald High. Why aren't you at school today? Davina asks, and I say it's a Baker Day. I suddenly wonder if all schools have the same Baker Days and a dart of fear goes through me: but Davina just says, Oh, and doesn't ask anything more. We sense she's going to usher us out now and before she can do it, Lisa asks what the baby's called, and Davina says, Melissa. That's a pretty name, I say, and Davina says thank you. So we admire the baby, her screwed-up little face and flexing fingers, and I think of having Mr. Knox's baby growing inside me, and a huge rush of heat goes through me. When Davina says, as we knew she was going to, Girls, as I'm sure you can see, I've really got my hands full here, and Lisa says, No, no, of course, we'll have to be going—and she's getting the giggles now, I can see them rising in her, the way the corners of her lips pucker and tweak—I say, Yes, of course, but do you mind if I use your toilet first? Davina blinks again, her red-raw eyes, as if she can sense a trap but doesn't know quite what it is, and then she says, No problem, but the downstairs loo's blocked. Wee Reuben has a habit of flushing things down it and they haven't gotten round to calling out the plumber, you'll have to go upstairs, it's straight up and first on the left. I can feel Lisa staring at me but I don't meet her eye, I just say, Thank you, and make my way upstairs.

The bathroom is full—just humming—with Mr. Knox. There's his dressing gown hung on the back of the door, his electric razor on the side of the sink, his can of Lynx deodorant on the windowsill. There's his toothbrush in a mug, and there's flecks of his stubble in the sink, and there's his dirty clothes in the laundry basket: I kneel and open it and recognise one of his shirts, a slippery pale-blue one with yellow diamond patterning. I reach over and flush the toilet, so the noise will cover my movements, and then I open the mirrored cabinet above the sink and run my fingers over the bottles on what must be his shelf, the shaving cream, the brown plastic bottle of prescription drugs, a six-pack of Durex condoms, two of them missing. The skin all over my body is tingling, tingling in places I didn't know could tingle, in between my fingers, the backs of my knees. I ease one of the condoms from the strip, tugging gently along the foil perforations, and stuff it into my jeans. Then I put the box back, exactly as it was, and close the mirrored cabinet. I stare at myself in the mirror. My face looks flushed. I wonder, again, what age she was when he first noticed her. I realise that I don't know how long I've been in here. I run the tap, and look around me one last time. And then, without planning to, without knowing I'm going to until I've done it, I find my hand closing around one of the bottles of perfume on the windowsill, and rearranging the others so the gap doesn't show. You're not supposed to keep perfume on the windowsill, anyway: even I know that. I slide it into the inside pocket of my jacket and arrange my left arm over it so the bulge doesn't show, then I turn off the tap and go downstairs where Lisa's shooting me desperate glances.

Outside, she can't believe what I've done. None of them can. We catch up with Donna and Tanya still waiting for us on the main road—although it feels like a lifetime has passed, it's only been ten minutes or so since they left us.

"You'll never believe what she did," Lisa says, and there's pride in her voice as she tells them how we knocked on the door and went inside, inside Mr. Knox's house, and talked to Davina, and touched the baby, and how I used his bathroom. I take over the story. The condom I keep quiet about—that's mine, just for me—but I show them the perfume. It's a dark glass bottle, three-quarters full, aubergine, almost black, with a round glass stopper. In delicate gold lettering it says, *Poison, Christian Dior*.

"I can't believe you nicked her fucking perfume," Donna says.

Tanya stares at me as if she's going to be sick.

Donna takes the bottle from me and uncaps the lid. She aims it at Lisa.

"Fuck off," Lisa says. "You're not spraying that shit on me."

"Spray me then," I say, and they all look at me. "Go on," I say, "spray me." I roll up the sleeve of my jumper to bare my wrist.

Donna aims the nozzle. A jet of perfume shoots out, dark and heady and forbidden-smelling.

"Eww," says Tanya, "that smells like fox. Why would anyone want to smell like that?"

I press my wrists together carefully and raise them to my neck, dab both sides. It's the strongest perfume I've ever smelled. The musty green scent makes me feel slightly nauseous. It doesn't smell like a perfume you'd imagine Davina Calvert choosing. He must have bought it for her; it must be him that likes it. I wonder if he sprays it on her before they go out. If she holds up her wrists and bares her throat for him.

"What are you going to do with it?" Lisa asks.

"We could bring it into school," I say, and all at once my heart is racing again. "We could bring it into school, and spray it in his lesson. We could see what he does."

"You're a fucking psycho," Donna says, and she laughs, but for the first time ever it's tinged with awe.

"You can't," Tanya's saying, "I'm not having anything to do with this," but we're all ignoring her now.

"Me and Lisa have Spanish tomorrow," I say, "straight after lunch. We'll do it then. Right, Leese?"

"What do you think he'll do?" Lisa asks, wide-eyed.

"Maybe," I say, "he'll keep us behind after class and shag our brains out on his desk." I say it as if I'm joking, and she and Donna laugh, and I laugh too, but I think of the condom hidden in my pocket and the tingling feeling returns.

That night I lie in bed and squeeze my eyes closed and play the scene of them meeting in Granada with more intensity than ever before: and when I get to the part where he undoes her halterneck top and eases her skirt off and lies her down on the bed, my whole body starts shaking.

* * *

The next day in Spanish we did it, just as we'd planned. Before class started we huddled over my bag and sprayed the Poison, unknotting our ties to mist it in the hollow of our throat. We were feverish with excitement. He didn't know how close to him we'd gotten.

I had his condom with me too. I'd slept with it under my pillow and now it was zipped into the pocket of my school skirt: I could feel the foil edge rubbing against my thigh when I crossed my legs.

Mr. Knox came in, sat on the edge of his desk, and asked us what we'd been doing over the weekend.

My heart was thumping. I suddenly wished I'd prepared something clever to say, something that would get his attention, or make him smile, but I hadn't and I found myself saying the first thing that came into my head, just to be the one who spoke.

"*Voy de compras,*" I said.

"I'm sure you go shopping all the time, but in this instance it was in the past tense." He looked straight at me as he spoke, his crinkled eyes, a teasing smile. He seemed surprised, or amused, to see me talking. I was never one of the confident ones who spoke up in class without prompting. "*Otra vez, señorita.*"

Señorita. I'd never been one of the girls he called *señorita* before. I imagined he'd called Davina *señorita.* His accent in Spanish was rolling and sexy. Hers would be too, of course. They'd probably had conversations of their own, over and above everyone else's heads.

"*Fui de compras,*" I said, locking eyes with him.

"*Muy bien, fuiste de compras, y qué compraste?*"

"What did I buy?" The cloying smell of the perfume was making me dizzy and I couldn't seem to straighten my thoughts.

"*Sí—qué compraste?*"

"*Compré . . . compré un nuevo perfume.*"

"*Muy bien.*" He grinned at me. "*Fuiste de compras, y compraste un nuevo perfume. Muy bien.*"

"Do you want to smell it, Mr. Knox?" Lisa blurted.

"Lisa!" I hissed, delighted and appalled.

"*Gracias, Lisa, pero no.*"

"Are you sure? I think you'd like it."

"*Gracias*, Lisa. Who's next?" He gazed around the room, waiting for someone else to put their hand up. I'd said it. I couldn't believe I'd said it. I felt the colour rising to my face. Lisa was stifling a fit of giggles beside me but I ignored her and kept my eyes on Mr. Knox. He hadn't flinched.

At the end of class we hung about, taking our time to pack our bags, and wondering if he'd keep us behind, but he didn't. We left the room and fell into each other's arms in fits of giggles—but we were both exaggerating, kidding ourselves that we weren't disappointed. Or at least I was. Maybe for Lisa it was just a big joke. I don't know what I'd expected, exactly, but I'd expected something: a moment of recognition, something.

My last lesson of the day was maths, where I sat with Tanya—none of our other friends were taking higher maths. We walked out of school together. Tanya lived up by Stormont and it was out of my way, but I sometimes walked home with her anyway. My mum had gone back to work since my dad moved out and I didn't like returning to an empty house. And today, there was the increased attraction of knowing that this was the way Mr. Knox must drive home.

We walked down Wandsworth Road, crossed the busy junction, then along the Upper Newtownards Road. When we got to the traffic lights at Castlehill Road, by Stormont Presbyterian, I kept us hanging about. I made sure I was standing facing the traffic. I was waiting for the Alfa Romeo to pass us: I knew in my bones that it would, knew that it had to.

When it did, I turned to follow it and didn't take my eyes from it until it was gone completely from sight. And by the time I turned back, something inside me had shifted.

I spent an hour that night learning extra French vocab and practising my Spanish tenses, determined to impress him the following day, to make him notice me.

The next day I walked home with Tanya again, and the day after that, and pretty soon I was heading home with her every day. It was a twenty-minute walk from school to hers, and most days by the time we reached the Upper Newtownards Road his car would be long gone. But I took to noting which days he held his after-school language club for sixth-formers, or had staff meetings, and on those days I'd try to time our journey; persuading Tanya to come to the mini-market with me and killing time there choosing sweets and looking at the magazines, then lingering at the traffic lights by the church in the hope of seeing his car. On the days that I did, even just a flash of it as it sped past through a green light, I'd feel like I was flying all the way home.

Lisa and Donna were friends again, and Lisa still didn't invite me on their Cairnburn nights, but suddenly I didn't care. Three Saturday evenings in a row I let my mum think I was going to Lisa's, and I walked the whole way to Mr. Knox and Davina's house, and I moved past two, three, four, five times, and saw both cars in their driveway and the lights in their windows and once even caught a glimpse of him in an upstairs room.

It had to happen. I knew it had to happen.

The days you were most likely to see his car, I'd worked out, were Tuesdays and Wednesdays: one Wednesday, as I kept Tanya hanging about at the end of her road, Mr. Knox's Alfa Romeo finally pulled up at the lights.

He was right beside us. Metres away. It was real: it was happening. For a moment, I couldn't breathe.

"There he is," I said, and Tanya followed my gaze and replied, "No, wise up, what are you doing?"

"Mr. Knox!" I yelled, and I waved at the car. "Mr. Knox!"

His windows were wound halfway down—he was smoking—and he ducked to look out, then pressed a button to wind them down fully.

"Hello?" he said. "What is it, is everything okay?"

"Mr. Knox," I said. "We need a lift, will you give us a lift?"

"Stop it!" Tanya hissed at me.

"Please, Mr. Knox!" I said. "We're really late and it's important."

The lights were still red but any moment they'd go amber, then green.

"Please, Mr. Knox," I said. "You have to, please, you have to." I had taken to wearing a dab of Poison every day I had a French or Spanish lesson—even though Lisa told me I was a weirdo—and I could still smell the perfume, Davina's perfume, on me, and I wondered if he could too, creeping from me in a slow green spiral.

He took a drag of his cigarette and dropped it out of the window. "Where are you going?"

Tanya hissed and grabbed my arm but I wrenched it free. The lights were amber and as they turned green I was opening the passenger seat and getting in. There I was, in Mr. Knox's Alfa Romeo. It was happening.

"Where do you need to go?" he asked again, and I said: "Anywhere." He looked at me and raised an eyebrow and snorted with laughter, and I thought he might tell me to get out, but he didn't, he just revved the engine and then accelerated away, and in the wing mirror I caught a glimpse of Tanya's stricken face, open-mouthed, and I looked at Mr. Knox beside me—Mr. Knox, I was there, now, finally, in Mr. Knox's car, me and Mr. Knox—and I started laughing too.

* * *

Afterwards, I couldn't resist telling Tanya. I told her how he kissed me, gently at first and his lips were soft, then harder, with his tongue. I told her how he undid my tie, and unbuttoned my shirt, and how his fingers were cool on my skin. I told her how he slipped his hand underneath my skirt and traced his fingers up, then hooked his fingers under my panties and tugged them down.

"He *didn't*," she said, big-eyed and scared, and I promised her, "Yes, he did." And her shock spurred me on, and I said how it hurt at the start. I said there was blood. I said it was in the backseat of his Alfa Romeo, in a cul-de-sac near the golf course, and he'd spread his jacket out first, and afterward he'd smoked a cigarette.

Once I'd told Tanya, I had to tell Donna, and Lisa, and when Lisa looked at me with slitted eyes and said I was lying, I got out the condom and showed them: as proof, I said, he'd given it to me for next time.

I hadn't counted on Tanya blubbering it all to her mother: all of it, including the time we went to his house. We got in such trouble for that, but the trouble he was in was worse.

Even though I cracked as soon as my mum asked me, told her that I'd made it all up, she didn't believe me—couldn't understand why I'd make it up or how I'd even know what to make up in the first place. In a series of anguished phone calls she and Tanya's mother decided Mr. Knox had an unhealthy hold over me, over all of us.

There's no smoke, they agreed, without fire.

They contacted the headmistress and that was that: Mr. Knox was called before the governors and forced to resign, and I was sent to a counsellor who tried to make me talk about my parents' divorce. And then, in the autumn, we heard that Davina had left Mr. Knox: had taken her babies and gone back to her mother's. It must have been her worst nightmare come true, the merest suggestion that her husband, the father of her two children, would do it again. She, more than anyone else, would have known there was no such thing as innocence.

I think she was right.

I don't believe it was a one-off.

What happened that day is that he drove me five minutes up the road, then pulled a U-turn at the garage, and drove back down the other side and made me get out not far from where he'd picked me up and said, "Now this was a one-off, you know," and laughed.

But I can still see his expression as he dropped me off: the half-smile, the eyebrow raised even as he said it wasn't to happen again.

It had happened before. And there's a certain intensity that only a fourteen- or fifteen-year-old girl can possess: I would have redoubled my efforts at snaring him.

If only I hadn't told Tanya.

I lifted my glass of wine and took a sip, and then another. Mr. Knox and Melissa were still giggling over the cocktail menu, flipping back and forth through the pages.

"Excuse me," I said, turning to the bar and addressing the nearest barman. He didn't hear me; carried on carving twists of orange peel. "Excuse me," I said again, louder.

He raised his finger: one moment. But I carried on.

"You see the couple over there? By the window? The man with the black hair and the blonde girl?"

He frowned and put the orange down; looked at them, then back at me.

"Can I pay for their drinks?" I blurted.

"You'd like to buy their drinks?"

"Yes, whatever they're having. All of it. I want to pay for all of it."

"I'll just get the bar manager for you. One moment, please."

My heart was pounding. It was impulsive, and utterly stupid. My friends hadn't even arrived yet; we'd still be sitting here when Mr. Knox asked for his bill in a drink or so's time, and how would I explain it to them, or to him: because the barman would point me out as the one who'd paid for it. Even if I asked them not to let on, not to give me away, my name would be on the credit card slip, so he'd know. Or would he? Would my name mean anything to him, all these years later? Surely it would. Surely it must.

I swivelled on my stool to look at them again. Melissa, with her blonde hair and pouting glossy lips and blue eyes, didn't look very much like him. She didn't look much like Davina either. They were mock-arguing about something now. She flicked her hair and cocked her head and put her hands on her waist, a pantomime of indignation, and he took her bare upper arms and squeezed them, shaking her lightly, and she squealed then threw her head back in laughter as he leant in to murmur something in her ear.

She had to be his daughter. She had to be.

"Ma'am. Excuse me." The manager was leaning across the bar, attempting to get my attention. "Excuse me."

"Sorry," I said, "I was miles away."

She had to be his daughter.

"I understand you'd like to buy a drink for the couple by the window?"

"No," I said. "I'm sorry, I was mistaken. I mean, I thought they were someone else."

"No problem," he replied, smooth, professional. "Is there anything else I can do for you?"

I looked at him. He waited, head politely inclined. I almost asked: *Can you find out their names?* Then I realised that, either way, I didn't want to know.

WET WITH RAIN

BY LEE CHILD

Great Victoria Street

Births and deaths are in the public record. Census returns and rent rolls and old mortgages are searchable. As are citizenship applications from all the other English-speaking countries. There are all kinds of ancestry sites on the web. These were the factors in our favour.

Against us was a historical truth. The street had been built in the 1960s. Fifty years ago, more or less. Within living memory. Most of the original residents had died off, but they had families, who must have visited, and who might remember. Children and grandchildren, recipients of lore and legend, and therefore possibly a problem.

But overall we counted ourselves lucky. The first owners of the house in question were long dead, and had left no children. The husband had surviving siblings, but they had all gone to either Australia or Canada. The wife had a living sister, still in the neighbourhood, but she was over eighty years old, and considered unreliable.

Since the original pair, the house had had five owners, most of them in the later years. We felt we had enough distance. So we went with the third variant of the second plan. Hairl Carter came with me. Hairl Carter the second, technically. His father had the same name. From southeastern Missouri. His father's mother had wanted to name her firstborn Harold, but she had no more than a third-grade education, and couldn't spell except phonetically. So Harold it was, phonetically. The old lady never knew it was weird. We all called her grandson Harry, which might not have pleased her.

Harry did the paperwork, which was easy enough, because we made it all Xeroxes of Xeroxes, which hides a lot of sins. I opened an account at a Washington, DC bank, in the name of the society, and I put half a million dollars into it, and we got credit cards and a checkbook. Then we rehearsed. We prepped it, like a political debate. The same conversation, over and over again, down all the possible highways and byways. We identified weak spots, though we had no choice but to barrel through. We figured audacity would stop them thinking straight.

We flew first to London, then to Dublin in the south, and then we made the connection to Belfast on tickets that cost less than cups of coffee back home. We took a cab to the Europa Hotel, which is where we figured people like us would stay. We arranged a car with the concierge. Then we laid up and slept. We figured midmorning the next day should be zero hour.

The car was a crisp Mercedes and the driver showed no real re-luctance about the address—which was second from the end of a short line of ticky-tacky row houses, bland and cheaply built, with big areas of peeling white weatherboard, which must have saved money on bricks. The roof tiles were concrete, and had gone mossy. In the distance the hills were like velvet, impossibly green, but all around us the built environment was hard. There was a fine cold drizzle in the air, and the street and the sidewalk were both shiny grey.

The car waited at the kerb and we opened a broken gate and walked up a short path through the front yard. Carter rang the bell and the door opened immediately. The Mercedes had not gone unnoticed. A woman looked out at us. She was solidly built, with a pale, meaty face. "Who are you?"

I said, "We're from America."

"America?"

"We came all the way to see you."

"Why?"

"Mrs. Healy, is it?" I asked, even though I knew it was. I knew all about her. I knew where she was born, how old she was, and how much her husband made. Which wasn't much. They were a month behind on practically everything. Which I hoped was going to help.

"Yes, I'm Mrs. Healy," the woman said.

"My name is John Pacino, and my colleague here is Harry Carter."

"Good morning to you both."

"You live in a very interesting house, Mrs. Healy."

She looked blank, and then craned her neck out the door and stared up at her front wall. "Do I?"

"Interesting to us, anyway."

"Why?"

"Can we tell you all about it?"

She said, "Would you like a wee cup of tea?"

"That would be lovely."

So we trooped inside, first Carter, then me, feeling a kind of preliminary satisfaction, as if our lead-off hitter had gotten on base. Nothing guaranteed, but so far so good. The air inside smelled of daily life and closed windows. A skilled analyst could have listed the ingredients from their last eight meals. All of which had been either boiled or fried, I guessed.

It wasn't the kind of household where guests get deposited in the parlor to wait. We followed the woman to the kitchen, which had drying laundry suspended on a rack. She filled a kettle and lit the stove. She said, "Tell me what's interesting about my house."

Carter said, "There's a writer we admire very much, name of Edmund Wall."

"Here?"

"In America."

"A writer?"

"A novelist. A very fine one."

"I never heard of him. But then, I don't read much."

"Here," Carter said, and he took the copies from his pocket and smoothed them on the counter. They were faked to look like Wikipedia pages. Which is trickier than people think. (Wikipedia prints different than it looks on the computer screen.)

Mrs. Healy asked, "Is he famous?"

"Not exactly," I said. "Writers don't really get famous. But he's very well respected. Among people who like his sort of thing. There's an appreciation society. That's why we're here. I'm the chairman and Mr. Carter is the general secretary."

Mrs. Healy stiffened a little, as if she thought we were trying to sell her something. "I'm sorry, but I don't want to join. I don't know him."

I said, "That's not the proposition we have for you."

"Then what is?"

"Before you, the Robinsons lived here, am I right?"

"Yes," she said.

"And before them, the Donnellys, and before them, the McLaughlins."

The woman nodded. "They all got cancer. One after the other. People started to say this was an unlucky house."

I looked concerned. "That didn't bother you? When you bought it?"

"My faith has no room for superstition."

Which was a circularity fit to make a person's head explode. It struck me mute. Carter said, "And before the McLaughlins were the McCanns, and way back at the beginning were the McKennas."

"Before my time," the woman said, uninterested, and I felt the runner on first steal second. Scoring position.

I said, "Edmund Wall was born in this house."

"Who?"

"Edmund Wall. The novelist. In America."

"No one named Wall ever lived here."

"His mother was a good friend of Mrs. McKenna. Right back at the beginning. She came to visit from America. She thought she had another month, but the baby came early."

"When?"

"The 1960s."

"In this house?"

"Upstairs in the bedroom. No time to get to the hospital."

"A baby?"

"The future Edmund Wall."

"I never heard about it. Mrs. McKenna has a sister. She never talks about it."

Which felt like the runner getting checked back. I said, "You know Mrs. McKenna's sister?"

"We have a wee chat from time to time. Sometimes I see her in the hairdressers."

"It was fifty years ago. How's her memory?"

"I should think a person would remember that kind of thing."

Carter said, "Maybe it was hushed up. It's possible Edmund's mother wasn't married."

Mrs. Healy went pale. Impropriety. Scandal. In her house. Worse than cancer. "Why are you telling me this?"

I said, "The Edmund Wall Appreciation Society wants to buy your house."

"Buy it?"

"For a museum. Well, like a living museum, really. Certainly people could visit, to see the birthplace, but we could keep his papers here too. It could be a research centre."

"Do people do that?"

"Do what? Research?"

"No, visit houses where writers were born."

"All the time. Lots of writers' houses are museums. Or tourist attractions. We could make a very generous offer. Edmund Wall has many passionate supporters in America."

"How generous?"

"Best plan would be to pick out where you'd like to live next, and we'll make sure you can. Within reason, of course. Maybe a new house. They're building them all over." Then I shut up, and let temptation work its magic. Mrs. Healy went quiet. Then she started to look around her kitchen. Chipped cabinets, sagging hinges, damp air.

The kettle started to whistle.

She said, "I'll have to talk to my husband."

Which felt like the runner sliding into third ahead of the throw. Safe. Ninety feet away. Nothing guaranteed, but so far so good. In fact bloody good, as they say on those damp little islands. We were in high spirits on the way back in the Mercedes.

The problem was waiting for us in the Europa's lobby. An Ulsterman, maybe fifty years old, in a cheap suit, with old nicks and scars on his hands and thickening around his eyes. A former field operative, no doubt, many years in the saddle, now moved to a desk because of his age. I was familiar with the type. It was like looking in a mirror.

He said, "Can I have a word?"

We went to the bar, which was dismal and empty ahead of the lunchtime rush. The guy introduced himself as a copper, from right there in Belfast, from a unit he didn't specify, but which I guessed was Special Branch, which was the brass-knuckle wing of the old Royal Ulster Constabulary, now the Police Service of Northern Ireland. Like the FBI, with the gloves off. He said, "Would you mind telling me who you are and why you're here?"

So Carter gave him the guff about Edmund Wall, and the appreciation society, and the birthplace, but what was good enough earlier in the morning didn't sound so great in the cold light of midday. The guy checked things on his phone in real time as Carter talked, and then he said, "There are four things wrong with that story. There is no Edmund Wall, there is no appreciation society, the bank account you opened is at the branch nearest to Langley, which is CIA headquarters, and most of all, that house you're talking about was once home to Gerald McCann, who was a notorious paramilitary in his day."

Carter said nothing, and neither did I.

The guy continued, "Northern Ireland is part of the United Kingdom, you know. They won't allow unannounced activities on their own turf. So again, would you mind telling me who you are and why you're here?"

I said, "You interested in a deal?"

"What kind?"

"You want to buy a friend in a high place?"

"How high?"

"Very high."

"Where?"

"Somewhere useful to your government."

"Terms?"

"You let us get the job done first."

"Who gets killed?"

"Nobody. The Healys get a new house. That's all."

"What do you get?"

"Paid. But your new friend in the very high place gets peace of mind. For which he'll be suitably grateful, I'm sure."

"Tell me more."

"First I need to check you have your head on straight. This is not the kind of thing where you make a bunch of calls and get other people involved. This is the kind of thing where you let us do our work, and then when we're gone, you announce your new relationship as a personal coup. Or not. Maybe you'll want to keep the guy in your vest pocket."

"How many laws are you going to break?"

"None at all. We're going to buy a house. Happens every day."

"Because there's something in it, right? What did Gerald McCann leave behind?"

"You got to agree to what I said before. You got to at least nod your head. I have to be able to trust you."

"Okay, I agree," the guy said. "But I'm sticking with you all the way. We're a threesome now. Until you're done. Every minute. Until I wave you off at the airport."

"No, come with us," I said. "You can meet your new friend. At least shake hands with him. Then come back. Vest pocket or not, you'll feel better that way."

He fell for it, like I knew he would. I mean, why not? Security services love a personal coup. They love their vest pockets. They love to run people. They love to be the guy. He said, "Deal. So what's the story?"

"Once upon a time there was a young officer in the US Army. A bit of a hothead, with certain sympathies. With a certain job, at a certain time. He sold some obsolete weapons."

"To Gerald McCann?"

I nodded. "Who as far as we know never used them. Who we believe buried them under his living room floor. Meanwhile, our young officer grew up and got promoted and went into a whole different line of work. Now he wants the trail cleaned up."

"You want to buy the house so you can dig up the floor?"

I nodded again. "Can't break in and do it. Too noisy. The floors are concrete. We're going to need jackhammers. Neighbours need to think we're repairing the drains or something."

"These weapons are still traceable?"

"Weapon, singular, to be honest with you. Which I'm prepared to be, in a spot like this. Still traceable, yes. And extremely embarrassing, if it comes to light."

"Did Mrs. Healy believe you about Edmund Wall?"

"She believed us about the money. We're from America."

The guy from Special Branch said, "It takes a long time to buy a house."

It took three weeks, with all kinds of lawyer stuff, and an inspection, which was a pantomime and a farce, because what did we care? But it would have looked suspicious if we had waived it. We were supposed to be diligent stewards of the appreciation society's assets. So we commissioned it, and pretended to read it afterward. It was pretty bad, actually. For a spell I was worried the jackhammer would bring the whole place down.

We stayed in Belfast the whole three weeks. Normally we might have gone home and come back again, but not with the Special Branch copper on the scene, obviously. We had to watch him every minute. Which was easy enough, because he had to watch us every minute. We all spent three whole weeks gazing at each other, and reading crap about dry rot and rising damp. Whatever that was. It rained every day.

But in the end the lawyers got it done, and I received an un-dramatic phone call saying the house was ours. So we picked up the key and drove over and walked around with pages from the inspection report in our hands and worried expressions on our faces—which I thought of as setting the stage. The jackhammer had to be explicable. And the neighbours were nosy as hell. They were peering out and coming over and introducing themselves in droves. They brought old Mrs. McKenna's sister, who claimed to remember the baby being born, which set off a whole lot of tutting and clucking among her audience. More people came. As a result we waited two days before we rented the jackhammer. Easier than right away, we thought. I knew how to operate it. I had taken lessons, from a crew repairing Langley's secure staff lot.

The living room floor was indeed concrete, under some kind of asphalt screed, which was under a foam-backed carpet so old it had gone flat and crusty. We tore it up and saw a patch of screed that was different than the rest. It was the right size too. I smiled. Gerald McCann, taking care of business.

I asked, "What actually happened to McCann?"

The Special Branch guy said, "Murdered."

"Who by?"

"Us."

"When?"

"Before he could use this, obviously, whatever it is."

And after that, conversation was impossible, because I got the hammer started. After which the job went fast. The concrete was long on sand and short on cement. Same the world over. Concrete is a dirty business. But even so, the pit was pretty deep. More than just secure temporary storage. It felt kind of permanent. But we got to the bottom eventually, and we pulled the thing out.

It was wrapped in heavy plastic, but it was immediately recognisable. A reinforced canvas cylinder, olive green, like a half-size oil drum, with straps and buckles all over it, to keep it closed up tight, and to make it man-portable, like a backpack. A big backpack. A big, heavy backpack.

The guy from Special Branch went very quiet, and then he said, "Is that what I think it is?"

"Yes, it's what you think it is."

"Jesus Christ on a bike."

"Don't worry. The warhead is a dummy. Because our boy in uniform wasn't."

Carter said, "Warhead? What is it?"

I said nothing.

The guy from Special Branch explained, "It's an SADM. A W54 in an H-912 transport container."

"Which is what?"

"A Strategic Atomic Demolition Munition. A W54 missile warhead, which was the baby of the family, adapted to use as an explosive charge. Strap that thing to a bridge pier, and it's like dropping a thousand tons of TNT on it."

"It's nuclear?"

I said, "It weighs just over fifty pounds. Less than the bag you take on vacation. It's the nearest thing to a suitcase nuke ever built."

The guy from Special Branch said, "It *is* a suitcase nuke, never mind the nearest thing."

Carter said, "I never heard about them."

I said, "Developed in the 1950s. Obsolete by 1970. Para-troops were trained to jump with them, behind the lines, to blow up power stations and dams."

"With nuclear bombs?"

"They had mechanical timers. The paratroops might have gotten away."

"Might have?"

"It was a tough world back then."

"But this warhead is fake?"

"Open it up and take a look."

"I wouldn't know the difference."

"Good point," I said. "Gerald McCann obviously didn't."

The guy from Special Branch said, "I can see why my new friend wants the trail cleaned up. Selling nuclear weapons to foreign paramilitary groups? He couldn't survive that, whoever he is."

We put the thing in the trunk of a rented car, and drove to a quiet corner of Belfast International Airport, to a gate marked *General Aviation*, which meant private jets, and we found ours, which was a Gulfstream IV, painted grey and unmarked except for a tail number. The guy from Special Branch looked a little jealous.

"Borrowed," I said. "Mostly it's used for renditions."

Now he looked a little worried.

I said, "I'm sure they hosed the blood out."

We loaded the munition on board ourselves, because there was no spare crew to help us. There was one pilot and no steward. Standard practice, in the rendition business. Better deniability. We figured the munition was about the size of a fat guy, so we strapped it upright in a seat of its own. Then we all three sat down, as far from it as we could get.

Ninety minutes out I went to the bathroom, and after that I steered the conversation back to rendition. I said, "These planes are modified, you know. They have some of the electronic interlocks taken out. You can open the door while you're flying, for instance. Low and slow, over the water. They threaten to throw the prisoner out. All part of softening him up ahead of time."

Then I said, "Actually, sometimes they do throw the prisoner out. On the way home, usually, after he's spilled the beans. Too much trouble to do anything else, really."

Then I said, "Which is what we're going to do with the munition. We have to. We have no way of destroying it before we land, and we can't let it suddenly reappear in the US, like it just escaped from the museum. And this is the perfect setup for corroboration. Because there's three of us. Because we're going to get questions. He needs to know for sure. So this way I can swear I saw you two drop it out the door, and you two can swear you saw it hit the water, and you can swear I was watching you do it. We can back each other up three ways."

Which all made sense, so we went low and slow and I opened the door. Salt air howled in, freezing cold, and the plane rocked and juddered. I stepped back, and the guy from Special Branch came first, sidewinding down the aisle, with one of the transport container's straps hefted in his nicked and scarred left hand, and then came the munition itself, heavy, bobbing like a fat man in a hammock, and then came Carter, a strap in his right hand, shuffling sideways.

They got lined up side by side at the open door, their backs to me, each with a forearm up on the bulkhead to steady himself, the munition swinging slackly and bumping the floor between them. I said, "On three," and I started counting the numbers out, and they hoisted the cylinder and began swinging it, and on three they opened their hands and the canvas straps jerked free and the cylinder sailed out in the air and was instantly whipped away by the slipstream. They kept their forearms on the bulkhead, looking out, craning, staring down, waiting for the splash, and I took out the gun I had collected from the bathroom and shot the guy from Special Branch in the lower back, not because of any sadistic tendency, but because of simple ballistics. If the slug went through-and-through, I wanted it to carry on into thin air, not hit the airframe.

I don't think the bullet killed the guy. But the shock changed his day. He went all weak, and his forearm gave way, and he half fell and half got sucked out into the void. No sound. Just a blurred pinwheel as the currents caught him, and then a dot that got smaller, and then a tiny splash in the blue below, indistinguishable from a million white-crested waves.

I stepped up and helped Carter wrestle the door shut. He said, "I guess he knew too much."

I said, "Way too much."

We sat down, knee to knee.

Carter figured it out less than an hour later. He was not a dumb guy. He said, "If the warhead was a dummy, he could spin it like entrapment, like taking a major opponent out of the game. Or like economic warfare. Like a Robin Hood thing. He took a lot of bad money out of circulation, in exchange for a useless piece of junk. He could be the secret hero. The super-modest man."

"But?" I said.

"He's not spinning it that way. And all those people died of cancer. The Robinsons, and the Donnellys, and the McLaughlins."

"So?" I said.

"The warhead was real. That was an atom bomb. He sold nuclear weapons."

"Small ones," I said. "And obsolete."

Carter didn't reply. But that wasn't the important part. The important part came five minutes later. I saw it arrive in his eyes. I said, "Ask the question."

He said, "I'd rather not."

I said, "Ask the question."

"Why was there a gun in the bathroom? The Special Branch

guy was with us the whole time. You didn't call ahead for it. You had no opportunity. But it was there for you anyway. Why?"

I didn't answer.

He said, "It was there for me. The Special Branch guy was happenstance. Me, you were planning to shoot all along."

I said, "Kid, our boss sold live nuclear weapons. I'm cleaning up for him. What else do you expect?"

Carter said, "He trusts me."

"No, he doesn't."

"I would never rat him out. He's my hero."

"Gerald McCann should be your hero. He had the sense not to use the damn thing. I'm sure he was sorely tempted."

Carter didn't answer that. Getting rid of him was difficult, all on my own, but the next hours were peaceful, just me and the pilot, flying high and fast toward a spectacular sunset. I dropped my seat way back, and I stretched out. Relaxation is important. Life is short and uncertain, and it pays to make the best of whatever comes your way.

TAKING IT SERIOUS

BY RUTH DUDLEY EDWARDS

Falls Road

Ach, Marty just takes things a bit serious," said Mrs. O'Gorman.

"But it can't be good for him to be stuck indoors all day, Maria. He needs to be with boys of his own age kicking a ball around the park."

Mrs. O'Gorman said nothing but bent her head and began to hunt for offending bobbles on her cardigan. As she located a couple and pulled them off, her sister Patsy, recognising they had moved into a familiar cul-de-sac, shrugged, gave her a peck on the cheek, got into her car, and drove away with a half-hearted wave.

Mrs. O'Gorman went back into her house and looked at her younger son, who was still hard at work updating his montage of photographs. Not for the first time, she gave thanks to Jude, her favourite saint, that the days of screaming fits about the frustrations of glue or Blu-Tack or pins were over since his Uncle Joe had given him an infinitely flexible press-on and peel-off adhesive. Carefully, Marty plucked an image from the left-hand side and stuck it on the right, but after a moment's consideration, he moved it back to where it had been. He showed no sign of knowing she was there.

"Are you sure you wouldn't like to go out for a wee while?" she asked eventually. "Aunty Patsy says your cousins'll be there for another hour or two. And then youse could all go to McDonald's. I'll give you the money."

He didn't raise his head. "Don't want to."

Despite her better judgement, she persisted: "But you've no reason to be doing that now. Didn't everyone say it was grand on Sunday?"

"That was last Sunday."

"So what's different?"

"This is for next Sunday."

"But isn't it only another wee procession?"

He looked up and his face darkened. "Don't call it that, Ma. They're commemorations."

"Oh, sorry, son." She paused and tried to get the language right. "I mean, why do you need to change your pictures about for another wee commemoration? Aren't they all commemorating the same wee army?"

The O'Gormans' next-door neighbour was on the phone when she heard screaming and the sounds of breaking china. "That nutter Marty's at it again," she told her daughter. "Shouting and breaking things. Why can't Maria just shut up instead of setting him off? If she's not careful he'll kill her one of these days."

Mrs. O'Gorman used the spare key Marty didn't know she had to sneak nervously into his bedroom. Although the taxi wouldn't be dropping him home till three, she could never shake off the terrible memory of the day he'd found her sitting on his bed when he'd been sent home early after he'd lost it badly with the special needs teacher. They wouldn't do that again without warning her, the head had promised, and since then she'd always had notice, but it would take only one mistake. It had taken weeks for her face to heal and for his wrist to mend that last time after he threw the laptop through the window. That had been a bit of a blessing, though, since he hadn't the strength to do any more wrecking.

She knew her need to check out his room every day seemed to be nearly as compulsive as one of his routines, but still, every morning at eleven, telling herself she shouldn't, she did. Somehow, there was comfort in being in his place with his things around her, without him there to get hysterical in case she touched something she shouldn't.

As usual, everything was in complete order. Like she sometimes said defensively to Patsy, she wasn't saying there weren't problems with Marty, but wasn't it a rare blessing to have a teenage boy who made his bed perfectly, hung up the clothes when she'd pressed them, coordinated his socks, kept his books and knickknacks neat, and didn't go out getting drunk or taking drugs or running after girls? She hadn't said "unlike your Conor," but they both knew that was what she meant. And neither had she said how much handsomer and cleverer Marty was than any of Patsy's three boys. Didn't the school say if he held it together he'd get some great exam results in maths and science?

The new version of the montage that had caused yesterday's trouble was in its place over Marty's wee shrine to his heroes. It was a miracle it hadn't been damaged along with everything else that had been within his reach. Mrs. O'Gorman shook her head. Poor lad. It wasn't his fault he had a syndrome. And now that she'd no wee treasures left, it didn't really matter that a few oul' mugs and plates got broke. Sure they were cheap to replace, so they were.

She took a closer look at the montage. All around the edges were the familiar photos of Patrick Pearse and James Connolly and the others who had signed that thing in Dublin in Easter 1916 saying we were free. What was it called? She caught sight of one of the mugs that hung beside her. Oh, yes, there were the same men beside a document with a big headline saying, *IRISH REPUBLIC*. The Proclamation, that's what it was. A dull-looking document she'd never read but she knew was like the Bible to Republicans. She should know what was in it, of course. Since Marty'd learned it off by heart he must have recited it to her a dozen times, but you couldn't really listen. Wasn't he always reciting?

The fellas who had signed it weren't much to look at, she thought. Not like that Big Lad, Michael Collins, swaggering in his uniform—now there was a fine figure of a man. Used to him being a constant, she was surprised to see him missing. In his usual place there was a skinny young lad in uniform with round specs she'd never seen before. And in the middle—in pride of place—there was just one of Marty's sketches, this time of a Celtic cross with white decorations; he'd written *Seamus Harvey* on one arm and *Gerard McGlynn* on the other. The names meant nothing to her, but she supposed they were two more young lads who'd died for Ireland. She recited her mantra—"Sure weren't they some poor mothers' sons"—and thought how lucky she was she'd never lost anyone that way. It was bad enough that she'd been widowed so early, but at least her husband had a peaceful end with that heart attack and he looked lovely in his coffin. Not the way he'd have been if he'd been shot or blown up or starved to death. Sure, Joe had done a spell in jail after he was caught with the guns, but it was a long time ago and being a community worker seemed to suit him. And though she was lonely for her Cormac since he'd gone to Canada, he was doing great and he was safe.

Had Marty bought anything new? She looked along the line of mugs with tricolours and Sinn Féin and IRA logos and slogans and saw a bright green one with a harp that said: *FENIANS*. It brought back the memory of that terrible scene after that eejit of a cousin of his gave him a red mug for Christmas that said . . . what was it exactly? Oh, yes: *I'm an unrepentant Fenian bastard.*

"I'm not, I'm not, I'm not a bastard!" Marty had screamed. "My ma was married to my da. Look at the photo on the sideboard." "Sure it's only a joke," wee Conor had babbled, but a minute later he was on the ground with Marty biting and kicking him, and she trying to pull him off. That had ended in A&E and it was only because they were cousins that the police weren't called.

Mrs. O'Gorman sighed, got up, smoothed the bedspread so there was no sign she'd been there, closed and locked the door, and got ready to go to the pound shop to buy new tea cups.

Marty had been ready an hour early, his trainers spotless and his jeans as creaseless as his new black T-shirt, which bore the legend, *IRA Undefeated Army*. When his uncle arrived, he was proudly shown the montage, which he viewed with apparent enthusiasm. Privately, he had misgivings. Why had Mick Collins been replaced with Liam Lynch? The war of independence would never have been won without Mick, and whatever you thought about the rights and wrongs of the treaty, Liam Lynch was an intransigent diehard who hadn't done the country many favours.

Marty's anxieties had ebbed on the journey to Castlederg. Uncle Joe had been on time, there wasn't any mess in the car, the case containing the montage fitted neatly in the boot, he could see from the instrument panel that there was plenty of petrol and oil, the speed limit was adhered to strictly, and the traffic was so light that he nearly stopped worrying they might be late. He'd never been on such a long journey before, but the doctor had said he'd be okay if he took his medication. And he'd consulted Google Earth as well as his uncle, knew exactly the route they would take, what the village looked like, and where they'd be parking.

All the commemorations he'd been to before were in Belfast, so this was very different. He'd read online that the Prods didn't want it. He couldn't understand why. "It's a mystery to me, Uncle Joe."

As Joe O'Gorman knew all too well and was constantly tormented about, an awful lot of life was a mystery to Marty, and most mysteries couldn't be explained to him. "You see, Uncle Joe, Seamus and Gerard weren't trying to bomb Castlederg. The customs post they were targeting was three miles away. " Having no sympathy anyway for those he considered Unionist cunts, O'Gorman wasn't going to embark on the hopeless task of trying to explain to his nephew why the Protestant inhabitants of Castlederg—who had had a fair few fatalities in the past—might feel annoyed by an IRA commemoration, even of an event from three decades ago. He switched off as Marty began to recite detailed statistics about the frequency of Unionist parades and changing demographics in Castlederg. "So the Prods have parades all the time, Uncle Joe. So can't they see it's fair we should have some too?"

"They're different, son."

Marty's face puckered. "I keep telling you I'm not your son, Uncle Joe. I'm your nephew."

As he saw the anxiety in the boy's big green eyes, O'Gorman cursed his own absentmindedness. Would he never learn to avoid the most obvious pitfalls? "Sorry, Marty. It's just that I love you as much as I would if you were my son." And, hastily, "Now what else have you learned about Castlederg and County Tyrone?"

As they drove into the village, Marty had almost finished reciting the dozens of names of Tyrone volunteers and dates of their deaths. O'Gorman parked, waited until he finished, and applauded.

"Do you think they'll play the ballad?" asked Marty.

"What ballad?"

"'The Ballad of Seamus Harvey and Gerard McGlynn.'"

"I never even heard of it."

"It's on YouTube. I've learned it. Can I sing it to you?"

O'Gorman listened patiently to Marty's quavering rendition of what seemed like a tuneless dirge. "Very nice," he said.

"The song said they died trying to free our country, Uncle Joe. That was a long time ago. Why isn't our country free yet?"

"We'll talk about that afterward, Marty. Now we should get going or we'll be late joining the procession."

A few months later, after another outing with his nephew, O'Gorman sat up in bed one morning. "I wish to God wee Marty had never got interested in Republicanism. It doesn't suit people with literal minds when we're at peace."

Paddy McCarthy turned over lazily. "Okay, tell me. Was there an outburst?"

"No. He's getting better in a lot of ways. For instance, he's learned many of the tunes the bands play, so the familiarity helps him deal with the noise and the drumming. And if I'm there, he's okay with crowds. And though he gets upset that people aren't properly dressed or don't walk in time to the music, he doesn't shout at them."

"If that's what he wants, Joe, maybe he should become an Orangeman."

O'Gorman's playful cuff took both their minds off the subject, which they returned to much later, over a couple of pints in a discreet corner of the local pub.

"So there were no disasters, but he's getting fanatical, and I blame myself for getting him involved in the first place."

"Why did you?"

O'Gorman took a reflective swig of Guinness. "I wanted to spend more time with him. The job takes me to lots of these events, and he could come with me. The lad is too much alone."

"You're very close for an uncle and nephew."

"I was always fond of the wee lad, but when my brother was dying, I promised him I'd do my best to be a father to him."

McCarthy picked his words carefully. "He's a bit of a handful, though. Must be tough."

"He's that and all, but you couldn't but love him. And he's the nearest I'll ever have to a son."

McCarthy checked there was no one within earshot. "You're not planning on doing an Elton John, then? No surrogate mother to provide Joe O'Gorman with a kid?"

"Jaysus, Paddy, the lads would stone me to death. That's if their mammies didn't get there first."

"So your Marty doesn't know about you."

"Not him, not his ma, not his aunt. And I'm not planning on coming out soon. Not that it's my biggest worry. What's really bugging me is that the wee fecker seems to be turning into a dissident."

"How do you mean?"

"He's getting hung up on Irish freedom. He keeps asking why the IRA stopped before we got it."

McCarthy yawned. "You know I've no interest in this stuff, Joe. It's just history to me. I don't care what you did twenty years ago. I don't even care what you believe." He left the table and went to the bar. After he had come back with the pints and sat down he looked at O'Gorman. "You're upset, aren't you?"

"Worried."

"Because he's going on about Irish freedom. Isn't that what your crowd have always gone on about? What's different?"

"He's wearing a T-shirt that says, *Britain Out of Ireland*. He got that off a dissident website."

McCarthy shook his head. "But isn't Brits out what you want?"

"They believe in achieving that through armed struggle. We want it to happen through the ballot box."

"So they're doing what you used to do."

"Yes, but circumstances have changed. We're in government and they're messing things up."

"Is that what you told him?"

"No, of course not. I said those people died for equality and that's what we've got."

McCarthy leaned over and patted O'Gorman's hand. "Look, Joe, as I said, I've no interest in this stuff, but even I know that's bullshit. Youse spent decades going on about a United Ireland and now youse pretend it was all about having road signs in Irish. Am I right?"

O'Gorman lowered his voice. "Yes and no. We were tired, we had lost, and we had to pretend we'd won. And I for one am grateful as it got me out of jail after three instead of ten years. But Marty's been reading about Irish history since 1916 and he's on the side of the ones who never compromised."

"Is it a good idea to take him to commemorations then? Aren't they mostly of people who died fighting?"

"How can I stop now? It would break his heart."

McCarthy shrugged. "You're stuck then. You'll have to hope he discovers girls. Or boys. Now for God's sake, lighten up and let's talk about where we'll go on holiday. I'd say Tel Aviv, but from what I've seen about how Sinn Féin view Israel, it'd probably have you court-martialled. Is Barcelona more like it?"

Mrs. O'Gorman was delighted to see her brother-in-law. "I was just passing, Maria, and wondered if there'd be time for a cup of tea and a yarn."

When they had settled at the kitchen table and caught up

on general family news, there was a brief silence. Then he said, "And Marty?"

"Doing well at school, but he spends most of his free time upstairs at the computer so I don't see much of him."

"Have you any idea what he looks at, Maria?"

"How would I know? He wouldn't tell me. And anyway, he doesn't want anyone to know. There was a scene when Conor was over last week and wanted to look something up. Marty said his computer was his private property and no one must ever touch it." She smiled. "It was so good of you to buy it for him. You're too generous. That boy worships you, you know."

Depression settled on O'Gorman. "I'd prefer if he'd have more to do with people his own age than an oul' fella like me."

"Go on with you, Joe. Aren't you a fine man and wouldn't any woman be proud to have you? Time you found one and settled down and reared your own children."

"I'm a bit busy for that at the minute."

"So you'll be picking Marty up on Sunday again? Where are youse off to this time?"

"Just Ardoyne."

"It's for another wee lad, isn't it? Marty's got a new photo of a lad in a leather jacket."

"That'll be Thomas Begley. Remember the Shankill Road fish shop twenty years ago? His bomb went off early."

Mrs. O'Gorman crossed herself. "God have mercy on their souls. There were a lot of them, weren't there?"

"Bootsy Begley and nine others."

"Some mothers' children" she said automatically. "Well, I hope the weather keeps fine for youse."

"I've got to give all this up, Paddy. It's not just that I can't get through to Marty but I'm wondering myself if there was any point to all that dying for Ireland. What did we achieve?"

Paddy McCarthy threw his arm around O'Gorman. "Living for it's certainly a lot more fun."

"Marty wouldn't agree. All the way back he was reciting what was on the plaque. Ending with: *It takes courage and devotion to your people to take the hard road to freedom.* A quote from Seamus Twomey."

"Never heard of him."

"He was a hard bastard, so he was. Did terrible things when he ran the Belfast Brigade. But Marty thinks he was great. *He wouldn't have sold out,* he said."

"So he really does agree with those dissidents."

"He won't let me use the word. Says they're the people who've kept the faith and it's Sinn Féin who are the dissidents. He had some long quote from Patrick Pearse about how you should never compromise."

"Doesn't sound good, Joe. Are you afraid he'll join up with those gutties?"

"I'd say he's too odd for them to take on. He's no team player. That poor lad Begley was a bit simple, but he'd have followed orders all right. Anyway, it's my hope they wouldn't have him. But I've tipped off a few of the lads I can trust to keep an eye out for him hanging round with anyone suspicious."

Marty had intensified his researches into his band of heroes and had identified Bobby Sands as the greatest of them. He had long been familiar with the huge portrait of him on the side of the Sinn Féin shop on the Falls Road, and had absorbed the accompanying quote: "Everyone, Republican or otherwise, has their own particular part to play. No part is too great or too small, no one is too old or too young to do something."

Having read a lot about Sands on the dissident websites,

Marty had come to the definite conclusion that Sands hadn't died for Sinn Féin to be governing a part of the United Kingdom.

"We must see our present fight through to the very end," he had said, and for Marty that meant a united Ireland. He cried out in anger and frustration when he read Sinn Féin leaders saying the war was over. How could it be? How could they betray Bobby like that?

Gradually, Marty came to realise that the part he must play was to target members of the apostate Sinn Féin party. His inspiration was Thomas Begley, who had intended to eradicate the leaders of the Catholic-killing Ulster Defence Association that Saturday afternoon. He'd had bad information—which was why he'd got civilians instead—but Marty was doing his own briefing. He identified a forthcoming commemoration in the Milltown graveyard that was guaranteed to have at least one member of parliament and three members of the assembly. And with the help of his pocket money from Uncle Joe and instructions from the Internet, he had the materials and the know-how to build a bomb and the rucksack to put it in. On a long canvas he had carefully written out and illustrated Pearse's line, "Life springs from death; and from the graves of patriot men and women spring living nations," which was now decorating the top of the wall facing his bed and which he looked at last thing before he switched off the light. *I'm going to die for Ireland*, he would tell himself in the watches of the night. *And my name will live forever.*

Marty knew that Uncle Joe disagreed with him, but he didn't want him hurt so he rang him to say he had too much homework to do that Sunday and couldn't go, and Uncle Joe said that was fine by him as he'd a sick friend he urgently needed to visit.

"Great news on two counts," O'Gorman said to McCarthy. "Marty's putting school work ahead of freeing Ireland—which gives me hope he's cooling a bit—and we can have a lazy Sunday together after all."

Marty left the house while his mother was at Mass and joined the parade as close to the front as he could get. He felt vulnerable on his own, but he wore his headphones, which helped him block out disturbing sounds. He was halfway to Milltown when his mother rang her brother-in-law to say she'd come home to an empty house and to ask if Marty was with him.

"No. Wasn't he doing homework? Maybe he's gone to the library."

"It's not open on Sunday."

"Or the shops?"

"He won't go to the shops except on a Thursday."

"Is he not answering his phone?"

"It's in his bedroom. And Joe, he didn't lock it. That never happens."

"I'm sure he's just gone for a walk. He's a big boy, Maria. Don't worry, he'll be back soon."

O'Gorman wandered to the kitchen window and tried to think what would make his nephew behave so out of character. "I don't like it, Paddy. When Marty says he's going to do his homework, homework is what he does."

"You're fussing," said McCarthy. "Get on with your breakfast. That plateful was fried with love and it doesn't deserve to get cold."

Ten minutes later, though, O'Gorman stopped eating. "I can't relax, Paddy. Just let me call a couple of the lads in case he decided to go to Milltown." A couple of phone calls later, he stood up from the table. "Sorry, Paddy. I don't get it, but Marty's been sighted in the crowd walking toward Milltown. I've got to go after him."

"When you're halfway through brunch? Why?"

"Because he's never done this before alone and he could get into a terrible state."

"There's got to be a first time, Joe. Maybe the lad wants a bit of independence."

"Maybe he does, and if he looks okay I'll keep my distance. But I can't take the risk something'll happen and he'll get into a row and do someone harm. Jesus, Paddy, prison would kill him." He grabbed his coat, muttered apologies, and ran for his car.

When crowds blocked the road, O'Gorman parked hastily and began trying to push his way through. Helped by another couple of calls, he knew Marty was now at the front, in the centre of the line just after the leading bands. He didn't sight him until the Tannoy was relaying speeches. It was seeing Marty wearing a beret that turned O'Gorman's worry into fear. "Do you have to be a volunteer to wear a beret, Uncle Joe?" was a question that the boy had asked only a few weeks back. The rucksack was unsettling. What could be in that? He thought of all Marty's chatter about the Begley bomb and he fought panic.

He was almost within arm's reach of his nephew when Marty jumped the wall that protected the dignitaries. As O'Gorman scrambled after him, his sister-in-law, her hand clasped to her mouth, was trying to grasp the implications of a montage that now had at its centre a photograph of Marty, wearing a black beret with a green, white, and orange badge that said, *Free Ireland*, and a smile of pure happiness.

PART II

CITY OF WALLS

LIGATURE
BY GERARD BRENNAN
Hydebank

I can't breathe.

Too many people here, sucking up the air. We're on top of one another wherever we go. Even the library seems full today. There's a buzz among the inmates and I can hear somebody crying. I follow the sobbing to the corner nearest the librarian's counter; away from all the rest of them. It's one of the girls, like me. She's not my friend or anything, but we've seen each other outside the counsellor's office now and again. Both of us are having trouble adjusting. We don't usually talk, me and this girl, but I think we could understand each other if we did.

"Hey. Hey you."

She snuffles, watery and loud. I feel bad because she disgusts me.

"Dry your eyes a second, will you? What's happening?"

The crying girl answers, her voice far too loud for the library: "A boy. There's a wee boy dead over on the young offenders side. Hung himself, so he did."

I know the word should be *hanged*. Meat's hung, people are hanged. My ma told me that one time, before she left us. I don't correct the crying girl, though. She's too loud and I know she'll get us in trouble, but I want to hear everything before they make her pipe down.

"He used a ligature," she says. "What's a ligature?"

I wrap the cord of my trackie bottoms around my index finger. "Just anything, really."

"I can't hear you," she says. "Speak up."

I spy a screw coming up behind her. One of the big, dour male ones who reminds me of the Bible-thumpers who used to hang around Corn Market waving signs with aborted babies on them, scaring the life out of you. Something about his eyes, maybe. One time I nearly told him that I didn't want a fucking abortion anyway. He gives most of the girls the creeps. I turn away to show him I'm not involved in the disturbance.

"You know, don't you?" Yappy-hole asks again. She just won't let it go. "What's a ligature?"

"It's nothing," I hiss. "Look, just shut it!"

I don't watch as the crying girl is led off by the big Bible-thumping creep, no doubt for a lecture where he'll tell her that abortions are wrong and that she needs to do something about her leaky lamps before somebody hits her a punch in them.

Or, he might be telling her just to chill out.

Everybody needs to chill out.

Especially on the boys' side.

Another one of them dead, like.

Doesn't seem that long ago since that first wee boy killed himself over there. It must be crazy on their side. They're all wee teenagers without an ounce of sense.

Sometimes they shout at us through the fence. It doesn't bother me as much as it bothers some of the others. I know what wee lads can be like, especially when there's a pack of them. Street-corner craic, like. But the eejits who work here take it all so serious. They say they have a duty of care, but they only care about themselves. Cover their own backs first, then tell us what's good for us.

Our side of the fence is for women, but we call ourselves *the girls*. Most of us are only out of our teens, like. They're the boys, we're the girls. And at their age the boys are all gagging for it. Sex. Attention. Love. All of that shite.

My head's filling up with too many thoughts.

I need to *move*. Do something.

So I take a dander to the common room. Don't even know why I went to the library now. The librarian doesn't have much time for me and I never liked books anyway. But then, when I get to the common room, I don't know why the fuck I came here either.

All the usual cliques are in place.

And I don't like the way that one bitch is staring at me.

"What's your fucking problem?"

It's out before I can prevent it. Too quick with the aggro.

I'm going to get in trouble again. Always being taught lessons, never learning them. At least it isn't a screw this time. It's the pretty blonde. Helen. She came in here last month and made friends with everybody. I don't know how she did it. It was like a magic trick or something. All of a sudden the loud girls wanted to talk to her. They never spoke to me before then, so it's not like I lost friends or anything, but I'm still annoyed about it.

"What's your problem?" I say it louder this time.

Helen wears "going out" makeup every day. That's the last thing any of us should be thinking about here. It's like she can't admit to herself that she's going nowhere. She probably thinks she's better than the rest of us.

The stuck-up bitch looks at me and touches her earlobe with her middle finger. Jangles a long earring. Can she not bloody hear me? Is that what that's supposed to mean? Or is she giving me a sneaky finger?

My palms are sore. I should have cut my nails last night. How am I supposed to swing a decent dig when my nails are so long? I could scratch her.

But I should probably just calm the fuck down.

In through the nose, out through the mouth.

Like the counsellor taught me. Silly bitch.

Blondie's smiling at me now. Looking me right in the eye. There's them other girls behind her, but they're creeping backward like shadows retreating from the sun; leaving the bitch to fight alone. And I'm white hot, ready to turn her to ashes.

"You girls all right in here?"

It's the big SO. I didn't know she was behind me. Like a lot of heavy women, she's very light on her feet. Dainty. I'm not going to look at her. She has a mean stare. Mean little black bead eyes. She didn't like it when I told her I hated the way she looked at me that time. Hate's a strong word, apparently. But that's fine. I'm no wee weakling, like.

"What's happening, Jo?"

She's pretending to be nice, but I'm not falling for it. I know I got her in trouble at the last landing meeting because I complained that she was smoking where we weren't allowed to. It doesn't matter that it was outside. If the staff can smoke anywhere then we should be able to as well. I didn't want them to stop the big SO from smoking outside, like. It would have been fine with me if we could all smoke in the same place at the same time. The principal officer agreed with me and said it was double standards.

"Jo!"

The SO's getting closer to me and Helen's sort of smiling like something bad is going to happen.

I won't turn around. They can't make me. Nobody can. Not even—

A hand on my shoulder.

I shrug it off like I don't care. The SO shouldn't touch me if I haven't done anything wrong. That's not fair. That might be a double standard too. *I do fucking care*, but you can't ever let on. That gets you in trouble. Blondes get you in trouble too. I remember my daddy said that once and I didn't understand it then. It makes a bit of sense now.

"She's nuts," Helen spoke first. I should be okay now. If she started it, I can't get in trouble.

I'm going to point at her and say: *You can't let her talk to me like—*
The SO's holding my wrist.

"Ow. That's my sore arm."

I peel back my sleeve and the SO flinches.

A wee part of me cheers, but only on the inside.

"Ach, Jo, you didn't? Not again, love."

"I told you she was nuts. Didn't I tell you?" Helen says, and looks at all the loud girls for confirmation. They're quiet now, though. Keeping their heads down. Another wee win for me. I'm clocking them up today, so I am.

"You look like a pigeon on the footpath, Blondie."

She doesn't understand what I mean, but she *does* look like that. Her head's all bobbing about like she's looking for a dropped pasty that an oul' drunk eejit couldn't hold onto. God, I'd kill for a pasty bap from our chippie. Anything from the outside, from Belfast.

Somebody's sniggering now. I hate that kind of laugh. It's sneaky and mean and for bullies. Best way to take care of bullies is to slap them. They're never expecting that. I spin around like Mickey Marley's Roundabout on Royal Avenue. If I catch the bully sniggering at me they're dead.

As soon as I know who I'm supposed to hurt I'll hurt them and then I can stop hurting myself. Easy.

But it's just the SO there, and mean as she is, she never sniggers. I hold up my hands to show her I'm sorry. The SO knocks them to the side.

"Don't touch me!"

"Settle down, Jo."

"I wasn't doing nothing."

The sniggering's behind me again. It was Helen. She threw her voice over my head the first time. Fucking bitch. I never liked playing piggy-in-the-middle. They made me be the pig every time. My eyes are hurting and it's like crying in the playground again. Somebody sniggered that day too.

God, I'm so sick of it. So sick of all this bullshit.

I'm done with it.

Helen. That fucking blonde bitch!

Now she's crying. Blondie's crying. No, worse . . . she's screaming.

Everybody's screaming now, except for me. But even though all of this is hurting my arms it's the good kind of hurt. Like when a blister gets ready to pop and you feel the sting and the nice at the same time.

I don't even care anymore that my nails are too long.

I feel them tearing something.

Clothes, skin, mine, hers, theirs . . . it doesn't matter.

More hands clamp my arms and legs. They heave me up into the air. More blisters pop and old scars split. I'm lighter than a feather now. That's another good feeling. It never lasts, though. I remember one time when my da let me stay home from school even though I wasn't really sick. I had to lie in bed because he thought I might be faking. That was okay with me. Bored in bed was better than bored in school. And he changed the blankets when I was still laying there, his mouth all straight because he was pretending to be hard, but his eyes were soft like the sheet floating down on me. Nice to have that feeling back again. I never feel like that anymore.

They throw me into the cell and I hear that *clunk-click* that makes me want to pee. You can't pee in the cell, but I can get out for a toilet break in an hour, I think. I'm not sure what time it is now. I don't want to look. That way I can pretend that it's not really a whole hour. And they'll maybe let me have a light for my fags then as well. If I'm really good, like. I'll try to be good. It can be hard when you're in the cell. Even if you have magazines and you can lie down and be bored in bed. It's not like it used to be. You can't catch that floaty-down sheet feeling.

Where's my blade?

I think there's still one left. One that I snuck in from the kitchen and hid very safe. There's not many places to hide things in these cells and they check them sometimes and you can get in trouble when they find stuff, but I'm sure they haven't got . . .

Sweet. It's there. But I'm not going to use it. Not yet. I put it back. They'll probably check on me soon.

I'll spend a bit of time at the window.

My cell looks out onto the road and I can see lorries and cars going to Purdysburn one way and down to Lisburn the other. They never speed, though. It's boring to watch cars drive slow, but what else am I going to do? I lost my TV privileges. Sometimes it's fun to think about me out there in the car. I go faster than them all. Whip up the handbrake and get the dizzy feeling with my heart in my mouth and my throat tightens to keep the food down and I'm free as fuck and flying off my head and I'm okay. Aye, I'm okay. The last time, the time I had to take some poor bastard's car to get away from the bad thoughts, the stinking cops ran me off the road. The bad thoughts came back.

It was one of those weekends: smoking, drinking, pill-popping. House parties all over Belfast, in streets I didn't really know. Areas I shouldn't have been. Started off with a gang of friends. That's the big rule for a party girl: never go anywhere alone. But

I dozed off when it was dark and woke up when it was bright. On my own. Which is a funny way to feel. There *were* other people there, just no one I knew.

It was near the river. New. Small. Not much bigger than this cell. Somebody had called it an apartment. Most of the others laughed.

"It's a fuckin' flat, mate. Where do you think you're from?"

Even the guy who'd said *apartment* laughed at that.

When I figured out how to get out of the building I couldn't even tell if I'd ended up in a Catholic or Protestant area. No flags or painted kerbs. No murals. Not even the graffiti gave you a clue. The writing on the wall was about things called *regeneration* and *fracking*. I didn't know what those words meant, but somebody with a spray can thought they were bad.

For a while I thought maybe I'd ended up in South Belfast—it's all a bit different where the money is—but I was only a five-minute shuffle from the city centre. Passed a wee dark-skinned man playing a weird-looking thing like a violin. He smiled at me, but I'd no money for his hat. Only thing in my pocket was a phone with no credit and a flat battery. I wondered if the wee violin-trumpet player had thought of taking some of his teeth to the Cash for Gold across the street.

"Watch out for the pink buses, mate. They don't slow down," I said.

He laughed at me, just. Fine. Let him find out the hard way, then.

With gold on my mind, I checked to see if my Claddagh pendant was on show. Almost tucked it under my T-shirt but thought, *Fuck it*. Once upon a time you'd get shot here for wearing the wrong football jersey. According to my uncles, anyway. But here, the way I was feeling, getting shot might have been an improvement.

If they'd all just left me alone, I'd have felt better in a bit.

But they never leave you alone.

Security guards followed me around CastleCourt Shopping Centre. I was only trying to cut through to get to the black taxi rank, but I didn't want them to think they'd chased me out. I went into the jewellery shop and wound up the girls behind the counter instead. Not everything's locked behind a glass door like it used to be. You can actually pick up some of the wee ornaments and clocks now. They really have to watch you since they got the place done up, and they're not shy about it either.

"You all right there, miss?"

"Can I help you, miss?"

"Are you sure you're all right there, miss?"

Miss. In the shops around my way they'd say, "How's you, love?" Even if they knew my name. Love is warm. These cold bitches with their good jobs and fancy clothes have no manners. I got my fingerprints all over the crystal until the security guards started shouting. They scared me, but I shouted back to hide it. That made them show their teeth like monsters in the dark. All I could see were fangs and no faces.

It was too much.

I ran out the side door to get a taxi. When I got to the depot there were so many people and they were all looking at me because my face was beetroot red and my chest was heaving up and down. The Claddagh pendant bounced with each breath. I should have felt safe, this was the Catholic taxi rank. The Prods go to North Street. But I didn't see any friendly faces there. Everybody looked at me with squinty eyes.

One party I went to, this lad I like was spoofing about the time he stole himself a black taxi and had a joyride around Divis. None of us believed him. The taxi drivers are tough as shite and keep hammers under their seats.

"For repairs," they'd say. "If the peelers are asking."

My cousin's a handyman and he reckons that you can't get arrested for having a hammer in your car if you've got screwdrivers and all as well, but sure, even screwdrivers are weapons. So a black taxi man can put holes in your head if you try and cheat him out of a quid and some shrapnel. But if I had one wee screwdriver in my pocket and got scooped, I'd be in some serious shite.

Double standard.

I didn't care about hammers and screwdrivers there and then, though. I knew a place up the road where I could get some Indian diazepam. They're not as good as the prescription ones, but you get more for less, like, and I only had that emergency fiver tucked into my shoe. Plenty to sort out my paranoia, if I could save on the taxi fare. Only, I was done with walking.

It'd be suicide to *take* a taxi the way the spoofer tried to tell us he did, but the oul' doll putting her shopping in the boot of her red Corsa looked distracted. You're not meant to park outside Iceland, even if you have a disabled badge. Maybe that's why she had the engine running. Or maybe she knew the black taxi men would start a war with the NCP parking attendants if one of them tried to give her a ticket. Either way, I always wanted a red car and this one was right there waiting for me. I just had to move fast and never stop.

It was a bad idea. Completely fucking stupid. I know that now. Knew it before the peelers forced me off the road and into the big blue fence outside the Royal, like. The firemen didn't get to use the jaws of life. One of the cops helped me out of the driver's window. He said I was some driver, and I think he meant it. But when I told him I couldn't remember getting that far up the road his eyes near closed. Told me I should have saved it for the racetrack.

Aye, dead on. See me at a racetrack. Sure I'd have to steal another car to get there.

I never got my diazepam. They led me through rooms, stations, and courts without anything to take the edge off. Had to beg for fags and tea, like. They said no to everything else, even paracetamol.

Then I ended up here with a list of offences as long as one scarred arm.

Every time I get lost in my wee daydream I have to wake up and realise that I'm still here. In my cell with no TV and only that barred hole in the wall that shows me what I don't have and how many other people are wasting it.

I miss my kids.

Where the fuck is the guard with my lighter? It's been—

No. I'm not going to look at the time.

It's definitely been more than an hour, though.

I wrap the cord from my trackie bottoms around my finger. Pull it tight.

Nobody looks in on me. They're supposed to make sure I'm okay. It's in the PAR1 form. Not doing their job.

The tip of my finger's gone purple. I unwind the cord and there's a rush in there that feels nice. Maybe that's what the boy was after today. He didn't mean to die, did he? They're only wee youngsters over there. Second one in a few months, like, but I can't believe he wanted to *die*.

Although . . .

The cord is around my neck now.

Tied to the door handle. That's the way to do it.

All I have to do is sit down. If I'm meant to, I'll be able to get back up and I'll feel that nice feeling in my head. Maybe it'll flush out some of the bad. And if I'm not meant to get up, sure

I can find the boy who just died. Ask him why he wanted to die. It's interesting, you see.

Well, I think it's interesting.

I can't breathe.

BELFAST PUNK REP

BY GLENN PATTERSON

Ann Street

Milky couldn't keep his mouth shut, that was the story, he was down on his knees in the subway, sucking this fella off, some big ugly fucker, which was somehow the point, and the fella was moaning and getting on, grabbing Milky's hand, trying to get him to squeeze his balls, and Milky couldn't help it, he went and laughed just as the fella came, and, well, whatever it was you called him before that, Milky was Milky from that moment on.

That was the story. Could have been Milky himself started it. He really couldn't keep his mouth shut.

I was writing this piece for one of the Sundays, premillennium, "Inflammable Material Planted in My Head: How Punk Nearly Saved Belfast from the '80s." I was back for a week from England staying with my father—a whole other story that—calling in to the latest incarnation of Good Vibrations, which is to say the one before the one before the one before the current one, talking to Terri, arranging interviews with guys who had been in bands and now oversaw Radio Ulster's daytime output. Nobody I asked there or in the bars where I spent my evenings—Lavery's, Pat's, The Rotterdam—seemed to remember Milky, and yet what he did in the subway had, to me, been the definition of punk.

This was one ugly, ugly fucker whose dick he was sucking. To-the-rotten-core ugly. The sort of ugly-to-the-rotten-core fucker who thought he would never in a million years be moaning and groaning in a subway while the likes of Milky sucked him off.

How could you not laugh?

Milky never did wash the jumper he had been wearing that night. Mohair. You can imagine. There was blood on it too. The ugly fucker had hit him a dig in the bake the moment he'd put his dick away. Took a front tooth clean out. Milky found it in among the fag butts and beer cans and pissy-smelling litter. He took it round to a fella he knew off the Ormeau Road and had it made into an earring, which he stroked when he was thinking, those odd times when he thought before he said or did anything.

It occurred to me, halfway through the week, I was maybe looking for him in the wrong places. The music had never really been Milky's thing as much as what the music unlocked. He would be a civil servant now, or a traffic warden, or a yoga teacher.

Finally, on my last day, last night, someone sidled up to me in the back room of Pat's. I hear you were looking for wee Milky? Used to hang about the subway?

The subway was where I had first met him. It ran from the town-side of a clapped-out street to the docks-side. There was a cop shop on the docks-side, cop fort, though fuck all use that was to anyone who wasn't actually in it, all they were interested in in those days was things coming over the wall, or through the wall. The subway was too far away for anything to come under the wall from that direction, so the cops left it alone.

You could get yourself a digging down in the subway or you could get yourself a ride: punishment or reward. You had to risk one for a chance of the other. It was organised religion given concrete form. And striplighted. Milky, of course, was in his element. Sometimes he got both on the same night, sometimes he got the same thing twice.

That's right, I said. Have you seen him around at all?

You mean you didn't hear? He's inside.

What for? I laughed. Being Milky?

Seriously, you didn't hear?

No.

Ahhh, well then . . .

What?

He clapped my back. You're the big journalist fella. (There are no wee journalists in Belfast, or even many precisely to scale. We're big, to a man and woman I would say, only it's always—clap on the back, tight smile—*fella*.)

I told the editor when I got back to London that I needed to make one more trip across.

Oh no, not on our expenses you don't, he said.

I knew better than to ask, I said.

And I knew better than to ask my father. (Some day I'll tell that one. Some day.)

I sent a letter care of HM Prison Maghaberry.

You probably won't remember me, but I'm writing this piece, would you mind if I visited?

He sent a letter back. It looked like he had got a child to write it for him. He remembered me all right, so, sure, why not?

January had leeched into February. As I waited in the visitors' centre for the bus to take me to the prison, I flipped through an old fanzine someone had sent me after the last trip. Belfast looking like another planet. Dystopia. Someone in the background of a crowd shot looking a bit like Milky.

You know you'll not be allowed to take that in with you, one of the other visitors said to me. That picture on the front.

It was a montage of a cop with a plastic-bullet gun and some woman's bare arse pointing at it. At least I think it was the arse doing the pointing.

They'll not like that.

I put it back in its clear plastic Ziploc.

The bus came, drove us the quarter-mile to the security hut where we were turned inside out old-school fashion. I kept the fanzine under my arm, front cover toward me. One of the guards held out his hand for it. He held the Ziploc between his forefinger and thumb up toward the ceiling light.

I don't think so, sunshine, he said. His mate smirked and shook his head.

Milky got to his feet as I came in, last. His hair was flat, thinning a little. Like I could talk: bald before I was thirty. He shook my hand. He had a dotted line tattooed round his right wrist—*CUT HERE*—the letters R, E, P inexpertly inked on the knuckles of his left hand. The earring had gone.

You're not who I was thinking you were at all, he said.

No, I said, I'm always being mistaken for him.

He was looking at the cigarette box I had set on the table. B&H. It was what we all smoked then, or No 6 if we were skint.

I didn't know if you were still on them, I said.

He rolled his eyes. Sat forward and took one out, like he was doing me a favour, cutting short my embarrassment.

He was halfway down it—the smoke a helmet round his head—before he spoke. What is it you want to know?

What happened?

Did nobody tell you? That big sloppy bake of his, minus more than the one tooth now.

What happened? Punk died.

Milky took the bereavement hard. I mean, there were wee cunts running about still with two-foot Mohicans, crusties all round Botanic strangling whippets with bits of old string, but the thing was over, gone.

The bunch of people he'd shared a house with fucked off to university, all seven of them: sociology, all seven. (I didn't let on I'd fucked off and done it too.) If they had told him at the start they were only having a holiday he'd have found somewhere else. He heard of a room going in a house in the Holy Lands, but by the time he got there it was taken. The girl who answered the door took pity on him and let him sleep in the bath. That went on for six or seven months until one of the other girls in the house got a new boyfriend who said there was no fucking way he was having some fella lying there watching her walking in and out of the bathroom in her bra and knickers.

Wise up, she said. He's a fruit.

It was news to Milky that he was anything.

Anyway, after that he hung around that part of town every night until he found a house with a party (it was the Holy Lands, there was always a house with a party) and went in and drank their drink and passed out on the floor.

This one night he picked up a Yale key from the floor and put it in his pocket and went back with it a couple of nights later and there was nobody in so he helped himself to a few things and never heard anything about it so then he did it anytime he went to a party house.

The first time he wound up in court, the lawyer described him as a crepuscular character: his own lawyer, that is. A crepuscular character whose predilections he was sure few in the courtroom would share. On this particular occasion, however . . .

Crepuscular? I said.

Milky made a fist of his left hand and held it out to me, thumb sticking out at a right angle. There was a C on the pad. Not R, E, P, then: CREP.

I had those four done before I realised I wasn't going to have enough fingers for the rest of the letters.

He turned the hand toward his face as though one or the other belonged to somebody else. Off my fucking tits.

The ugly fucker from the subway turned up on the TV years later, telling everyone him and his ugly mates were going to stop doing what nobody had asked them to do in the first place and looking to be thanked for it. They were part of the solution now. The future. Tony Blair called him courageous.

At least, Milky was 99 percent certain it was him. He would know how to prove it, he said. Said it quite a lot, in fact. Him and his mouth. Him and his mouth and a mole your man was supposed to have. He had drawn a picture of it on the subway wall.

That's where the cops found him. (They weren't so worried about things coming over their wall anymore, even bothered occasionally to respond to 999 calls.)

Milky heard one of them say to an ambulance man, Jesus, they wiped the floor with the fucker.

Actually, it was the walls. Four fellas, one on each arm and leg, dragging him the length of the subway one way, dragging him the length of the subway again the other, grinding his face into the tiles.

Where? they were shouting at him. Where's that fucking graffiti, you cunt!

One of the spides who had used to give him grief in the subway had become a wine buddy. (And innocent grief too, it seemed now in comparison.) He told Milky about a mate of his who had been kneecapped one time for taking the wrong person's car. Worse than kneecapped: he had the whole eight joints done: knees, ankles, wrists, and elbows. Bastards had to stop in the middle of it to reload. One of them was eating a Yorkie bar.

The day they let him out of hospital he stole a car and in the middle of that night drove it to the door of the man who had given the order for him to be shot. He wedged one crutch against the horn and hopped off up the street on the other.

That was all you could do, show the fuckers you weren't beat.

Milky asked around—quietly, for once—and found out where the top man lived. He took the bus out and—holy fuck—let's just say he hadn't done too badly doing what he hadn't been asked to do all these years. Reminded Milky of when he was a kid (Milky was a kid once), a house—*mansion*, him and his brothers called it (Milky was a kid with brothers)—big orchard out the back. They used to take a tree each in apple season, climb up into it, and strip it from the inside.

There were three cars in the top man's drive, an Audi, a—actually, Milky had no idea what the second was, but like an Audi, and like an Audi expensive—and a Land Rover, or Range Rover, with a couple of guys sitting in it. They were too far away for him to see if they were two of the ones who had used his face as an eraser.

He took the bus up twice more before he worked out how to get in: a tree overhanging the railings at one end of the long garden. Whoever did the gardening needed sacked.

The fourth time he caught the bus it was night. The Land Rover or Range Rover was in the driveway again when he passed on the far side on the street, the two guys in it both, by the looks of them, asleep. Fifty yards up the road he doubled back and crossed to the other side. The tree was wee buns compared to the apple trees Milky had used to climb in and out of as a wee lad.

He let a couple of hours go by, time enough for his eyes to adjust, get the lie of the land. An extension ran right along the back of the house, about twenty feet away, flat roof, spotlight mounted on the wall above it. Milky chose a twig within easy reach: one hand to yank, one hand to muffle the snap. He wedged his back against the trunk and threw. It didn't have to be especially accurate to break the spotlight's beam. The guys from the Land Rover or Range Rover came round and thrashed about a bit below him in the garish light. As soon as they were gone Milky did it again. They came back again.

The third time they started saying maybe it was the light. They got a ladder, one of them climbed up. He took out the bulb, put it back in. Must be the wiring! he shouted down. We'll check it in the morning.

So when Milky climbed out of the tree and up there and the light came on, they moved so slowly that he had the bulb out before they arrived.

I told you it was the wiring.

Milky leaned across the table. You see, just because I act the prick, people think I'm stupid. I'm not stupid.

Not stupid, but tired all the same. He fell asleep up there. When he woke there were voices, far off. It was the middle of the morning. He could see someone down in the garden. He climbed off the roof and stood in the open doorway. Whoever was down there had no idea he was behind them. He walked inside. Black-and-white floor tiles, chrome. Like an abattoir. He took a bite of an apple he found in a crystal fruit bowl and spat it out. He picked up a little paring knife. He turned with it in his hand. There was a teenage boy standing there. Son, grandson, Milky couldn't have worked it out. His hair was bleached. He had a stud in his ear, another in his nose.

He looked at Milky a long moment. Who the fuck are you? I'm Milky.

The boy's lip curled. Well, you're fucking dead, he said.

I don't think so, Milky told me he said to him, then: It doesn't sound like much, does it, a paring knife?

I stopped writing, dropped the pencil in fact. I didn't pick it up.

Tell me you're spoofing.

He shook his head, reached for the cigarette box again.

I pulled it back out of his way. What were you thinking?

For a moment his forefinger and thumb went toward his ear, or to a point a front tooth's drop below it.

He had a nasty mouth on him, he said. Speaking to me like that.

I kept my hand on the cigarettes then pushed them back across the table.

Milky had his arms folded. His lips were drawn tight.

You can keep the rest of the box, I said.

You know, if yon boy ever gets out they'll kill him, the guard told me on my way back to reception. Safest place for him is in here, you know that, don't you?

His mate gave me back the fanzine in its Ziploc bag. My wee brother was a goth, he said.

Good for him, I replied.

He raised an eyebrow and the other guard told him there was no use bothering with some people.

I had a couple of hours still before getting my plane out of City Airport.

I got the taxi to drop me in town and went down to the subway. The useable city was spreading down toward the docks, or where the docks used to be. It was all trendy pubs and boutique hotels now. Soon they'd do something with this too, turn it into an arcade, a bar maybe.

I walked from one end of it to the other, three, four times, but there was twenty-odd years' worth of other shit scrawled and sprayed up there, even supposing Milky's story was true.

Even supposing.

THE RESERVOIR

BY IAN MCDONALD

Holywood

He wears the suit like a man who does not wear suits. It falls badly around him, ill-fitted, too short in the sleeve, too long in the leg, too low in the crotch, too tight around the thighs. A grey suit. A supermarket suit. An F&F suit. He is a short, thickset man, carrying weight on his upper belly, heart-attack fat, uncomfortable not just in the suit but in the skin beneath.

He slips into the church. The bride has processed. Every eye is on her. An usher cuts him off as he heads for the side aisle. Hand on his chest.

"What the fuck are you doing here?" Whispering, because you don't say *fuck* in church. Whispering, because you don't want the bride to look around.

"Come to see my daughter get wed. What else?"

"You're not coming in here."

"You going to try and stop me, and wreck her day?"

"If she sees you, her day's already wrecked."

"My Emma loves her da. Which is more than she ever did you, when she had that weekend with you when Ross was away at the Everton game."

The usher's mouth works like he's catching flies. Snatch an order of service, slide past. A wave of consternation moves down the church. Heads turn in each row he passes. Whispers. It's him. Can't be. It is. Fuck, aye, it is. In a suit. Where'd he come from? I thought he was gone for good. I thought he was in England. I thought he was in Spain, I thought he was dead.

But it's true. He's back. In a suit.

In the front row: Karen. She hears the whispers and he sees her freeze, knowing she has to look round, knowing what she will see if she does. Dreading that. Then she freezes, and so he can study her. The line of her jaw, the set of her cheekbones, the corners of her eyes, lifted and frozen with Botox. Good toxins, friendly poisons. The Botox battles the ultraviolet: her skin brown and crackled as parchment from the tanning salon. Still the Sunbed Queen of Lord Street. Still firm-skinned, firm-bodied. Still a toned bird. Pilates Monday, Body-pump Tuesday, Hot Yoga Wednesday, '80s Retro-Aerobics Thursday, Beach Body Friday, nails and hair with Lee Saturday, Sunday sweat out the Saturday hangover in the sauna. Saturday night was always going-out night on the road. To be so deeply into yourself; to be so knowledgeable and careful of every part of your body that you know what's right with it and what's wrong with it and what needs doing to it. He still can't understand that. There had been lads in jail deep, deep into gym, so obsessed with their bodies, and those of their gym buddies, it had almost been sexual. He could never understand that either.

That white suit shows off the tan. Skirt still way too short. And that ape Jim with her. He'd been that ape once. She went for a type. But he never had the neck tattoo. That's never classy. At least it's not a spiderweb. Psychos get the spiderweb.

Ape Jim is fast for an ape. Three fingers on his chest.

"Where the fuck do you think you're going?"

"Everybody asks me this. In here." The pew behind. "Don't you worry, I'm not going to show her up. I'm not going to embarrass her or anything. Mother of the bride? She's the important one here. Marriage'll be over in six months, but at least Karen'll have had her big day. So I'm not going to make a fuss. And I'm not going to tell her about how you killed Robbie Wright." With every word his voice had dropped. Now it was a whisper. "Everyone thought Andy Boyd did it. But it wasn't. It was you."

"You can't know that."

"Oh no, I can't. I forgot. I was in England or Spain. I even heard I was in Australia. That would've been good. Weirdest was Dubai. That's a good one. Dubai, or dead. But you killed him, Jim-bob. Smacked his skull open with a baseball bat for one hundred grams. It's a strong bone, the skull. Has to be. Saw that on *Discovery*. You need some force to crack a skull. Smash it like a pumpkin. You've been working out. No, I won't tell her. Has she told you about the quarter of a million?"

Now he slides up the polished wood bench behind Karen, leans over the front of the pew to whisper in her ear.

"Nice church. Good church. I'm glad she went for a proper church. Those modern ones, they look like a Lidl. And all they do is sing to those fucking ying-ching-ching guitars. This is good. Classy."

"What the fuck are you doing here?"

"Like I said, come to see my daughter get wed. I've already had a wee word with Jim. You didn't hang around."

"We all thought you were dead."

"Why would you think that? Most people thought I was in England. Anyway, I believe the legal limit to get someone declared dead is seven years. It's only been five. You're looking good, Karen. He's got a good one."

"I'm not going to apologise or make excuses."

"Of course not. You're a good-looking woman, Karen. Still got it. Still have needs; I understand that. I've always understood that. It never bothered me the way it would bother him. I wouldn't have minded that personal trainer. Jim, well, he mightn't be so understanding. Of your needs, and all that."

"Fuck you, you can't—"

"I did mention the money to him. I presume you told him. I mean, a quarter of a million, it's kind of hard to keep that hidden in an open, caring, trusting relationship. Buys a good wedding, though."

"I never had—"

"You did. You did. Don't lie. It's bad luck to lie on a wedding day. Actually, it's not, I just made that up. You never could lie to me. You know, I think maybe I made a big mistake mentioning the money to Jim. Oops. They're starting."

A chord. The congregation stands. A hymn. "Love Divine, All Loves Excelling." No one knows the tune or understands the words. They mumble through three verses. The singing at weddings is always shite.

No West End musical, no St. Peter's High Mass, is so tightly choreographed, so intensely scripted, as an East Belfast wedding. Recessional: Robbie Williams. "Angels." Jesus, he whispers. Guests file out: bride's side to the right, groom's to the left. He waits, admiring the flowers, a thing he has never done before and which convinces no one. It keeps him away from questions. When the place is empty, that's when he'll slip out, while the next act of wedding script is being performed. He can get away in the confusion of the photographs. But steps instead into a smoke break: Emma and her bridesmaids beside the church railing, smoking furtively. As if God sees, as if it is sin. They are careful to keep ash off their dresses and lit ends away from light veils and lace.

She sees him.

"Daddy."

She takes him aside. Ross looks over, she exchanges eyelines with him: *It's all right, I'll handle this.*

"Why didn't you say? Where were you? There's no dinner for you."

"I'm sorry, love. I was away. Somewhere . . . else. I wanted to see you. See you get married. See everyone."

"Why didn't you tell me? Facebook or something? Even just lift the phone."

"That's not so easy where I was."

"Were you inside again?"

"No. Nothing like that."

"At least be in the pictures. Come on."

Ross looks over, the photographer looks over, Karen looks over. Time and efficiency. Bride and bride's parents. They're waiting; squinting in the bright sunshine, hot in their good dresses and cheap suits.

"Emma, before I went . . . you wouldn't have known, you were only, what was it? Jesus. Fifteen. Before I disappeared . . . there were things that weren't right. With us. All of us. We weren't good people. There were things going on you didn't see. We kept them from you. Ross was in it too. Things were left unfinished. Hanging. I need to tie things up."

"Daddy, I know. Ross told me, but I knew then."

"He didn't tell you, love."

"I trust him. I just married him."

He winces. "He didn't, because he couldn't. He couldn't because he doesn't know it. Emma, love, did he fix his little straightener-up before he went down that aisle? Cut himself a little line or two for wedding-day bravery?"

For a moment, Emma is close to tears. She glances over at Ross, he sees her distress. In a second he will come over. That confrontation will happen, but it's not for now.

"Don't answer that, love. I'll come around later. After the speeches and the photos. I won't be in the photographs, you know?"

"Come on, Emma!" Karen calls. When Emma looks back, her daddy is gone.

He doesn't smoke: never has. Lungs. Even secondary smoke makes them feel as if they are turning to stone. People always remarked on that. He doesn't smoke. Only a fool would smoke, though a final fool smokes to look hard. But the smoking space is where you meet people. The hotel has a tasteful little gazebo: wooden uprights and cross members covered in climbing wisteria so you think you're in Los Angeles and not Moneyreagh. There's even a gas heater. His bald patch feels like it's frying in its own grease. Bald patch. It's all bald patch now. Monopatch. This is a clear night. Belfast is a sulphur-glow beyond the dark treeline, defeating all but the brightest stars. You're not really in the country out here.

That's a right racket coming from the room. The mobile disco is still cranking out the tunes for the old dolls. "Birdie Song," "Pride of Erin Waltz," "Tennessee Waltz." He's always loved that one. His ma used to sing it round the house. They'll get onto the kids' bangers when the old ones have gone. Four-to-the-floor, *bang bang bang bang*. There'll be a fight. There's always a fight at weddings like these. He's avoided a few. Not this time. There will be blood tonight. That's the entire point.

He's not surprised none of the bridesmaids know about him. Karen with a new man in a new house in a new area; Emma with new friends. Best they didn't. He would hate them to think other of Emma because of who he was. The bridesmaids are chubby and lippy and if he was thirty years younger he would have a swing at them, probably all of them together. Make it sound exotic and daring. Book a room to make it look a little less trashy. They stay for a flirt, a drink and smoke, and go back to the party.

"Da."

Emma always called him Daddy. Kier called him Da.

"I waited out here because I knew you'd be out for a fag eventually. It's simpler if I don't go inside."

"You came back."

"I didn't get round everyone I needed to get round this morning."

"That's not what I mean."

"Oh, I know. Still, you gave her away really good."

"It should have been you."

"It should have been all sorts of things, Kier. Does he have any respect for you at all, son?"

"Who?"

"Ross. The Beast from the East. I hear he calls himself that."

"It's true. But he's not . . . you."

"Glad to hear it. It should have been you."

"I do all right. We're still making money."

"Selling shit."

"You had the cocaine."

"I did. Can't deny that. I can give you any number of excuses—it was a one-off, I was just easing over the transition, adjusting to the Good Friday world—but the moment I touched it I knew I was fucking scum. You don't even have to put it into yourself to know it will feel like dirt. In your veins. Dirt in your veins. Crack now, isn't it?"

"Ross wants to move into crystal meth. It's cheaper and easier."

"Listen to yourself. You make it sound like Tesco home delivery. Meth: now that fucking *is* dirt. That's like someone shit in your heart."

"Is it worse than getting protection from the wee shops, like you did? They was honest, hard-working people. With crack it's only players involved."

"Yeah, well, that's a fine moral hair you're splitting there. But I'll tell you this about the drugs: it showed us what we really were. We thought we were heroes and soldiers and protecting the community and getting on like we're out of some Andy McNab book or Vin fucking Diesel movie, but all it takes is a half-kilo of white shit to show that we are thugs. Cheap fucking thugs."

"What did you do with that cocaine?"

"I never touched a gram of it, son."

"You ran off with it to England."

"Who told you that?"

"Ross."

"And you believe him? Maybe he *should* be the Beast. You're too fucking stupid."

And in a whisper of movement, the burning tip of Kier's cigarette is over his eyeball. He doesn't blink.

"The reservoir, Kier. Did he ever tell you about the reservoir? No? Then listen."

"Do you know what they call this?" He's sitting on the stone bench in the little leafy temple for wedding photographs. The club hits from the dance floor are a series of soft detonations. "The Grassy Knoll. I heard one of the waiting girls say it. It's one of those things that once you get it into your head it doesn't get out again."

Ross smells of beer. Everything tight about him has been loosed: tie, collar, cuffs, button on his pants. As if he was swelling up like a beer balloon. But he's not drunk, and he is quick and fast. Two handfuls of collar. Up close. Hair-dryer close. His breath is rank. Meat between the teeth. Spittle flecks.

"What the fuck are you doing here?"

"What kind of way is this to treat your father-in-law?"

"What the fuck are you doing here?"

"Like I said, come to see my Emma get wed."

"What the fuck are you doing here?"

"Meet a few faces I haven't seen in a long time. Pull a brides-maid at the disco. Wedding stuff."

"What. The. Fuck. Are. You. Doing. Here?"

"Do you want to know? Do you really want to know?"

"I don't. I don't care about anything you want or have to do or see or say. I just want you to tell me what the fuck you are doing here. Because you can't be here. Because I saw that car go into the reservoir."

"I'm a good swimmer. There's a trick to it, I saw it on the Discovery channel. You have to open the windows, let the water in. It's all to do with pressure."

Ross shakes him, like a dog with a rat.

"I put two clips into that car before I put it in the water."

"You're not as good with that gun as you think you are."

"I'd fucking kill you now—"

"It's not that much, is it, a quarter of a million? You get that just for opening a box on *Deal or No Deal*. Game-show money. Won't even buy you a house. Half a million would—half a million, that's money—but you had to split it, didn't you? Half for the setup, half for the delivery. Did you sample the goods? You should never do that. Sell your half and then spend it all buying it back again and snorting it up your sinuses. You can piss it away pretty damn quick in that game. Did Ems even see a penny of it? Just buy her a nice ring and a honeymoon in the Seychelles. Even that?"

"If you fucking told her—"

"You'll do what? Kill me again? It's not just you. It's all of you. I set you up like dominoes. One takes out the next, takes out the next. All the way to the end. All it takes is one wee tap. Two wee words."

Ross drags him out of the belvedere, away from the lights and the music, away from the floods in the car park, away from the open door of the kitchens where the chefs smoke, into darkness.

"I'll fucking make sure you never say even one word," Ross says. This is the night of fast, whispering moves: a flicker and Ross has a knife in his hand.

"You brought a knife. To my daughter's wedding. A knife." He laughs. The laugh scares Ross. It's wrong, it's not what should happen here. It's an unscripted laugh. "I thought Kier was thick as pig shit for believing you, but man, you take it to a whole new level. You want to deal, you want to be a player? You need something in here, son." He taps Ross's temple. "Do you think I'd have told you any of this if I thought there was a chance of you stopping me? I said those two wee words five minutes ago. Do you know what I said? I said: the reservoir."

Car headlights glare up the Grassy Knoll. Ross lifts a hand to shade his eyes. He slips out, under Ross's knife, away from the Beast. Kier stands by the open car door. His eyes are fixed on Ross. His voice is low but the words carry over the Balearic thud from the dance floor.

"You fucking traitor."

The oldest, dirtiest insult: disloyalty.

He walks past the car. Karen is in the backseat, her white suit bracketed by men in dark suits; a groomsman on one side, Jim on the other. He'd been right about that spiderweb tattoo. Psycho. Loyalties, disloyalties. Karen's sunbed face is grey. Grey as a ten-day drowned corpse. Her eyes are black holes. She's crying. Mothers of the brides always cry at weddings. She looks at him, he opens his mouth to speak. Beg. Plead. Spit. None of it will make any difference now. Backlit by disco lights, Emma is a hollow ghost in a white dress at the hotel door. Her mouth is open.

Sorry, love. I did wreck your big day after all.

Now Kier and one of the groomsmen wrestle Ross to the front seat. Kier has the knife. He turns back to watch the end game.

"You! Fuck you!" Spit flies from Ross's mouth. He is crazy with rage. "You are dead! Dead!"

He walks out into the dark.

"Where the fuck do you think you're going?"

"Back," he says.

It's a hot summer; the last thing anyone expected; the hottest summer a generation can remember. There are water panics. Reservoirs reveal their pale, dirty scum lines as levels drop. Three fishermen, camping out in the hills up behind Holywood, cooling beer in the water, notice the shape below the surface. It looks like a car. Police and a bright red tow truck haul the shadow out of the reservoir: the slimy skeleton of an Audi. 2008 plates. Riddled with bullet holes. Behind the wheel, human bones in the remains of a cheap supermarket suit. Forensics go to work. They calculate the bones have been down there four, five years. Old bones. But the suit; the suit is split new.

PART III

CITY OF COMMERCE

THE GREY

BY STEVE CAVANAGH

Laganside, Queens Island

M y client, Mickey Fuck, pushed his chair away from the table and said that there was no fuckin' way, on God's fuckin' green earth, that he would fuckin' do six fuckin' months for murder.

No. Fuckin'. Way.

I should say, purely for the sake of accuracy, that the surname *Fuck* does not appear on Mickey's birth certificate. That particular document bears the name *Michael Padraig Pearse Flannigan*. It was Mickey's predilection to season even the most basic of sentences with a liberal, and at times bewildering, peppering of *fucks* that earned him his infamous moniker.

"Mickey, it's murder," I said. "Not to put too fine a point on it, but you're fucked, so to speak. At the moment, the prosecution aren't treating this as a paramilitary killing within the scope of Good Friday. We're trying to persuade them otherwise. If they agree to treat it as a Troubles killing, then under the terms of the Belfast Agreement the maximum sentence will be two years, but at the moment they're pleading it as a straight killing and that's twenty-plus on conviction. You're sixty-three, you don't have twenty in you. Think about it, please."

"I don't fuckin' have six months either, Mack. Six months? Tell 'em to get ta fuck. Fuckin' six months, fuck," said Mickey, casting his eyes around the white, sanitised consultation room.

Most of my clients these days called me Mr. Mack. The

younger ones, anyway. Mickey was a client of old. We'd grown up together in the law. Not that Mickey was a lawyer, no, he was a window cleaner by trade, but his real talents lay in cunning and not-so-cunning fraud. I'd first met Mickey forty-odd years earlier, when I was a white-wigged barrister fresh out of pupillage with not a penny to my name and even less experience. At that time Mickey already had an impressive juvenile record and I'd been chosen as the jockey for his debut in the Crown Court. The venue was court one in the Crumlin Road Courthouse. I'd arrived at the court early that morning, having slept little the night before. Terrified that I would be delayed by security checks or bomb scares, I got there just after eight o'clock only to find the wrought-iron gates and bomb-proof barriers firmly locked with no sign of life inside.

My instructing solicitor was a kindly sort who was doing my pupil master a favour by giving me a decent brief to kick off my career. In those early days of the Troubles you found your feet as a barrister pretty quickly. Due to the huge number of terrorist trials there simply weren't enough criminal barristers in the Bar Library to serve the demand from clientele. Several of my brothers at the bar collected their enrolment papers, the ink still wet from the lord chief justice's pen, and walked straight into supergrass trials or murders without the faintest notion of how to conduct even the most basic of careless driving pleas in the Petty Sessions.

Mickey and I popped our Crown Court cherries on a charge of fraud. The genesis of the charge lay in a brace of loyalist bomb attacks on pubs in known Catholic enclaves of the city; the first bomb went off at 4:03 p.m. in the Clifton Bar on the Cliftonville Road, a public house affectionately known to the locals as the Suicide Inn. The second went off at 4:09 p.m. in the Hole in the Wall on Baltic Avenue, just off the Antrim Road. Mickey submitted a criminal injury compensation claim to the Northern Ireland Office stating that he had been hurt in both attacks. The difficulty arose due to the fact that both bombs went off within minutes of one another, on the same day, several miles apart, and unless Mickey had hijacked a passing Chinook with the aid of his trusty ladder, there was no way he could've been in both locations when the attacks occurred. Mickey had submitted two separate application forms for the separate incidents and if both applications hadn't fallen across the same desk of the same diligent civil servant, Mickey might have gotten away with it. So Mickey held the hands up and after a nervy, but thorough plea in mitigation delivered by yours truly, he walked out with two years' probation and a fine. A result. Within a few years, several solicitors' practises were sending me work and one even remarked, "If your client's in trouble with the peelers, just phone The Mack."

Mickey's current trouble was much more worrying. Murder was a serious business and, it has to be said, out of character for a career criminal like him. Although a diehard Republican, Mickey stayed out of the paramilitary ranks.

"The judge has decided that this will be a jury trial," I said. "She'll be pissed off because she bent over backward to give me the nod to six months on a plea in a Diplock court. If you turn that down, she'll hammer you in sentencing if you're convicted after a fight in front of a jury."

My young instructing solicitor, Mr. O'Neill, nodded in agreement.

Mickey ran his hands over his thinning Cliftonville football shirt. Where once bright tattoos adorned his forearms, now only faded remnants clung to flaccid skin. The tattoo of a Celtic badge on his wrist now appeared to resemble a poorly realised quiche. Phlegm whistled through his breath, the result of a lifetime of smoking dog-ends and roll-ups.

"It's like Noel fuckin' Edmonds says, no deal," replied Mickey.

Gathering my brief together in readiness to depart, I was about to remark that the *Deal or No Deal* presenter, Noel Edmonds, although undoubtedly wise when it came to opening mysterious boxes, might not in fact be the best person from whom to take counsel when one was faced with a murder charge, when I felt a jagged pain in my left hand. The sharp end of a brass fastener, which held my brief together, must've raked across my skin. I sucked hard on the cut at the base of my index finger and tasted metal, not knowing if it was from the brass or the blood.

Mr. O'Neill and I left the holding cells beneath Laganside Courts, the heavy cell door closing behind us with a resounding *clang*.

"We'd better go and tell the prosecutor and judge that the deal's off. We'd better check who the—" began Mr. O'Neill, before I interrupted.

"Whoa, hang on there now. Let's not kill ourselves here. We'll get a coffee and a smoke first."

Standing in the paved garden outside Laganside, I pondered my client's predicament. The prosecution would put forward a strong circumstantial case: our man's van was seen parked outside the victim's flat a week before the murder and, worst of all, they had a DNA hit.

The murder of Willy Stoke had gone unsolved for over thirty years. The historical enquiries team reviewed the case some months previously; a single droplet of blood on a photograph, found near the body, which had never before been tested for DNA, revealed a precise match for Mickey. What had been a ropey circumstantial case thirty years before now looked strong. Back in 1982, just days after the body of Stoke had been found in his living room by his wife Betty, the Royal Ulster Constabulary had hauled Mickey in for questioning once they'd traced the van back to his address. At the time, the van and the droplet of blood, which was of the same type as Mickey's, along with several hundred thousand others, simply wasn't enough to sustain a conviction.

Unfortunately, Mickey initially denied ever knowing or meeting Willy. Mickey had lied to the police. He had known Stoke and admitted as much when he was interviewed again thirty years later. The DNA changed everything. Trying to explain how your blood came to be on a Polaroid found beside the body of a dead man was difficult enough. With Mickey's false statement to the police, conviction looked inevitable.

As far as judges and juries are concerned, the innocent don't lie and DNA is king.

"What do you think?" asked Mr. O'Neill.

"I think he's foolish turning down six months. But if he says he's innocent, we're obligated to take his instructions and do our best to challenge the prosecution. We just need to sow some reasonable doubt in the minds of the jury. Easier said than done."

My instructing solicitor was in his midtwenties, passionate, and skilled. As a young lawyer he still worried about his clients, about their lives, about their fate. He hadn't yet learned the self-preservation of detachment, but having said that, I too felt deeply worried for Mickey because I believed him to be innocent. And that creates its own unique pressure.

A low December sun glimmered from the revolting face of Belfast's latest office building—a monstrous mixture of ugly metal and concrete newly adorned with *To Let* signs partially obscured the view of the Waterfront Hall which was, by contrast, a beautiful structure.

It was all part of the new Belfast.

Following the Good Friday Agreement, the state had either pulled down or let rot their old institutions of justice such as the Crumlin Road Courthouse, the Maze Prison, and the old Petty Sessions building, as they were seen by some as houses of oppression, as monuments to the past conflict, and reminders of the horrible, public wounds we had visited upon one another. Now, in this part of the city centre, it was all about the new grey, the new shining pillars of justice and rejuvenation; as if the city was wiping itself clean and starting afresh. So the new Laganside Courthouse had been erected, officially opened, officially declared too expensive, and officially left to deteriorate. It sat opposite the Royal Courts of Justice and the Bar Library—both clothed in sterile, neutral, independent stone, brick, and glass.

That was how it had to be.

The city centre had to be for all religions, and so the ubiquitous, shining grey had quickly become the nascent colour. Whereas the Ardoyne rejoiced in tricolours and every shade of green, so too the Shankill kept their houses and kerbs in the Union Jack, and each side of the divided city painted their gables and drenched themselves in the rich colours which formed their history, their protection, their identity, their flag, and they lived under the terrible weight that came with it.

In Belfast, colour was joyful, territorial, and frightening. And so the heart of the city embraced a comforting blanket of grey. That grey served as my comfort too, my goal in every case; it was my job to shade the prosecution's black-and-white into wonderful, doubtful grey. Whilst I sought out that pallid doubt, I too remained colourless, cloaked in grey, so that I could invite all people from every shade of the conflict to my door.

"Come on," said Mr. O'Neill, "we'll seat the jury."

* * *

"Appearances, gentlemen," said Her Honour Judge Henrietta Booth, a rather plump woman with a keen legal brain and about as much common sense as a root vegetable.

"I appear for the Crown," said David Fossett QC.

"If it please Your Honour, I appear for Mickey Fu . . . er . . . I mean, I appear for the defendant, Mr. Flannigan."

Court Fourteen in Laganside sat at the top of the house. The courtrooms of the fourth floor were reserved for the most serious of criminal trials, and the sheer size of the rooms added drama and gravitas where none was needed. A small public seating area at the back of the court seemed almost an afterthought to the designer. The space was reserved for the accused in a long dock which could hold perhaps twenty defendants and then three rows of legal benches: solicitors at the back, junior barristers in the middle, and Queen's counsel closest to the highly elevated judiciary. If you sat in the public gallery, even if you were able to see around the dock, the judge would appear as if he or she were sitting atop Mount Olympus.

Jury selection isn't what it used to be. In the last few years the government had done away with the defendant's right to challenge the selection of a juror without cause. Prior to the change, one would be supplied with a list of potential jurors which included their names, addresses, and occupations, and the defendant enjoyed the privilege of challenging up to twelve jurors without having to state a reason. The challenges normally took the shape of a religious parade; one would not want Billy Wilson from the Woodstock Road sitting as a juror when the defendant was Bridie Connolly from the Lower Falls. This perceived religious bias was not enough for a challenge for cause anymore. Since the change in the law the defendant can only challenge for just cause and jurors are selected anonymously, by number, at random. Justice by lottery.

With twelve random souls seated, the prosecutor, Mr. Fossett QC, opened the case for the Crown. Fozzy, as he was known, bore a startling resemblance to a flustered duck. As he reached his peroration, his robes fluttering with bold sweeps of his arms and his yellow jowls flapping about his pouted lips, he told the jury that the defendant's DNA had been found in a droplet of blood smeared on a photograph discovered beside the body of the late Mr. Stoke. He continued, "The photograph, ladies and gentlemen, is of the deceased's wife, Elizabeth Stoke, but that need not concern you. What is of concern is the blood. It is the prosecution's case that the victim was probably holding the photograph when he was attacked and bludgeoned to death by the defendant. In the ensuing struggle, as Mr. Stoke fought bravely for his life, he must have injured the defendant in some way and the defendant's blood found its way, quite by chance, onto the photograph, leaving for you, members of the jury, the key to the identity of the killer."

I flipped open my brief and found a copy of the photograph. Betty Stoke had been an attractive woman; she stood in the sunlight, on a wintry beach, hugging her coat about her beneath a dark sky. She looked happy. Fozzy wasn't interested in the photograph itself, or why the deceased might have been holding it, but that became the key question in my mind and one which I felt might hold the answer to my client's case.

Fozzy let his last statement sink in before finishing his speech with a final and surprising nail in Mickey's coffin: "Members of the jury, the motive for this brutal killing is known. The killer believed the victim to be a police informant. You will see, in photograph four, the living room where the deceased was found. Scrawled on the wall, in fresh paint, is the word *tout*. The paint was obtained from the airing cupboard in between the kitchenette and the living room. Photograph five is a picture of the open airing cupboard where we believe the paint to have been stored. The jury will note, as I have already stated, that the defendant initially denied ever having met the deceased. Yet, members of the jury, the defendant's thumbprint was found on the inside of the airing cupboard door, left there, we say, in a moment of carelessness whilst he fetched the paint to scrawl the motive for his heinous crime on the living room wall for all to see . . ."

I was on my feet in a flash. "Your Honour, a matter has arisen." Judge Booth sent the jury out.

"Fozzy, you fuck, you've not served any forensics on a fingerprint," I said, fuming.

"Oh, haven't we? I'm sure that I directed service. The partials obtained during the initial investigation have only just been matched with your client. We found some partials on the photo too, but not enough for a match to your man. After the DNA hit I directed a full forensic review. You know what the cops are like—they get a DNA match and they think they're home in a boat."

"Gentlemen?" said Judge Booth.

I explained that the fingerprint evidence had not been served. Fozzy apologised and a prosecutor handed me a brown envelope containing the forensic report. Even though it had not formed part of discovery, it was relevant and there was no way of excluding it.

Turning to face Mickey in the dock, I began scratching at the cut on my finger which had become red and itchy.

Behind Mickey, in the public gallery, his long-suffering wife Agnes bit at her hanky, her small hands trembling.

Mickey was going down and she knew it.

The next morning I drove along the Ormeau Road, on my way to court, thinking about the photograph of Betty Stoke. That image clawed at my memory, but its significance continued to elude me. The traffic calmed as I made my way past the old Gasworks. The beautiful Victorian brickwork façade and clock had been preserved when the site went through redevelopment. For some reason the developers had failed to keep up maintenance on the clock, which always seemed at least an hour slow.

The radio distracted me. A heated discussion had begun amongst commentators arguing over the latest political bomb-shell by someone or another who had proposed, in all but name, an amnesty for historical crimes committed during the Troubles. One commentator, a representative from a victims' group, argued that it was the right of the victim or the victim's family to determine whether or not they would forgive past crimes or seek truth and justice through an inquiry or prosecution. To balance the argument, a politician, if one were willing to stretch the definition of that title to fit this individual, who regularly appeared on early-morning radio, presumably having been prodded with a stick by the producers until he reached his seemingly habitual state of apoplexy, argued that murder was murder and that all crimes, political and historical, should be prosecuted to the full extent of the law. I found a parking space on Cromac Street, let out a sigh of relief as I killed both the engine and the radio.

My relief was twofold: I was glad that I didn't have to listen to such a heavy argument on a full stomach of bacon and black pudding, and secondly, I'd realised the significance of the photograph.

Stepping out of the car into the biting December air, I called my instructing solicitor.

By an ingenious technological feat, when one telephoned Mr. O'Neill's mobile, instead of a ringtone one was treated to the theme tune from *The A-Team*. The call went to voicemail, "You're through to the voicemail of Sean O'Neill, the People's Champion. I'm probably fighting with the police at the moment, leave a message and I'll get back to you when justice has been served."

"Mr. O'Neill, it's Teddy Mack, I'm on my way to court. I've had a thought, a possible game changer for our good friend Mr. Fuck. Meet me at the cells. We need a consultation right away."

Disconnecting the call, I threw my red velvet bag which contained my wig, collar, and gown over my shoulder, hefted my briefcase, and stepped brightly toward the day's labours.

It was Friday and I saw the vans and cars of stall holders parked outside St. George's Market. There had been a fish market at this site for over three hundred years with fishermen selling their catch straight from Belfast Lough. They sailed up the River Lagan right into the heart of the city and anchored just a stone's throw away from the marketplace. In the late 1800s a beautiful indoor Victorian market had been built with a paned-glass roof and it still operated today, although it had changed much over the last twenty years. When I first came to Saint George's, as a young barrister seeking a Friday cod, I would have to fight my way through the old millies who operated the jumble sale at one end of the market. A milly was a heavily built middle-aged woman, draped in shawls and dragging a shopping basket, who'd grown arms like thick steel cables from years working in the linen mills. In those times, during the summer, the market stank of fish and mouldy clothes. Not so today. Smartly dressed members of a jazz band hauled a double bass through the doors and I could already smell the fresh fish and the wondrous aromas of curry, exotic fruits, paella, and slowly roasting meat. The market had become trendy with boutique stalls that sold paintings and Art Deco furniture. Sadly, there was not one milly in sight.

Mickey held his head in his hands. Beads of sweat sat precariously on his unkempt and somewhat wild eyebrows.

"That fuckin' judge has it in for me," said Mickey.

"Forget about the judge," I responded, "I want to know about the photograph, the one of Betty Stoke on the beach."

His head came up. Fear in his eyes.

"I was listening to the radio this morning. They were talking about the Troubles and what should we do about the past. I think it's time your past came out, Mickey. I remembered our little case all those years ago. Our first case—the pub bombings? That got me thinking about our past. And our second or third case, if I remember rightly? Another fraud conviction. That time you got nine months, and with 50 percent remission and time on remand you were out in a month and a half. But you weren't worried about doing the time, you were worried about—"

"Fuck that, no way."

"You have no choice."

Rubbing his head, he swore.

"Why didn't you tell me?" I said.

"It's ancient fuckin' history, for fuck's sake. I didn't . . . I didn't want to put Agnes through all that, not again."

"It's the only way."

Eventually, Mickey relented. Even though he faced twenty years for murder, he would rather do that time than hurt his wife any further. I had to admire him for that, at least. But now it was time for the truth to emerge, with a little unwitting help from the prosecution.

Before court began, I sent Mr. O'Neill on an errand to the offices of the *Belfast Telegraph*.

Fozzy looked at me like I'd suffered a minor stroke. He questioned witness after witness—scenes of crime officers, photographers, police officers—and elicited damning evidence against Mickey from each one before turning them over to me, at which point I would politely shake my head, having no questions to ask.

"Are you feeling all right, Mack?" asked Fozzy.

"Fuck off," I said.

He called his final witness, a seemingly minor individual who was there simply to prove documents. He was Arthur Hamill, a records officer with the Department of Justice. Earlier that morning Fozzy had sought to introduce bad-character evidence against Mickey—in other words, his criminal record. He wished to show the jury that Mickey was a dishonest man and therefore a dishonest witness, having been previously convicted of over one hundred crimes of dishonesty. I agreed that Mickey's record could be shown to the jury on the understanding that we would be provided with a copy of the deceased's criminal record in return. Fozzy agreed, thinking that I had made a grave error; nothing is more likely to increase a sentence than attacking the victim during the defence case, and Fozzy wanted to give me full reign to hang my client by assassinating the character of a murder victim.

After Mr. Hamill, a rather bored civil servant in a blue suit was sworn in, Fozzy took the jury through our client's record, highlighting the number of convictions for theft and fraud, but not going into the facts of any of the prior cases.

"Nothing further," said Fozzy.

"I have just a few questions, Mr. Hamill," I began.

The jury seemed surprised to hear my voice, as if I was going to spoil what had been up until then a fairly straightforward affair.

"Mr. Hamill, you will see that the defendant was convicted of fraud on the 18th of October 1981 at Belfast Magistrates Court. There is, I believe, a short narrative below each record of conviction to give a little more detail of the crime. Would you please read out that narrative for the 18th of October?"

"Yes. It states, *Pleaded guilty to twenty-three counts of obtaining electricity by fraudulent means. Fined one hundred pounds, with time to pay, and sentenced to nine months' imprisonment on each count, sentences to run concurrently.*"

"Thank you. Now, I believe you also have a copy of the victim's criminal record?"

"Yes, I do."

"Mr. Stoke, the victim, had five convictions for violent crime?"

"It appears that he did, yes."

"And three of those were for common assault?"

"Yes."

"One of those convictions was for assault occasioning actual bodily harm roughly three years before his death?"

"Yes."

"One conviction for assault occasioning grievous bodily harm just six months before his death?"

"Yes."

"In actual fact, he spent two and a half years on remand before that conviction for GBH and was released just a week before his murder?"

"It seems so, yes."

"Mr. Hamill, the narrative for each of those convictions records the identity of the victim of all five of those violent assaults, does it not?"

"It does."

"And the victim is identical in each and every case of assault committed by the deceased?"

"Yes. The victim was Elizabeth Stoke."

"The deceased assaulted his wife, regularly, throughout a five-year period?"

"Yes. It appears that he did."

Several jury members shook their heads. Two female jurors appeared horrified. It was as good as I could've hoped for.

"Thank you, Mr. Hamill."

Fozzy flapped to his feet and said, "That is the prosecution's case."

The rear doors opened and Mr. O'Neill reentered the fray. I was pleased to see a thick bundle of papers tucked beneath his trusty arm.

"Your Honour, we call the defendant, Mr. Michael Flannigan."

The custody officer opened the glass-covered dock and let Mickey make his way toward the witness box. As he passed me I whispered, "Remember what I told you."

He nodded. "I know, tell the truth, don't say *fuck*."

I winked and patted his shoulder.

"Mr. Flannigan, did you know the deceased, Mr. Stoke?"

"I did. We were from the same area, I would have spoken to him the odd time in the street or in the bar."

I fetched the copy of the photograph found next to Mr. Stoke's body.

"Do you know the woman in this photograph?"

"Yes, that's Betty Stoke. Willy's wife."

"And did you know Betty Stoke?"

"Yes." He hung his head.

"How did you come to know her?"

"I did a bit of work for her."

"When you say *work*, what do you mean?"

"I fixed her electric meter so she wouldn't have to pay for any electricity."

"So we can all follow what you're saying—you mean you tampered with her electric meter illegally?"

"That's right."

From my brief, I removed Mickey's criminal record. Fozzy wasn't in the least bit interested. The jury members were paying close attention.

"I have your criminal record here. In 1981 you pleaded guilty to a number of counts of obtaining electricity by fraudulent means. Tell the jury exactly what happened."

Mickey turned in his seat and looked at the jury while he spoke, just as I'd told him. "I figured out a way to stop your meter turnin' when you put in your money. If you opened up the electric box and slotted a wee piece of card into the right place, like, the meter wouldn't turn. So you could put ten shillins into the meter and it would last you all year."

"And did you offer this electrical-engineering expertise to your fellow neighbours?"

"Aye, I wasn't workin' so I would do your meter for a couple of quid."

"How was your little enterprise discovered?"

"Wha'?"

"You were arrested, yes? How did the police discover your crime?"

"Well, turns out the IRA tipped off the peelers. The Ra' robbed the electric man the odd time, after he'd been round the houses, emptying the meters. After I started up they robbed him expecting to get a few hundred quid, but they only got about £4.50 and then they caught on to what I was doin'. They threatened me with a punishment beatin' but I was too well liked in the area. So they shopped me to the peelers—I mean, the police."

At that moment Mr. O'Neill placed into my hand the first of the clippings from the *Belfast Telegraph* that I had sent him off to find. The paper keeps all its past editions on microfiche and sends them across the road to the Central Library.

"The *Belfast Telegraph* learned of your exploits and a particular facet of your case became widely reported. Please read out, for the benefit of the jury, the headline of this piece from the 5th of November 1981."

He coughed and read aloud, "*Electricity Fraudster Is Secret Love Rat.*"

"We shall let the jury read the article in a moment, but give us the basics, please."

"I'm not proud of that, Mack, you know I'm not. At the time, me and the wife weren't gettin' on the best so some of the wee jobs I done in houses, on the meters, like, the women couldn't pay any money. So they paid me in other ways, you know. Voluntary, like—I'm not a rapist!" he added emphatically.

"Not one of the housewives ever said that you were. But, on those occasions that you weren't paid with money, when you were paid . . . in kind, shall we say, in what way were those jobs different to the jobs in which you were paid cash?"

"Well, I found out that the best thing to use to stop the meter was a Polaroid photo. It was just the exact size that you needed to stop the mechanism. So in those wee jobs, I would bring my camera and take a photo of the woman. Just a cheeky photo, like. And I'd put the photo in the meter. They liked that, some of them. They got a wee thrill knowin' there was a sexy photo of themselves stuck into their electric meter and their husband knew nothin' about it."

I paused as Mr. O'Neill handed copies of the article around the court. My finger itched like mad. The cut looked angry and swollen. Glancing over my shoulder, I saw Mickey's wife Agnes, her face drawn tightly together by her set lips. She didn't want this brought up and I guessed she knew where we were headed.

"And the photo of Betty Stoke, did you take that?"

Tears formed at the corner of Mickey's eyes and he seemed to grow pale.

"Aye, Betty was different. I loved her. She put up with so much from that oul' bastard she was married to. He beat her for years. Even when she started reporting it to the peelers, he kept on. But she loved him, she always took him back. I wanted to change her mind so I took her to Newcastle, the week before he got out. We were goin' to run away. She got afraid and said that he'd find us. When we got back to the flat, I put the photo in her electric meter and took out the bit of card I'd used before. I just . . . I just wanted her to know that I loved her, that somewhere in that house there was a wee bit of her that he didn't know about. I must have cut my finger, and that's how my blood came to be on the photo. And I opened the cupboard door, so my fingerprints would be on that too."

"He found the photo?"

"Aye, I got a phone call from Betty, not long after he got out. I drank in the Hatfield on a Thursday and she phoned the bar, she was screaming and crying. He found the picture, he was going to kill her, he'd almost killed her the last time, broke her jaw and everything. But this time, he was really going to kill her. She told me she had lifted the coal shovel and hit him over the head. He was dead when he hit the floor. She told me all this on the phone, in hysterics. I told her to write *tout* on the wall, get rid of the paintbrush and the shovel in the Lagan, and get out of the house, go and stay with her sister."

The jury, who up until then had only theory and conjecture, felt like they were getting the truth; I could see it, they were riveted to every word.

"Did you see her afterward?"

"No, she wouldn't see me again. She blamed me, you see, for the photo and what happened after."

"Why didn't you tell this to the police?"

"I didn't want to hurt my wife. Jesus, I'd put her through

enough in our marriage. I just wanted the past to stay buried," he said, his voice breaking with emotion.

"What happened to Betty Stoke?"

"She killed herself a year later; hung herself in her sister's bathroom."

Mickey broke down and the courtroom seemed to pause in the silence that only comes from the deafening truth. Then sound flooded the room: Mickey crying in the witness box and Agnes sobbing in the gallery.

The jury saw the pain. It had been a cruel thing to do to Agnes. I hadn't given her any warning of this because I wanted the jury to see her reaction, her pain, and feel it themselves, making it real.

Mr. O'Neill handed round the last paper clipping, from 1983, just three sentences:

A Belfast woman committed suicide yesterday. She was found by her sister. Police are making no further enquiries.

The clippings added corroborative force to Mickey's evidence. Mr. O'Neill and I had done all that we could. Fozzy did his best to catch Mickey in a lie during cross-examination, but his evidence remained consistent because it was the truth.

Closing speeches were short, and the jury took less than an hour to bring in a verdict of not guilty.

Mickey turned in the dock, desperately seeking out his wife, but Agnes had gone.

Within ten minutes of the verdict I put a pint of Guinness and a shot of whiskey in front of Mr. O'Neill and Mickey respectively, as we took our seats in Rumpole's just a couple of hundred yards from the courthouse. The pub no longer bore that name, but for me it remained Rumpole's. Its clientele consisted exclusively of hard men from the markets, lawyers, and judges, whom would all frequently join forces to throw the police out of the bar whenever they attempted to evacuate the area because of a bomb scare.

Mickey sniffed and supped his Powers, his head low despite the acquittal.

"I've lost her," he said.

"She'll come round, it was thirty years ago," said Mr. O'Neill. Technically, he was correct, but Mickey and I both knew that for Agnes, the betrayal was fresh, public, and brutal.

Blood dripped onto my beer coaster. I'd opened the cut on my finger.

"If you keep fuckin' pickin' at that cut it'll never heal," said Mickey.

Glancing through the window, I sucked at the fresh blood. At that moment, snow began falling on the city, covering everything in a clean, white veil.

ROSIE GRANT'S FINGER

BY CLAIRE MCGOWAN

Titanic Quarter

As soon as she walked into my office, I knew I was in trouble.

Well, okay. I don't have an office. Ma's front room. But I knew it all the same. It's not every day a good-looking older lady wants to see me, and she's crying.

I tried to be professional. "How can I help you, madam?" I thought she'd like that. She was in her early forties, I'd say, and wearing more jewellery than a Turf Lodge wide boy after a ram-raid at Lunn's.

"Are you the detective?"

"That's right. Aloysius Carson, private eye."

"It's your ad in the phone book?"

"I doubt there's another PI of the same name."

"I was expecting someone older."

"Most people are. Older. But lots are younger too."

She looked round the front room/office, none too impressed. I've tried to get Ma to move the baby pictures but she isn't keen. "I suppose you might know where young people go? Being one yourself."

"I might," I agreed. "We go all kinds of places. School. The bus. McDonald's. Are you missing a young person?"

"This is my daughter Rosie," she said. From her bag she took out a photo in a frame. That was a bit weird. Nowadays people normally show you something on their phone.

"Why's it in a frame?"

She gave me a funny look. "I didn't want to take it apart."

"Can I hold onto it?"

"The frame's silver."

I put it down carefully on Ma's coffee table. I often think that if I had a nice big desk I'd get a lot more respect from people. "Rosie's missing?"

"We haven't seen her for two days. It's not like her."

"Called the police?"

She shook her head. "We're afraid she might be in some kind of trouble."

"How old?"

"Eighteen."

That was the same as me, but I didn't say. I thought it might not inspire the necessary confidence in my abilities.

Rosie smiled out of the picture. It was a posey one, where she was leaning on her hand, but even so she was the kind of girl I would stare at all the way home on the bus and not be able to say a word to. Gavin would call her a *grade-A hottie*, but he watches too much American TV. She had that reddy sort of hair that Ma says is called strawberry blonde.

I took out my notepad and tried to look businesslike. "You said she might be in trouble?"

She made a face. "There's a boyfriend."

"There's always a boyfriend," I said wisely.

"Not with Rosie, this is the first. His name's John Joe. John Joe Magee."

And that name told me the situation was about to get a whole lot stickier.

You might ask yourself how I came by such a name as Aloysius Carson. The truth is, my parents had what we call a *mixed mar-*

riage. He was a Prod, God rest him, she's a Taig. Love across the barricades, that sort of thing. They still cared about that in the '90s, decade of my illustrious birth. So I'm not really one or the other. Usually, people like me to be, and which one depends on who I'm taking to. So I could see the problem Mrs. Grant had right away. I could tell the family were of my father's persuasion, shall we say, and Rosie's fella wasn't just a Taig, he was the nephew of super-Taig Nasher Magee. You know the name? If I showed you a picture of a top UVF man called Charlie Forster, all shot up like a colander, you'd remember. Nasher did that, while he was banged up inside the Maze. They still don't know how.

So I did what I always do when there's a difficult case: I promised Mrs. Grant I'd get right on it, and when she'd gone I ate a Pot Noodle. Would you not let me make you a sandwich? Ma always says, but I like it. The hard twisty bits getting soft and untangled. That's what solving a case should be like.

The next thing I do is some meticulous in-depth research. As long as you persuade your ma to get broadband then you're laughing. I was on Google in seconds and learned that Rosie Grant was the daughter of "successful tyre magnate and member of the Orange Order Harry Grant." That explained the jewels dripping off the mother; they were loaded.

Then I looked up Nasher Magee. He'd been out of jail since the Good Friday Agreement and owned a pub off the Falls Road. John Joe was Nasher's favourite nephew. Only son of his only brother, who'd been shot by an army patrol in 1993. He'd brought the boy up as his own, given him a stake in the business. I wondered how in the world someone like Rosie Grant, at her posh Protestant girls' school, had even met a body like John Joe Magee.

I decided onsite research was best, so I told Ma I'd be back for dinner—shepherd's pie—and I hopped on my bike. It's got ten gears, so it's pretty speedy.

The pub was called Wolfe Tone's, even though oul' Wolfe was actually a Protestant fella, which just goes to show nothing ever makes sense in this place. I got off and sidled round the walls. All the windows were barred, and from inside came the sound of a football match in Irish.

"Who might you be, son?" I was being watched by a white-haired man smoking a cig. He had tattoos all down both arms like a long-sleeved vest, if you could get a vest that was made of Celtic crosses and pictures of the Virgin Mary.

I knew immediately I was in the presence of Nasher himself, so I called on my detective training to blend in. "Just admiring the unusual signage, sir. Fascinating example of mural art."

He stared at me. "You a fruit or something?"

"Eh, don't think so, no."

"Well, get on out of it. You're attracting attention."

I pedalled on, noting that Nasher had seemed quite hostile and reluctant to let anyone near the pub. Was Rosie being held there?

Every PI needs a computer expert in their corner. Did you know that nowadays over 90 percent of cases are solved online or by CCTV? That puts the amateur like myself in a wee bit of a bind. Luckily I have Gavin. I met him on the first day of primary school, when he'd dismantled his Etch A Sketch to see how it worked. He lives in his mum's basement off the Lisburn Road—it's got its own door, so it's pretty cool really. He's filled it with several computers so there's always this sucking noise, and there's no light, but he doesn't mind. He doesn't mind much of anything except when the wrong actors get cast in the films of his favourite comics.

"If the elves live forever, how do they die?" he said as I went in.

I quickly realised we were on *Lord of the Rings*. "Um, I think they just retire. What you working on?"

"Hacking into the Pentagon," he said, taking a honk of his asthma inhaler. He had an open packet of Frosties on his knee and was scooping them up, spilling crumbs on his dinosaur T-shirt.

"Here, I brought you a sandwich. You need proper food."

"What's those funny green bits?"

"It's called *salad*, Gav. It's good for you."

"Hmm." He started picking the lettuce out, but ate the ham and bread.

"Rosie Grant," I said. "Need to find her. Any ideas?"

"Background?"

"Subject is eighteen. Father is Harry Grant. Owns some tyre business."

Already Gavin's left hand was tapping as he ate the sandwich with the other. "Protestant?"

"Yes."

He nodded. It's all the same to Gavin, just a keystroke in a different column. "Royal Belfast Girls School?"

"That's her." I was impressed. He was already in her Facebook profile, a big smiling picture of her making the peace sign like girls do when they're trying to be hippies, and lots of messages off other girls with smiley faces and bad spelling. "I need to know who might have taken her. She's going out with Nasher Magee's nephew."

Even Gavin raised his eyebrows at that. "Where'd she even meet him?"

A good question. Gavin would make a useful assistant, if only he'd wear trousers more often.

"I'll get you it all," he said in a bored voice. "You want police records? Bank statements?"

"Er—only if it's relevant. And don't get arrested again, Gav."

He sighed. "It's not my fault if they won't build proper firewalls around things."

I decided it was time to check out Rosie's friends, and thanks to the Internet I knew who to go to first.

It was child's play to track down Chrissie, Rosie's best friend according to Facebook. She put her entire life up there, so I knew she'd be leaving school at four p.m. after her first aid class. I recognised her blonde curls and short school skirt as I pulled up beside her on my bike with a bit of a screech, pretty cool.

"Chrissie Carr?"

She gave me the sort of look girls like her give to boys like me. "Who're you?"

"Aloysius Carson, private eye."

She chewed very slowly on her gum, showing the inside of her pink mouth. "Who?"

I explained Rosie's mother had asked me to find her. "She's been missing for several days."

"I thought she was off with her fella, like."

"Are you worried?"

"I dunno." She seemed to think about it. "Should I be, like?"

"Her mother seems to think she's in some danger."

"You talk funny," said Chrissie, wrinkling her nose. "Rosie is grand, I'm sure. She's always going off with fellas. Here," she added, looking me over, "what kind of name is Aloysius? You a Catholic too?"

For a moment I tried to think what she might want to hear—yes or no. "No," I said, and she lost interest.

"Pity. It'd wind my da up something desperate. Tell Rosie to text me if you find her, all right?"

* * *

I cycled home through town, past City Hall and the shops. I like cycling, it helps me think. I like hearing the spokes go round and the *whicka-whicka* noise. I was going past the Opera House when I realised what Chrissie said didn't make sense. Rosie was always going with boys? According to Mrs. Grant, John Joe was her first boyfriend. I smelled a rat, only it smelled like Impulse body spray and bubble gum.

At home, I chained up the Raleigh and let myself in. "Ma? Are there any Pot Noodles?"

She was hovering in the kitchen doorway. Behind her I could hear the theme tune of *Coronation Street*. "There's someone to see you."

A man rose up from the sofa—sitting in my office space, cheeky article. "Aloysius, is it?"

"It's Mr. Carson," I said coolly.

He laughed. "And I'm His Lordship Detective Sergeant Sam Taylor."

A peeler. I kept my face the same. "And?"

"And you've been getting up the nose of some important people, son."

It's hard to be dignified with your ma standing there. "Thanks, Ma, could you let us have a moment, please?"

She sniffed. "Your shepherd's pie's almost ready."

Taylor was still laughing as she shut the door. "I won't stop. Just take this as a wee friendly warning. You don't want to be snooping round certain pubs on the Falls Road anymore."

"I don't know to what you are referring."

"I think you do. Now I don't know what your business here is, and it's fine by me if you want to play Number One Boy Scouts' Detective Agency, but we've been watching Mr. Magee ourselves for quite some time, and we don't need schoolkids getting in the way."

"I've never been in the Scouts."

"Keep it that way," he winked. "What's a wee fella like you doing with a detective agency anyway?"

"There aren't any jobs. And there are lots of crimes the police can't solve," I said pointedly.

"Working on one at the minute?"

"I can't say," I said, thinking of Rosie. Her family wanted to keep the peelers out of it.

"You got a phone, Mr. C? Let me see it a wee minute."

"I don't have one," I said, stalling for time. "I, eh . . . don't believe in them."

"Do you think I came up the Lagan in a bubble? Don't make me use my stop-and-search powers, Aloysius." He gave me a threatening look and I handed over the phone. It's a smartphone—I convinced Ma I needed one as a legitimate business expense. He fiddled with it for a minute. "There's my number. You find out anything you shouldn't, you give me a wee phone."

"How will I know if it's something I shouldn't?" I said sulkily.

"Just be prepared. Dib-dib-dib, son." He patted my shoulder in a patronising way and left. How rude! I'd been out of school for *five whole months*.

I thought about what he said. Did this mean the PSNI were mounting surveillance on Nasher's pub, maybe checking out his lucrative side industries of drug dealing, arms trading, and extortion? Surely they'd have seen Rosie if she was there. But then the Grants hadn't reported her missing.

I was mulling it over with a Pot Noodle (they were on special offer in Dunnes, Ma said, but I wasn't to eat too much and spoil my tea), when my phone started ringing. "Aloysius Carson, PI." Gavin says I should answer with "Carson's the name, crime's the game," but he is very immature.

There was a sound like a deflating balloon on the other end. That was odd. "I've got voice-recognition software," I lied.

"Please . . . come . . . come now." It was Rosie's ma.

"Are you all right, Mrs. Grant?"

"Rosie . . . her finger . . . please . . ."

"Her *finger*?"

"Please!"

"I'm on my way."

"The address—"

"No worries, I have it." No need to explain Gavin had hacked into their tax return data. I wiped my chin, hopped on my Raleigh, and pedalled toward the Malone Road, Ma shouting after me that she wasn't making any more dinners to be ruined if I couldn't stay to eat them.

The Grants' house was the biggest on a street of big houses. It took me a good few minutes to bike up their drive, getting my tyres stuck on the gravel. The door was opened by a teenage girl, the spit of Rosie but with glasses and heavy dark makeup. "Yeah?"

"I'm the detective."

She sighed. "In there." From the living room came the loud sound of crying. "Are you going to take your shoes off? The carpet cost like ten grand."

I was wearing my Spider-Man socks. "I'll keep the shoes on. It's part of my process."

She rolled her eyes. "Go on then. She's too busy bawling to notice."

It was a swanky room, with a big fire and nice squashy sofas, but I didn't have time to take it all in because Mrs. Grant was on one of them, crying her eyes out. A red setter sat at her feet, looking up sadly. Standing by the fire was the sort of sports jacket-wearing fella you see in golf clubs. He was holding a big glass of what I thought was whiskey.

"Mr. Grant, I presume?"

He looked at me like the dog had done something nasty. "You must be the PI fella. Wee bit young, are you not?"

"Lots of people are, sir. What seems to be the trouble?"

Mrs. Grant started talk-crying and it sounded like, "Ba-ha-ha-ha finger, oh my Rosie."

On the table lay a lot of bubble wrap and a big envelope. In the middle of it was some cotton wool, and on that was, as she'd said, a finger. It had on pink nail varnish and a gold ring. It was, I'd guess, the middle finger. "Rosie's?"

"It's her ring," said her father, gripping the glass. "Her eighteenth birthday present."

"Please," sobbed the wife. "They want money. Half a million, look!"

It was a typed note, which unfortunately had got a bit stained with red. They'd been touching it, the eejits, but I was careful not to. I saw it was all spelled right. "Is there a name?"

"No. It's that Magee family, I'll bet. Bunch of ne'er-do-wells and not above kidnap."

That was true, but I wasn't sure Nasher could spell a word like *imminently*.

"Why do you think it's them, sir?"

"He rang here once, that dreadful man. Said he wasn't having his nephew going round with a stuck-up Prod. They must have taken her."

"Did you call the PSNI?"

Mrs. Grant panicked. "No! We can't do that. They said they'd kill her if we called the police."

"Gurriers," growled Mr. Grant. "I'll take my shotgun to them."

"Oh don't, Harry!" she cried even harder. "Just give them the money."

"It's negotiating with terrorists, Marjorie!"

"It's our daughter!"

In the corner of my eye I saw the other girl—the sister, she must be—had crept in. She was pretty under all the goth makeup. Same hair as Rosie. She was staring at the finger.

"Madeleine!" snapped her father. "I told you not to come in here."

"Is that Rosie's?"

"No, no, it's just—a Halloween toy."

"It's February."

"Maddy, will you please go away!"

"All right, whatever." She went.

"Look here," said the father. "There's a time and a place given for the ransom. We want you to take it to them. There's a key to a shipping container, in the docks."

"Me?"

"Yes. You're involved now. They said they'd give Rosie back if we send the money. Here." He went behind the sofa and pushed out a pink wheeled suitcase, like the type girls take on planes.

"Are you telling me there's half a million pounds in there?"

"Of course. I don't like it but she is, as my wife says, our daughter. Now take it down to the docks and do the swap. Call us as soon as you have her."

"But . . . wouldn't you be better with the police?"

"No, it has to be you. I'd go myself but I'm a very important man. Thousands of people depend on me for their livelihood."

"But, but—"

"Mr. Carson, if you don't do this, our daughter's blood will be on your hands."

Their daughter's blood was on their coffee table but I didn't say this. "Can I go to the toilet first at least?" I needed time. Not knowing what to do, I took the case with me.

I heard Mrs. Grant call, "Would you take your shoes off if you're going upstairs?"

I pretended not to hear.

On the stairs I found Maddy, painting her nails black. That gave me an idea. "Was your sister wearing polish when she went missing?"

"Doubt it. We're not allowed at school. They make you clean it off."

"Can I see if it's in her room?"

She shrugged and we went upstairs. Rosie's room made me dizzy, all posters and perfume and underwear hanging over chairs. Gav would have an asthma attack. I tried to focus. There was a whole drawer of varnishes, but no pink. Interesting.

"Do you think it's her finger?" Maddy pretended to blow on her nails.

"You don't seem bothered if it is."

"It's Rosie."

"Meaning?"

"She never gets in trouble. She's smart, you know. Like really, really smart. And mean. When I was ten my hamster bit her, so she drowned it, then told Mammy he'd escaped. I was never allowed another pet."

I looked at her. "How old are you?"

"Sixteen," she said. "Why, how old are you?"

"Eighteen. Well, nearly."

"Can you drive?"

"No."

"Oh."

"I've got a bike."

"Huh."

"Look," I said, "I've got an idea. I need to go to the docks and check things out. Only I can't ride my bike with a case."

"Get a cab. There's money in there, right?" She unzipped it before I could stop her. "Wow." We blinked at the piles of crisp notes. "They'd hardly miss a tenner for a taxi."

She was right, so I went outside. Part of me had been hoping I wouldn't get one, and I'd have to give up, but just my luck one was sitting right in front of the house, its light on. I got in, clutching the case to me like a baby. "The docks, please."

"Hello, son," said the driver, meeting my eyes in the mirror.

It was Nasher Magee.

This was bad. On a scale of one to bad, this went up to eleven—a joke Gavin would appreciate, but he wasn't here, and even if he was, he'd have been too busy crying and wetting himself to laugh.

"Where's my nephew?" Nasher was driving nice and slow through the evening traffic.

"I don't know! I'm trying to find Rosie. Her family think you have her."

"What would I want with some uppity Malone Road cow?"

"Money?" I was hugging the little pink case to me.

He laughed. Not in a nice way. "Son, I've more readies stashed than Mr. Golf Club could ever dream of. I just want my nephew away from the meddling little bitch. So where are they?"

"She's been kidnapped. Honest, they cut off her finger!"

"Did they now? Who did?"

"Eh . . . you? That's what they think."

"And what do you think, son?"

"I don't know."

"Smart lad. You only know what you don't know, is that right?"

"Eh . . . please, Mr. Nasher. I need to go to the docks. It's where they have her."

"In a minute."

Soon the cab was stopping, but not at Harland and Wolff like I'd asked for. "This is your pub! I need to get to Rosie!"

"Never you worry about Miss Grant. I'd worry about yourself more."

Then someone was opening the door and stuffing a black bin bag over my head and I was dragged out. There were steps. I know because I fell down them. There was a door, a metal one, which my head banged off. "Ow!"

"Shut your trap, son."

When the bag was ripped off, I was tied to a chair in a concrete basement. I tried shuffling but my hands were bound up. In the room were Nasher and two other men, both in black with balaclavas on. Nasher was smoking a cigarette and sitting on a table. He had on a Celtic top and grey tracksuit bottoms.

On the other chair was someone else with a bin bag round their head. I could see their mouth sucking in and out panicky breaths. Bin bags are actually porous, but they probably wouldn't find that too comforting. One of the gorillas ripped the bag off, but by that stage I'd already clocked the red Converse and I knew it was Gavin before I saw his face, white and scared.

"Al! What's going on?"

"Calm down, Gav," I said. I hoped I sounded it. "It's just a misunderstanding."

Nasher tapped his fag. "I wouldn't call it that. You boys have been following me. First you sneak round my pub, then your wee pal here's nosing in my bank accounts."

I gave Gavin a disappointed look. "You promised!"

"I was trying to help, Al! I thought he might have rented somewhere to keep Rosie."

"You eejit, Gav. Look, Mr., eh . . . Nasher. I'm afraid my associate doesn't know what he's doing. He's like Dustin Hoffman. You know, in that old film. *Rain Man*."

"Didn't he play a fruit once?"

"I don't know, sir. That's not the point. It's really not Gavin's fault."

Nasher moved off the table and I saw two things on it. One was the pink suitcase—open. Empty. The other looked like a bolt cutter.

Nasher ambled over to me. The cigarette dangled close to my left eye. With my right I glanced at the bolt cutter, which the second gorilla was weighing in his hands. "You better start talking, son."

I looked at the glowing end one inch from my eye and the bolt cutter and Gavin starting to wheeze and shake. So I told the whole story, about Mrs. Grant and John Joe and the finger in the box—"The money's to ransom her, see"—and how it looked like Nasher had been set up.

"Set up?"

"I think so, sir. Clearly you know nothing about it, but it's been made to resemble your, eh, trademark skills."

"I did used to do a lovely kidnap," he said nostalgically. I tried to move my face away from the flame. "So if you went with this case to the docks, you'd maybe find John Joe?"

"Um . . . definitely. Almost for sure."

"All right then." He moved, and quick as a flash the first goon cut my ropes. He cut me too, a bit.

"And Gavin?"

"He stays till you find John Joe."

"Can I take the money?"

"I said take the case, son. Not the contents."

"But how will I get her back without the ransom?"

"I'm sure you can improvise, smart boy like you." He tossed the car keys. "Take the taxi. On the house, son."

"Maybe you wouldn't smoke," I ventured. "Gavin's asthmatic, you see." I could hear them laughing and Gavin wheezing as they shoved me out the door.

I can't drive. Not even a bit. All I know is from playing on the Wii with Gavin. But I kept my eyes straight ahead, and ignoring the many, many beeps of other cars ("Hurry up, you fecking arsehole!"), I somehow found my way to the shipyards. The pink case was beside me on the seat of the black hack. I heard its wheels squeak behind me as I parked and walked away, then it was just me in the dark. A salty wind blew in from the lough, the lights of the city glittering all round me, like little winking eyes.

I ducked under the security barrier and found the gates of the shipyard unlocked. No one stopped me. I was walking amid a city of shipping containers, rusted and hulking. The key that had come with the finger had a number on it: *341*. I found this after a lot of wandering about in the dark. It was a bottom one. Green metal. I listened but heard nothing except the wind.

I put the key in the padlock. It turned, rusty, and I pushed the door open. "Eh . . . hello?"

No answer. I switched on the torch I always keep in my jacket, like any good PI should. The space was maybe eight metres long. In the pool of light from my torch was a chair, and a girl was tied onto it. Her head slumped forward, and in the light I could make out that her hair was that shade of red people like to call strawberry blonde.

"Rosie," I whispered. The torch beam was no match for the inky shadows in the place. I needed to add double-A batteries to Ma's shopping list. "Are you okay? I'm the PI. Your parents sent me."

She groaned. "Please . . . help . . ."

"Stop."

I moved the torch and saw coming out of the darkest corner a massive fella like the proverbial shithouse made of brick, pointing a knife at me. "John Joe Magee!"

He seemed confused, then put his menacing expression back on. "Yeah, so? You stay back."

"Eh . . . I've got your money."

"Oh. Well, put it down over there."

I parked the case, handle sticking up. "What happens now?"

"Em . . . you give me the money and you fuck off." His knife cast long glinting shadows.

"And Rosie?" Her head twitched.

"Eh . . . she can go with you?" John Joe sounded like he was asking a question.

"Is she all right? How's her hand?"

"Hand?"

"You cut off her finger. That wasn't very nice of you." I was trying to look at her hands, see if she had polish on them, but they were tied behind her.

He paused. "Look, stop talking, yeah? Give me the cash and fuck off." He raised a hand to scratch his face and I saw it was wrapped in some kind of fabric. The idea I'd had took shape in my head. In my pocket I felt for my phone, trying to count. How many names did I have saved? Where would S be on the contacts list? One, two, ten . . . I pressed the button, hoping it was the right one.

"Untie Rosie, and then you can have the money."

He moved over to the girl. Her eyes fluttered and she moaned something. John Joe suddenly straightened up, as if a thought had entered his brain and was clanging around in the empty space it found there. "Here, I need to count the money first."

Oh feck. "Um . . . it's all there. I think. Half a million. The ransom you wanted for *Rosie Grant*."

He went to it, tucking the knife under his arm. He seemed to struggle with the zip, fumbling. I was about three seconds from a good stabbing. I realised several things in that moment that saved my bacon. A good PI is 80 percent planning, 20 percent reaction, you see. 10 percent luck maybe. Is that more than 100?

I saw Rosie move in the corner of my eye, and just as John Joe was saying, "There's fecking nothing in here!" and letting the knife fall clumsily from under his arm, I threw myself into the shadows behind him and discreetly grabbed it. At the same time I chucked my phone into the darkest corner, its screen still lit up to show it was transmitting. I hoped to God the right person was listening.

Rosie stood up. The ropes had fallen off her and she was holding a gun. I saw clearly that all her fingers were exactly where they should have been—on her hands. I also saw that the reason for John Joe's clumsiness was that *his* left hand was bandaged. I imagined if we looked there'd be a bottle of pink nail polish somewhere around the container.

My back was against the container wall, cold and damp. "Now," I said, speaking clearly, "there's an explanation for this. There's a reason we're all here *at the docks*."

"You stole the money, you little bastard." Rosie waved the gun.

"No, no. It's being looked after. By John Joe here's uncle. While we're here *at the docks*."

"Uncle Nasher?" John Joe looked perplexed. "What's he got to do with it?"

"He's found us out, you moron," said Rosie, starting to pace. "I told you he didn't like me."

It was true so I didn't disagree.

She pointed the gun at me. "What'll we do with this one?"

I held onto the knife tight. If John Joe'd had any sense he could have squashed me like a grape. Luckily he didn't seem to. "Look, nice as it is here *at the docks*, I think we should—"

"We'll have to go to plan B. Get rid of him, send his ear to my parents."

They don't do a lot but I'm fond of my ears all the same. "Now, look, I'm sure all of us here in *container 341, at the docks*, could do with calming down a bit."

Rosie continued: "They'll send someone who's less of an eejit with more cash. We take it and scarper to the ferry as planned. Done. Or else we send your other finger to your uncle."

"Aw, Rosie. It really hurt last time."

"It worked, didn't it? Bit of nail polish and my ring—they're such eejits. I'm always right."

I cleared my throat loudly. They both turned to look at me. "Now," I said slowly, "why don't we come up with a different plan? There's not much we can do while we're here in *shipping container 341*, is there? Your uncle has the money, John Joe. Why don't we go and visit him?" Surely I could manage to get the gun off them in that time, and rescue Gavin, and get past Nasher's henchmen, and . . . ah, feck.

Rosie hoicked up the gun. "I want that money," she said to me. "If we bump you off, it'll look more convincing, won't it? And we could send them any number of body parts off you."

I panicked. "You could send them my shoe! That'd work just as well!" Oh bollocks. I whipped out the knife, hands shaking. "Now just stop right there."

Rosie threw back her lovely head and laughed. "I've got a gun, you fecking eejit. Who's going to stop me?"

"I reckon I could have a go." A different voice, harsh as a hundred cigarettes a day.

I blinked in a new beam of light. Nasher was at the door, grabbing the gun from Rosie's hands. "You didn't even take the safety off, you daft little cow. Here she is, Sammy." And there was his mate, DS Sammy Taylor, slapping cuffs on Rosie as another officer frisked John Joe.

"Sorry, Romeo and Juliet. Love'll have to be across the prison wings now, never mind the barricades." Taylor stopped in front of me.

I tried to drop the knife surreptitiously but it made a terrible clang. "Er, hello, DS Taylor."

"So you did phone me after all, Magnum PI."

"I felt the situation had . . . escalated."

"Lucky I put that wee tracker on your phone then, eh?"

"*What?*"

"How do you think we got here so quickly? Though your chat was handy to find the right place. *We're here in container 341! Gas.*" He laughed heartily.

"That's, that's . . . a violation of my human rights! I'll be contacting the police ombudsman."

The other officer was now in front of me, handcuffs dangling. "What about this one, sir?"

"Not him," said Taylor, still laughing. "He's an eejit, but sadly they've yet to make that a crime. Take him home, his mammy's worried."

Once everything was sorted out, Nasher gave the money back to Rosie's parents, who hopefully saw it as some comfort. Far from being missing, they now knew exactly where their daughter was: in the women's wing of Hydebank prison. DS Taylor got a promotion for catching the two extortionists, and I kept my mouth shut about the fact he was obviously in cahoots with Nasher. I spent my reward money on renting out some office space. There's even a desk for Gavin, though he's been strictly warned about hacking during work hours. I also took Ma out for dinner, so she didn't have to cook at least one night. She said it was nice but she didn't like to get too behind on *Coronation Street*.

There's a bit left over, so I might see if Maddy Grant wants to go to a film sometime. I get half price on a Wednesday. I think she'll like that.

OUT OF TIME

BY SAM MILLAR

Hill Street

Karl Kane's mobile began ringing on the bedroom table, just as the tablets he had consumed four hours earlier were starting to lose their cosy effectiveness. He could tell it was early morning because of the particular quietness from outside: no drunken louts or screaming teenagers spilling out from nearby pubs and clubs in and around Hill Street in city centre.

He let the mobile ring for a few more seconds while glancing at the luminous alarm clock on the table. It was the dangerous side of four in the morning and phone calls at four in the morning, in Karl's profession, only ever meant one thing: trouble.

Reaching over, he hooked the phone with a finger and thumb before staring at the number.

Lipstick. What the hell now?

"Karl?" said the groggy voice of Naomi by his side. "What's wrong?"

Naomi was dark-skinned, drop-dead gorgeous, with large hazel eyes and wild black hair. Despite the Northern Irish cadence in her voice, it still commanded a strong Southern resonance.

"Sorry, my wee darling. Didn't mean to wake you."

"Who . . . who is it?"

"Lipstick."

"Lipstick? I hope she's not in some sort of trouble."

"Trouble? Lipstick?" he said sarcastically. He hit the button on the mobile. "Okay, Lipstick, what's wrong?"

"Karl? What kept you?" Lipstick whispered, edginess in her young voice. "I've been waiting ages for you to answer."

"Sorry, like most law-abiding citizens I was in bed, trying to sleep."

"Say you won't get mad."

"That's a bit like when someone tells you not to get nervous. The first thing you do is get nervous."

"I need your help."

"Where are you?"

"Locked in a bathroom."

"What the bloody hell? You call me at four in the morning just to get you out of a—"

"In the Europa."

"The Europa?"

"Yes."

"I take it you're whispering because you can't speak too loud, in case someone hears you."

"Yes."

"A disgruntled client?"

"If that means ugly and angry, then yes. He's screaming through the door right now that he's gonna kill me. I'm scared, Karl. He means it."

"Room number?" Karl quickly swung his legs out of bed, before parking his impressive bulk on the edge.

"Fourteen."

"Has this creep got a name?"

"Calls himself Graham Butler. He's from London. He . . . he wanted me to do things I hadn't agreed to. He wouldn't pay me for what I already done for him, so I took his Rolex in exchange."

"I'll be there within ten minutes. Hold tight."

"Karl?"

"What?"

"Look tough."

"At four in the morning and wearing pyjamas?"

Naomi waited until Karl killed the connection. "What's she got herself into now?"

"Something I hope to get her out of, before I get too deep into."

He quickly put on a pair of socks while searching for his loafers.

"You can't keep putting yourself in danger every time she calls."

"Tell me how to say no to the person who saved my life, and I'll do it."

"Get off the guilt trip. You've repaid her a hundred times. She's ripping the arse clean out of it."

"I know she is, and it's *my* arse taking the hammering. I won't be long." He gave Naomi a quick kiss, and headed out the door.

Karl arrived outside the Europa in less than the promised time. Residing a few streets away definitely helped. Attacked thirty-three times, the grand old building had earned the unenviable sobriquet of the most bombed hotel in Europe. Or as Belfastians flippantly referred to it: *That blasted hotel.*

The last time Karl had been in the hotel was in the mid-'90s, helping Brad Pitt hone his accent for his role in *The Devil's Own.* The elocution lessons—or *spaking Balfast* as Brad liked to call them—went well enough, but the promised part for Karl in the film never materialised. Still, he couldn't complain. The pay off financially had been sound, and seeing his name on the screen credits at the end of the film went a long way to soothing his wounded ego. Naomi, of course, was enthralled by the tale, though he grudgingly had to admit she seemed more interested in Brad Pitt than Karl Kane.

Usually the area around the hotel was buzzing with tourists and the homeless looking for a place to kip, but at this time of morning, foot traffic had wisely disappeared. Even the notorious adjacent cul-de-sac—"Blowjob Alley" (more rubber used than a Michelin tyre factory)—was strangely deserted. Outside the hotel, a sleepy fleet of taxis lurked in the shadows.

Karl entered through the revolving doors leading into the marble-and-cherrywood reception of the grand foyer and was almost immediately eyed by a young concierge. "May I help you, *sir?*" he said disdainfully, looking a dishevelled Karl up and down.

"No, you're okay, son. Just heading up to see my old school friend Graham—Graham Butler—up in room fourteen." Karl made a movement toward the lift, but was nimbly blocked by the adolescent.

"You can't go up until I call Mr. Butler on the phone. That's hotel policy."

Karl glanced at the young man's name tag: *Raymond.*

"Hotel policy, Raymond? Is it hotel policy to turn a blind eye to janes and johns?"

Raymond's face reddened. "I . . . I don't know what you're talking about . . ."

"No? I never forget a name. A friend of mine, who's in trouble right now as I waste time speaking to you, happened to mention a Raymond to me. Likes to have his palms greased for turning a blind eye to illegal nocturnal manoeuvres of the sexual kind."

"I . . . don't know what that means."

"No? Okay then, we'll discuss the birds and bees later. Right now, be a good lad and hold that pose. I'll be back down in less than five minutes. No one will be any the wiser. And here's a score for forgetting." Karl slipped a twenty-pound note into Raymond's waistcoat jacket. "Oh, if I find out you phoned Butler, it'll not be your palms I'll be greasing when I return."

Raymond, looking faint, quickly moved out of the way.

Twenty seconds later, Karl stepped out of the elevator and immediately took stock outside number fourteen. A muffled, but angry voice could be heard inside.

Standing back a good three inches, he studied the door. He considered trying to kick the formidable-looking structure in, but quickly realised the implausibility of such a ridiculous act. He calmly rang the bell instead.

After a few seconds, a harsh male voice shouted, "Who the hell is it?"

"Room service, sir."

The door opened, revealing a nude, sweating man covered in tattoos. He was stocky, gym-manufactured, fake-bronzed, with ridiculously white teeth. He stood six-one, and was in his late forties auditioning for thirty. His hands were enormous—unlike his cock.

"What the fuck're you on about? I didn't ask for any fucking room service," Butler snarled, trying to sound like a tough guy.

"Facial masseur," Karl replied.

"Huh? I don't need a facial—"

Karl's uppercut caught him below the jaw so hard, Butler staggered backward over a sofa, before finally spreading out in crucifixion formation on the floor, moaning.

"You will now."

Quickly walking over to the bathroom, Karl banged on the door.

"Lipstick! Open the hell up! It's me, Karl."

The door opened, revealing a young matchstick-thin girl, early twenties. Her features were a portrait of heroin-addiction misery. She was nude, awkwardly trying to cover up her private parts.

"Is he gone, Karl?"

"Let's just say he'll be out for some time . . . What the hell happened to your face?"

Lipstick's eyes were turning an angry purple, partially closing. Bloody drool dripped from her busted mouth.

"He got angry because I wouldn't do anal for him. You know
I don't do anal, Karl."

Karl made an uncomfortable face. "I wouldn't let Naomi
hear you say it like that. She might get the wrong impression.
Hurry up and get dressed. I'm taking you to the hospital."

"But I don't need to go to the hospital. It's just a few smacks
in the gob."

"Do as I say. I'm not in the mood for debate." Karl turned,
walked over to the moaning Butler.

"Tough guy, eh? Like picking on wee girls?"

Blood was smearing Butler's mouth. It looked vulgar. Smirking, he peered up at Karl. "You . . . you don't know . . . who you're
fucking with, mate, you and your little whore."

"They say you should never kick a man when he's down, but
in your case I say name me a better time, eh?" Karl kicked the
smirking face twice before placing his formidable weight down
on Butler's exposed balls.

"*Fuuuuuuuck!*" Butler screamed.

"You don't look so tough now, not where I'm standing, *mate.*"
Karl applied more pressure.

"*Fuuuuuuuck!*" Butler's face knotted inward with pain. He
vomited a grey and yellow substance.

"That's enough, Karl!" Lipstick shouted from the bathroom,
hurriedly getting dressed. "No need to hurt him more."

But the rage was with him, and Karl continued ball-pressing.

"I said that's enough!" Lipstick snapped, appearing beside
Karl, pulling him away.

"You're too forgiving, kiddo. How many times have I told
you to toughen up?"

"Toughen up like you, the biggest softy on the planet? Besides, I got this." Lipstick dangled an expensive-looking Rolex in front of Karl's eyes, almost as if trying to hypnotise him. "He'll hate losing this more than any kicking you can give him. He's that sort of bastard."

Karl sighed. "*I'm* getting way too old for this kind of shit, Lipstick, and you're way too young to be doing the kind of shit *you* do."

She put her thin arms around his thick neck and kissed his cheek, leaving her trademark shimmering on his skin. "I love you, Karl Kane. You know that, don't you?"

"Everyone loves me when they're in trouble."

"Not like me, they don't," Lipstick said. "I *love* you."

"C'mon, kiddo. Let's get the hell out of here. We'll grab a taxi to the Mater. It'll be quicker than trying to get my car from Billy's garage."

"Do . . . do we really need to go to the hospital? They might start asking awkward questions." Then, uncontrollably, Lipstick started giggling.

"What the hell's so funny?"

Lipstick pointed at Karl's legs. "You really *are* wearing pyjamas . . ."

"Look at the state of you," Naomi said, placing a steaming cup of coffee by the sofa Karl was stretched out on. "What time did you get in?"

"About an hour ago," Karl replied, yawning, reaching for the coffee. Black circles were developing under his bloodshot eyes.

"Couldn't you've at least phoned, let me know where you were? I was worried sick when you didn't come back."

"If you remember, I was in a hurry. I left my bloody mobile behind. Now, can I drink this coffee in peace before it goes cold?"

Naomi's face flushed. She looked on the verge of intensifying the verbal jousting. Instead, she clicked on the digital radio, sat down at the breakfast table.

A song on the radio ended and seconds later the local news came on: "*A man, said to be known by police, was shot dead in his flat in the Sandy Row area of the city this morning. A quantity of drugs were discovered at the scene, and—*"

Naomi turned the radio off. "More grim news."

"Is there ever anything else in this bastarding place? Even when the sun shines, it's dark. Belfast is God's own private joke of perverse nastiness."

"Why are you so cranky this morning?"

"Possibly because *this morning* I've had little sleep, waiting in a sardine-filled emergency room with Lipstick."

"What? Why didn't you say something?"

"You didn't give me time, did you, with your interrogation?"

"What . . . what happened?"

"A steroid-induced scumbag beat the crap out of her, over in the Europa. That's what happened."

"God, Karl, is she okay?"

"Her face looks terrible, but the doctor said she should be okay in a couple of weeks. She's lucky not to be scarred for life. Lucky to be alive, if you ask me."

"What about the thug who did it? Was he arrested?"

"Lipstick didn't want the cops brought into it. I even had to make up a cock-and-bull to the nurse, who probably thought I was the one who did it. Sitting in the waiting room wearing pyjamas didn't help, either. The looks I was getting, as if I was some sort of perv."

"Did the thug get away?"

"Let's just say I had a ball of a time with what little balls he had to boast about. He'll be pissing glass for weeks. If it hadn't been for Lipstick appealing to my gentler nature, he would've had more broken bones than Evel Knievel."

Naomi's forehead furrowed. "Where's Lipstick now?"

"In the spare bedroom."

"*What?* Couldn't you've told me this before now?"

"Don't start all that again. Anyway, bringing her back to her place wasn't an option. She took a couple of painkillers. Hopefully she's sleeping."

Naomi got up quickly. "I'll check she's okay."

Karl eased his tired body off the sofa. Took a deep gulp of coffee. "I'm away to get a wash and shave before we open up for business. I just hope the day gets a lot better."

Saturday afternoon, Karl was just leaving the office to place a quick bet on a sure-hit-impossible-to-lose horse, when a car pulled up alongside him. The driver beeped the horn before getting out. He was young, hair combed back in a fashion long gone. Despite his age, there was something world-weary in his demeanour.

"Didn't you see the sign at the corner?" Karl said. "This is a no-noise zone. I should call the cops. Oh, sorry, I forgot. You *are* a cop, Detective Chambers."

"I need to talk to you, Mr. Kane. Urgently."

"It'll have to wait. I only have a minute to get this bet done." Karl pointed at the William Hill betting shop across the street.

"That's okay. I can wait here for you to return."

"I bet you a fiver you can't." Karl smiled.

"What's that supposed to mean?"

Just then, a female traffic warden came up behind Chambers. "Which of you two gentlemen owns the car?"

"It's mine," Chambers said. "Why?"

"Can't you see the double yellow line?"

"You don't understand—"

"No, *you're* the one who doesn't understand. You can't wait or park here."

Chambers's hand went to his inside pocket and produced a small brown wallet containing his police ID. "I'm a policeman."

"Then you should know better. Now, move the car right now, otherwise I'll have it towed."

Karl let out a loud laugh. "Belfast doesn't know the meaning of the word *protocol* when it comes to making money."

A chastised Chambers got back inside and started the car.

"That's a fiver you owe me," Karl said, making his way quickly to the bookies.

Ten minutes later, Karl reappeared, tearing up a docket.

"Any luck?" Chambers asked.

"The nag went down at the first hurdle. A hundred quid gone like a fart in the wind. Talking of farts, what little harassment operation has my devious ex-brother-in-law sent you on?"

"Inspector Wilson has nothing to do with this. He's in Edinburgh at the moment."

"Hope the bastard stays there."

"This is an off-the-record meeting. Can we go back to your office and talk?"

"So you can eye Naomi? Not a hope."

Chambers's face flushed. "We got a complaint from the Europa. A guest by the name of Graham Butler got a bad beating during the night. Apparently, Mr. Butler didn't want it disclosed, but when the day-shift manager returned this morning, he immediately reported it to us as required by law."

"Long story short?"

"What?"

"Get to the point. I've a hundred quid to get back from Billy Hill."

"I checked the hotel's CCTV. You were seen clearly on it, you and Miss Sharon McKeever—or Lipstick, as she refers to herself."

"Is there a crime in that?"

"I suspect Miss McKeever was there for a sexual encounter."

"She's an adult. She can do whatever she damn well—"

"I believe something bad happened in Butler's room, and you were called in to help her, knowing the history between you two."

Karl bristled. "History? What the hell's that suppose to mean?"

"She saved you from being killed by Peter Bartlett. That's more than enough for you to be indebted to her."

Karl glanced at his watch. "Unless you're planning to arrest me, I'm going back inside and—"

"Graham Butler is a very dangerous individual. A well-known criminal boss from the East End. At the moment, he's suspected of meeting with drug dealers over here, hoping to extend his so-called empire."

"I appreciate what you're telling me, and sticking your neck out."

"Just make sure you avoid him. We're hoping to send Butler back to London, first chance we get."

"I doubt Butler will come anywhere near me. He doesn't look like *that* stupid a man."

"One other thing. A journalist from the *Sunday Exposé* has been talking to some of the staff at the hotel. Don't be surprised if the newspaper contacts you."

"I doubt very much they'll contact me. Only interesting people help them sell more copies of their rag."

Chambers turned to leave.

"Aren't you forgetting something?" Karl said.

"Forgetting something?" Chambers looked puzzled. "What?"

"The fiver you owe me."

Sunday morning. Bucketing out of the heavens. Inside Karl's bedroom. Karl sitting at the table, typing his latest unappreciated manuscript on his beloved Royal Quiet DeLuxe typewriter. Actually, there was little typing being done as Karl continued staring blankly at a blank page. His fingers hovered nervously over the keys, like a helicopter trying to land on a house of cards. A couple of times his fingers landed briefly on the keys, only to quickly pull away, as if touching acid. Behind him, Naomi sprawled out in the middle of the bed, reading the morning newspapers.

"Do you have to make so much noise turning those pages, Naomi? How am I expected to concentrate with such a racket going on?"

She peered over the page she was reading, grin hidden. "Writer's block, my love? Can I help?"

"You can start by dumping those rags you're reading and get me a cup of coffee."

"I enjoy reading these. There's always some juicy gossip to be found."

Karl made a disapproving sound with his throat. "And the coffee?"

"You didn't say please."

"You didn't have to say please when I went out into the cold-and-wet this morning just to get you your *juicy* reading."

"True, but you were only expressing your love and deep gratitude for all the other things I've done for you." Naomi turned a page. "Karl! *Sunday Exposé* has an article about you and Lipstick."

"What?" He pushed away from the table.

"It's not a bad photo of you."

"Never mind that, let me see what the bastards have made up. Chambers warned me about this."

"Chambers?"

"You know who I'm talking about. The loverboy detective who fancies you."

"Stop being silly."

"Why're you blushing then?"

Naomi laughed. Patted the bed coaxingly. "Sit beside me. I'll read the article to you."

"I don't really have a lot of time for this . . . but okay." Feigning reluctance, Karl sat down on the bed, edging over beside Naomi. Her subtle perfume and body warmth tickled his nostrils. He hoped this wasn't all that would be getting tickled before the morning was over.

"*Local PI Takes on Notorious London Crime Boss*, says the wee headline." Naomi cleared her throat, and continued reading: "*Local private investigator, no-nonsense-taking Karl Kane, sorted out one of London's most feared crime bosses at the Europa last week, according to one of our inside sources.*"

"*Inside sources*, my bollocks. It was that greasy little worm Raymond."

"*The crime boss—who can't be named for legal reasons—was left with a broken nose, missing teeth, and a face his own mother wouldn't kiss.*"

"They can name me, but can't name him?"

"*Apparently, one of Kane's best friends, a Ms. Sharon McKeever, was left badly beaten, and Kane decided to quid-pro-quo by giving the London thug a good old Belfast punishment. Police say no charges have been brought against Kane because no one has come forward with a complaint. Sunday Exposé hopes the big bad crime boss has learned his lesson about beating up defenceless women in Belfast and elsewhere. Bon voyage back to London, and good riddance.*"

"Let me have a look at the picture," Karl said, secretly chuffed at the report not making him the villain for a change.

"I like it." Naomi handed over the newspaper. "You're almost smiling that roguish grin of yours."

"What roguish grin?" Karl asked, flashing his roguish grin.

"Hopefully this'll get us some extra business, Karl. Everyone reads *Sunday Exposé*, even those who pretend they're too intellectual to be seen dead with it."

"Before you start getting all philosophical on me, how about that coffee you still owe me?"

Naomi eyes twinkled mischievously. "I've something a lot tastier."

"Does it come in a cup?"

"Two." Naomi smiled, slowly unbuttoning the shirt she was wearing belonging to Karl. Next came her bra, unhooked from the front, leaving her breasts fully exposed. "Irish coffee or café mocha?"

"Irish." Karl snuggled closer, kissing her left breast gently and lovingly. "*Bonne bouche.*"

"I love it when you talk dirty *and* French at the same time. Whisper more to me," Naomi said, helping Karl remove what little garments he was wearing on a rainy Sunday morning in Belfast.

Despite the lousy weather outside, things inside were starting to look sunny for Karl. Very sunny, indeed. Of course, in Karl's world, sunshine never lasted very long.

"Any calls while I was out earning a crust on a dreary grey Monday?" Karl began, opening up the day's mail parked in a wire tray.

"The phone hasn't stopped. A lady called looking to find out if her husband is cheating on her, and would you investigate it. She's from the Malone Road, and read the article about you. See, even the well-to-do read *Sunday Exposé*."

"I'm beginning to think you've shares in it, the way you keep harping on."

"Another was from a man claiming his landlord is slowly poisoning his goldfish, just to get him out of his rent-controlled flat. I told them both to call back later in the afternoon."

The chime on the outside office door jingled. Through the frosted glass of the office, Karl saw a shadow come in and sit down in the reception area.

"Hopefully that's not the one with the goldfish. I'm not in the mood to listen to a lonely man's paranoia. I can do that anytime by myself."

"Stop being so uppity. That's our bread-and-butter you're talking about."

"I'm well aware of that, but I'm the knife who has to carefully slice the bread and spread the butter, sorting time-wasters from genuine clients. Now, if you don't mind?" Karl indicated with his chin toward the reception.

Naomi lifted her ample derrière off the desk, and headed out the door. A few seconds later, she returned.

"A Mr. Carlisle needs to talk to you. Face looks messed up, pretty ugly. Says he's hoping for help in locating a missing person. Shall I show him in?"

"You explained of course that we normally don't see anyone without an appointment, because of how busy we are?"

"I'm not in the mood to go along with your charades right now."

"Okay, give me a few seconds, then send him in."

Karl quickly picked up the phone and started talking into it, just as a man walked in.

"No, I'm sorry, Lord Mayor, but right now I can't take any

new cases for at least a month or . . ." Karl's voice trailed off. He set the phone down and glared at the man standing before him. "I didn't recognise you with your clothes on."

"Didn't think you'd want to see me if you knew who it was." Graham Butler sat down on a chair. His face was ballooned in black and blue. His left eye was totally closed by hyphens of stitches, and his off-kilter nose had an enormous sticking plaster on it.

He looked dreadful. Karl looked pleased.

"And there's me telling the cops that you wouldn't be stupid enough to come searching for me."

From an inside pocket, Butler removed a large envelope. Opened it. Produced the clipping from the *Sunday Exposé*. Slid it across the desk. "I've become very interested in this man."

Karl held the clipping in his hand. "Good-looking guy. Looks the type you wouldn't want to fuck with."

"I didn't know who you were until one of my associates showed me this. Now you have no hiding place."

"Who's hiding? The only hiding I remember is the one I gave you, *mate*."

Butler's face gave an almost imperceptible twitch. "You Irish have a saying, Kane: *Every dog is brave on its own doorstep*. Describes you perfectly. There'll be a time you'll face me on equal terms, not taking me by surprise or when I'm naked and defenceless."

"There's another part of that old saying you forgot to mention: *Only a stupid dog leaves its doorstep*."

Butler tried smiling, but it was obvious he was in pain. "In a strange way, I like you, Kane. You've got balls."

"More than I can say about you." Karl pointed at the door. "Now, if you don't mind, I've got to see a man about a goldfish."

"If this were London, you'd be dead by now. You understand that?"

"In all honesty, I wouldn't be seen dead in London. I was courteous to you in the hotel. Beating up wee girls doesn't go down too well over here, sparks something in our dark psyche. If I were you, I'd get on the next plane home, across the water, before some nasty vigilante comes searching."

"I've a couple of gentlemen not too far away, waiting in a car. They wanted to come in here, smash the place up, put you in hospital. Perhaps even worse. But I said no, Karl Kane is a smart man. Someone I can do business with. Am I right or am I right?"

"Wrong on both accounts. And as for your two gentlemen in the car?" Karl leaned over the desk. Stared directly into Butler's eyes. "This is *my* kingdom you're visiting. A whistle and I'll have forty not-so-fucking-gentle gentlemen here in five minutes, hoping to repay the many favours I've done for them over the years."

Butler shook his head in disbelief. "Okay, have it your way, but that little whore has a very expensive watch belonging to me. It's—"

"If you use the word *whore* again, I won't be responsible for where my fist lands—"

"—a Rolex Yachtmaster. It holds a lot of sentimental value in my heart. Twenty thousand quid worth of sentiment."

Karl almost swallowed the desk, but managed to remain calm, cool, and collected. From his pocket, Butler removed another envelope. Slapped it loudly on the desk.

"There's five hundred quid in there. See that the little . . . see that she gets it along with the message that she has twenty-four hours to return what doesn't belong to her. Otherwise . . ." Butler stood. "Well, you fill in the blanks. I'm sure you remember where I'm staying? See you soon, one way or the other . . ."

Karl waited until Butler left the room before quickly making his way upstairs. Rapped on the door of the spare bedroom.

"Who is it?" Lipstick's voice said.

"Me. Are you decent?"

"I'm always decent. You know that." She laughed. "Come in."

Karl opened the door and peered inside. Lipstick was sitting up in bed, a copy of Naomi's *Glamour* magazine in her tiny hands. Her face was healing a hell of a lot better than Butler's.

"How're you doing, kiddo?" Karl asked, forcing a smile.

"Feeling really great."

"Really?"

"Really."

"This is for you." Karl placed the envelope on the bed.

"What is it?"

"Five hundred quid, apparently."

"Five hundred?" Lipstick hungrily tore the envelope's stomach and spilt out its contents. "Where'd this come from?"

"Butler."

"Butler? How did he know I was here?"

"He doesn't. He's on a fishing expedition at the moment. He wants his watch back. He's sentimentally attached to it, apparently, as is his bank manager."

"What will we do, Karl?"

"*We?* We will do nothing. But you, on the other hand, need to return the watch. This thug isn't going away until he gets it."

"I'm not giving it back."

"I suspected that."

"And I'm keeping the money you just gave me."

"I suspected that too."

"Well? Aren't you gonna try and force me?"

"I've never tried to force you to do anything. I'm not going to start now."

"Good, because I'm going to enjoy spending that bastard's money and wearing his watch."

"Isn't it a bit big for a wee wrist like yours?"

"My wrist is, but not this." In a flash, Lipstick shoved a leg out from beneath the bedclothes, the watch attached halfway up. She began snaking the leg seductively toward Karl. "What do you think?"

"What *you* need to think is what could've happened in that hotel room. It was a warning most young people in similar situations don't get. Someone saintly must be looking over you. But even Saint Karl's patience is limited."

He turned and left, wondering what the hell Butler would do once he found out he'd have to add five hundred quid to his increasingly expanding Lost List of All Things Lovely.

Downstairs, Naomi waited, arms folded.

"Are you going to tell me what's going on, or do I have to wait and read about it in the papers? That was that nasty piece of work, Butler, right?"

"Right."

"You've got to call the police, Karl, tell them he was here making threats."

"How many times do I need to tell you to stop earwigging?"

"If I didn't listen in, I wouldn't know half of what the hell's going on in here at times."

"Well, this was one of those times."

"Are you going to call the police or will I?"

"I have ways of dealing with Butler."

"Yes, I read about those ways in last week's paper. I also overheard him talking about the gang in the car."

"He's threatened Lipstick. You want me to turn my back on the wee girl?"

"For God's sake! Stop with the martyrdom complex! She's *not* a wee girl, she's a woman, fully in charge of her life. You can't keep being her knight in shining armour each time she—"

Naomi stopped in midflow. Looked over Karl's shoulder. "Lipstick? What are you doing dressed and out of bed?"

Lipstick smiled. "I'm fully recovered, and raring to go."

"Go?" Karl said. "I hope you're not thinking of leaving, especially the way things are at the moment."

"Look, I love you both to death, but I'm not staying to see you arguing over me."

"No one's arguing over you," Karl said.

"That's right, Lipstick," agreed Naomi. "This has nothing to do with you. We were only—"

"My face has practically healed, and anyway, I've got to get back to work eventually. It took me a long time to get my clientele list, and I'm not ready to throw it away, at least not for a couple more years."

Karl spread out his arms in an appeal. "C'mon. You don't need to go to work. Wait a couple more days. I promise it'll be sorted."

"You don't need to sort anything, Karl. As Naomi said, I'm a woman, not a wee girl."

"I . . ." Naomi fumbled. "I only meant . . ."

Lipstick walked over to Naomi, and kissed her gently on cheek. "I know. And you're right. I'm a woman, not a wee girl, as Karl seems to think."

"You've Butler's watch," Karl quickly interjected. "If you don't intend to hand it back, you could sell it. Surely the money you'd get could keep you free from working, at least for a couple of months?"

"I'm keeping the watch for a future investment, or for someone *very* special," Lipstick said, giving Karl a cheeky wink, and then a kiss on his cheek. "Now, I really must be going. I have an appointment with a client, a nice one this time."

* * *

Tuesday evening. Naomi was just closing for the day when Detective Chambers, accompanied by Detective Harry McCormack, appeared at the door. A one-time heavy with Special Branch, McCormack was a six-three pillar of brick-hard, shit-house muscle, baptised in the fire of broken-bones, strap-your-balls-on street fights of Belfast. His ungodly face was as welcoming as a kicked-in door, and his bald head gleamed with lamplight sheen.

"We waited until everyone had gone, Naomi, so as not to cause a scene." Chambers sounded apologetic. "Karl's in, I take it?"

"He's had a hard day. What's this about?"

McCormack, chomping at the bit, said, "Why don't you just get Kane, and *we'll* tell him what it's all about, love?"

"Love?" Naomi's face went into battle mode. "Who the hell do you think you're talking to? What's your name?"

The man smirked. "Detective McCormack."

"Oh, now I remember. Detective McPiggy. Isn't that what the other officers call you?"

"What?" McCormack looked as if he'd had a dick-in-the-zip moment.

"Don't *ever* make the mistake of patronising me again."

A hand touched Naomi's shoulder.

"Easy, tiger," Karl said, appearing out of nowhere, smiling. "We don't want the big bad detective getting tough with you."

"Ha! Just let him try it!" Naomi glared at McCormack, before walking back in and heading up the stairs.

"We need to ask you some questions, Mr. Kane," Chambers said. "We're enquiring about the disappearance of Graham Butler, and any information you may have with regards to—"

"Whoa. Hold on a sec. Why're you asking me about that scumbag?"

Chambers pulled out a small notepad. "According to our information, he was last seen leaving here yesterday. He was to return to his hotel for a meeting, but never made it."

"Another one added to your long list, Kane," McCormack snarled. "Seems people who get too close to you either end up murdered or disappear into thin air."

"If you truly believe that, shouldn't you be frightened?"

"Frightened of *you*? God, what I'd give to have you alone for—"

"Detective McCormack?" Chambers said softly but with authority. "Can you go back to the car, please? I'll finish this report."

McCormack seemed on the verge of ignoring Chambers's request. Then, as if thinking better of it, he complied.

Chambers waited until his colleague left. "You don't make it easy for people to like you, do you, Mr. Kane?"

"I'm not running for election."

"Is there anything you can tell me, now that Detective Mc-Cormack has left?"

"Have you checked out the drug dealers Butler was dealing with? They should be your prime suspects."

"They are the prime suspects, that's why we want to be able to eliminate you from our enquiries, so that we can focus entirely on them and not waste time."

"Off the record?"

Chambers nodded. "Off the record."

"I detest Butler. He is a cowardly thug who likes to beat up on young girls. Will I lose any sleep if something appalling has happened to him? No. Have I anything to do with his disappearance? Unfortunately not. Satisfied?"

"For now." Chambers closed the notepad. "If you remember anything of importance, will you contact me?"

"My birthday's in a few days. How's that for importance?"

Chambers turned and walked away.

* * *

Saturday morning. Early. *Too* early for some. The doorbell sounded in Karl's office. Four impatient rings.

"What the hell . . . ?" Karl moaned from beneath the warmth of the duvet. "Naomi?"

She turned onto her side, a pillow jammed against her ear.

"Naomi? Can you get that? My head's killing me."

"Your feet aren't, so get it yourself. I warned you last night about drinking so much Hennessy."

Tamed, Karl proceeded trance-like down the stairs.

Four more rings.

"All bloody right! I hear you!"

Opening the front door, he was greeted by Sean, the postman, holding letters and a small package. "Morning, Karl."

"Never mind that oul' shite, Hans Brinker. Do you like sticking your bloody fingers in holes that don't belong to you?"

"Who the hell's Hans Brinker?"

"Read a book and find out."

"You look rough, like you've been boozing and cruising when you should've been snoozing—"

Karl snapped the mail from Sean's hand before slamming the door in his face. Made his way upstairs. Yawning.

Once back inside, he sat on the sofa. Checked the senders' names on the envelopes. Tore up four as junk. The other was from the bank. He wanted to rip that up as well, but thought better of it. Left it on the table. Began opening the package.

Inside, a small see-through plastic sleeve used for storing stamps and the like. He eased it out. A small opaque shadow could be seen within the sleeve. Holding it to the light, he scrutinised the contents.

"A double-headed mermaid . . . ?" Then it struck him

what it was; more importantly, where he'd seen it. "Oh shit . . ."

"I suspect that at one time it belonged to Graham Butler. His left forearm, if my memory serves me correctly. Someone has peeled it from his skin."

"How can you be so certain this is Butler's skin, Mr. Kane?" Detective Chambers asked, sitting alongside McCormack at Karl's desk.

McCormack was studying the tattoo, gripping the tiny envelope with tweezers. He seemed absorbed in the ghastly slice of inky flesh.

"I don't want to go into particulars, but you have my word on that."

McCormack made a mocking sound with his throat. "*Your* word?"

"That's right. My word, McCormack. Don't forget, I could easily have thrown the tattoo in the bin. No one would have been any the wiser."

The corner of McCormack's upper lip curled with contempt. "You called it in because you were afraid that down the line, word would eventually get out that you had destroyed evidence. Self-preservation. That's you in a nutshell. You're up to your neck in something. I can smell it."

"That's your body odour you smell," Karl said.

"Why would someone send it to you?" Chambers asked.

"How the hell would I know? Ask the people who made him disappear. Butler was probably bringing too much heat down on them with all the bad publicity he received in the media. Perhaps they were telling me case closed. I don't know."

Chambers seemed unconvinced as he walked to the door. "I'm sure we'll be in contact again, Mr. Kane. Good day."

McCormack stood there for a few seconds before moving

toward the door, a cynical smile on his overgrown face. "Oh, we *will* be in contact. Soon, Mr. Kane."

Two days later, leading drug dealer Nelson Roberts was charged with the abduction and suspected murder of Graham Butler. Yet Karl took scant interest in the arrest, having more pressing matters to contend with . . .

"Happy birthday, big fella," Naomi said, kissing Karl while handing him his birthday present.

"I told you I didn't want any fuss made. Why doesn't anyone listen to me?" Karl said grinning, quickly unwrapping the box like a kid on Christmas morning. "What the hell . . . ? A bloody phone? I already have a phone."

"Not like this you don't. It's an iPhone. The latest model."

"For God's sake, Naomi. You know I'm not into all these new gadgets. Too complicated."

Well, you'll just have to get used to it, instead of that ugly brick you call a phone. You've got to move with the times."

Karl sighed. "All I asked for was some Old Spice aftershave. Something simple, like me."

"Would you stop grumbling, and pretending you don't like—"

The door opened, revealing Lipstick, smiling. She gave Naomi a hug before walking over to Karl and planting a big kiss on his cheek.

"Happy birthday, Karl. Hope you like it," Lipstick said, handing him a small, package covered in birthday paper.

Before he unwrapped the package, Karl could tell from the shape what it was. He dreaded what he would have to say to Lipstick, refusing to accept a dead man's stolen watch, no matter how expensive. Her feelings would be hurt, terribly, but that couldn't be helped.

"Well? Do you like it?" Lipstick asked, as he slowly brought the watch out of the box, studying it.

"A Timex . . . ?"

"You don't like it?" Lipstick said, disappointment in her voice.

"No! No, I love it . . ."

"I thought it perfect for you, especially after reading its wee saying inside the box."

Karl tilted the box, read the Timex motto engraved on the inside, grinned, and then read it out loud. "*Timex. Takes a Licking and Keeps on Ticking.*"

DIE LIKE A RAT

BY GARBHAN DOWNEY

Malone Road

For every story a newspaper publishes, there are nine more it will never print. This is one of them . . .

Spotty John Norway's weirdly disfigured corpse was found nose-down in the pool of the Oxfordian, a private health club hidden away off one of the Malone Road's leafy laneways. The burn marks were largely confined to Norway's face and forehead, though there were also some patches on his neck and upper chest, presenting Inspector Jim Cotton with a problem.

"It's strange enough, Rex, that he was a member of that club in the first place," Cotton said. "A court clerk like him would earn what? Twenty grand a year? And I know he made a bit on the side—say another ten, tops. But a club like this would run you five, easy. Why would a man voluntarily hand over a sixth of his income, particularly when—and I mean no disrespect to the dead here—Spotty John would have needed every red cent he had to pull any colour of a girl?"

I looked down at the morgue tray and tried hard not to breathe in.

"Don't think even John would have argued with you on that score."

On his best day, Spotty John would have been too hideous to play the "before" guy in the *Blitz Those Zits* ad. But this evening, his head looked for all the world like it'd been parboiled then dipped in a deep-fat frier. Smelled like it too.

And people wonder why I won't eat bacon.

Cotton, fair play to him, had called me in to do the identification and spare the Norway family the nightmares. He knew the chances of me getting a decent night's sleep, after ten years on the crime beat with the *Belfast Standard*, were slimmer than my pay packet. Way too many carved-up bodies and scenes like this.

"The burns," he said, "are probably from scalding water. Steam, maybe. But he's clean as a whistle from the chest down, which means that whatever else, he wasn't fried in the pool. Otherwise we'd be looking at the full lobster effect. Oh, and there's no scalding in his throat or on the inside of his mouth."

"Probably killed somewhere else and then dumped in the pool," I nodded.

Cotton shook his head. "So you'd think, Rex," he said, raising a finger knowingly. "But the strangest thing is that the burning didn't kill him at all."

"How then?"

He took a beat then grinned. "He drowned. And the forensic guys at the scene are pretty certain it happened at the pool. Preliminary water samples seem to match."

"Tortured first, then held under?" I suggested.

"Possibly. Except there are no restraint marks on his body. And we scrubbed him for any other DNA but found nothing."

I couldn't resist: "Next thing you'll be telling me is that you've no idea why it happened to him."

Cotton laughed mordantly and at long last pulled the sheet back over the corpse. "No mystery there, I'm afraid. Little weasel had it coming."

Spotty John was a small-time blackmailer and had become

quite renowned for it. His job at the magistrates' court, while undoubtedly menial, gave him licence to put the bite on all manner of petty criminals. For a small fee, he'd make sure a defendant's name and address would be withheld from reporters, thus sparing the client considerable public embarrassment and community retribution. But should a chosen client decide not to divest himself of this small fee, you could guarantee that the juicier insides of the file would be leaked to a willing hack and distributed to tens of thousands of homes across the North before you could say *punishment shooting*.

John had given me dozens of stories in my years with the *Standard*—and held back hundreds more.

"He obviously put the squeeze on the wrong guy," said Cotton.

"Either that, or this is the worst-thought-out suicide ever."

Despite being a cop, Cotton sometimes found it difficult to suppress his inner decency, and the following evening he rang me at my flat, midgame, to give me a headstart on the pack.

"Kiddie-fiddlers," he said, by way of hello.

"Excuse me?" I replied.

"Spotty John. He was trying to shake down a couple of child abusers. Their names were being withheld from the papers by order of the judge. Until the trial ends at least. And there's a good chance they're going to beat the rap. But you know yourself, when the names get out, the public assume the worst, and you're ruined anyway. These particular gentlemen have a big amount to lose and that's even before the concerned vigilantes come a-calling."

"Off the record . . ." I said. But there was no need for wheedling. Cotton didn't do foreplay. It was all duck or no dinner with him.

"Billy Black and Sami Zucker," he went on.

"Not *the* Billy Black?"

He laughed. "Billy Hairless, one and the same, and yes, *the* Sami Zucker as well."

Jesus. Sami Zucker was one of the five richest men in Cherry Valley. The current chairman of Belfast Chamber of Commerce, he'd risen from nowhere over the past decade to own hotels right across Europe. Billy Hairless, on the other hand, was a ten-bob hood, who ran tarts and protection at the roughest outreach of the Golden Mile.

"What the hell are those two doing together?" I asked.

"Yeah," Cotton chuckled. "It's like Cliff Richard in bed with the Pussycat Dolls. Apparently Mr. Zucker has been feeling a bit lonely since trophy wife number two left the nest, and Billy's been finding him other chicks to keep him company. Except one of the chicks was under the bar."

I whistled quietly. "Much under?"

"A month or so—not that it matters. Zucker said he was certain she was twenty-one, as Billy had told him. Billy says Zucker knew all along."

"Charges gonna stick?"

"Fifty-fifty," he sighed. "You know yourself, big money has a way of buying its way out of trouble."

"But you have the girl and Billy Hairless's statement."

"Yeah. A teenage prostitute and an unconvicted serial killer, against a man who has four different judges on speed dial. Though in saying that . . ." He paused knowingly, to let me salivate a little.

"You have something else?" I ventured.

"You could say that," he laughed, ending the tease. "According to his bank, Zucker withdrew two hundred thou, in cash, a week ago. And from what we can see, he hasn't deposited it anywhere else. But you'll never guess, coincidentally, who bought himself a new car, two days before he swallowed the bath."

"No kidding."

"Nope. We figure, though, that Spotty John had been a bit more discreet this time—and set up the whole scam anonymously. Insisted on the hush money being delivered to a PO box somewhere—maybe even got a third party to lift it. Zucker probably had his suspicions. He hears every blade of grass that bends. And when Spotty John drove past in his new Mercedes coupe, Sami added two and two together and made one thieving rat."

My editor, Mike Mortimer, was, as per usual, caught halfway between ecstasy and a bad pill when I filled him in.

"Best ever," he declared, and slapped his fake-wood desk with a vengeance. "We'll nail sleazy Sami to the front page." But within five seconds, Mike had his manager's hat back on and was frowning like his numbers had come up a week too early. He looked at me slowly, picking his words. "Got to be very careful with this one, though, Rex. We print one wrong syllable and he'll close us down. He'd love nothing better too. He took a quarter mil off one of our sister papers across the water, few years back, when they claimed he'd stolen the patent for the Asshole Chip. Last thing the bosses here want is to hand him another big payday. Before you write a single word, you'd want to make sure everything is tighter than a row of teeth."

"He was the man behind the Asshole Chip?"

"Yeah." Mike swung his feet up on the desk, smiling like a smug chipmunk. "That's how he made his first mil. Surprised you didn't know that."

The controversial Asshole Chip for cars had been withdrawn from sale not six months previously after being cited in two separate road-rage killings in Britain. A beautifully simple device—little more than a transmitter and receiver—it allowed you to send text messages to any other car thus equipped, using just its plate number. It had originally been piloted as the "D-Mate," a fun device which was supposedly a safe alternative to mobile phones. But despite its phenomenal popularity, research showed that within its first year, a third of the messages from driver to driver had consisted of the solitary word *asshole*, so the Asshole Chip it had remained ever since. And then you had the pitched battles on the motorway bottlenecks, the two tyre iron–related deaths—and the ban.

I remember reading somewhere that the D-Mate's owners had taken a serious bath. Though obviously not as serious as the one Spotty John had taken.

"Sami had long since sold it on," said Mike, reading my thoughts. "He had to stay one step ahead of the patent police. No doubt he stole it, though. The other guy had the blueprints—and was about to produce them for the court."

"So how did Sami wind up keeping it then?"

"You'll appreciate this," said Mike. "The other guy was beaten to death with a baseball bat in a suspected road-rage attack in Cultra. Ironically, his own car wasn't fitted with the chip."

"Could Mr. Zucker have had anything to do with it?" I asked.

He smirked again. "Could Dolly Parton hold a pencil with no hands? Nothing could be proved, though. And as soon as the water was clear, Sami sold on the patent for a mil and a bit and bought his first hotel."

We sat silently in the cluttered little room for a minute—paperless office my hairy hole, as Mike was wont to say—gazing out through the glass wall at the maze of reporters' desks in the newsroom.

"We're dealing with an exceptionally cunning animal here,"

said Mike, scratching his beard. "Might be best to go in with some sugar first, rather than the stick."

He pulled his feet back off the desk and assumed his business face. He'd thought of an in. This is why he was the boss.

"We'll get him to turn on Billy Hairless," he said. "Tell him we know it's a setup. That we've a picture of Billy collecting the girl at school. That two other businessmen have been caught in the same scam."

"And then?"

"We'll put a hidden wire on you—round the rim of your boxers probably best—and get Sami to incriminate himself on the girl. Then we'll take it from there—see if we can squeeze the rest of it out of him at a second run. The way it is in this town, most people would be happier to cough to a murder than a sex offence. Even if it is just a matter of a month too early."

"Angry mobs rarely stop to ask," I agreed.

"Indeed and they don't. Listen, I know Zucker slightly. I'll set up a meeting at the Berkshire Hotel for tomorrow lunchtime. Wear your good suit—and see if you can persuade that poor girl of yours to run an iron over the rest of you."

It is not every day you get to call on eighty million dollars, so the next morning I made the supreme effort and bought a new shirt. The suit had been cleaned just two weeks before, for a wedding I had managed to duck out of at the last minute, so it was still crease sharp and minty fresh.

Before I'd left the *Standard* the previous night, Mike had pointed out to the empty news editor's desk right outside his door and told me that if I brought this one home, the seat would be mine. Five grand a year more in the bank, and no late nights or mangled bodies.

I have to say I was tempted. The downside was that the extra dough could put ideas into other people's heads—marital ideas, that is. And I'd been getting enough of that lately, without any extra help. Also, the company would get to own you body and soul. Like they owned Mike. Still, I was flattered with the offer. But I also knew he was warning me not to upset the big money.

Before I left the flat for the meet, I rang Jim Cotton at the cop shop to let him know what I was at. I didn't want my visit getting back to him from one of the minions at the Berkshire. And it was also possible that Jim might hand me a smoke grenade to lob at Sami.

"Try and get him to turn on Billy Hairless," said Jim. "Tell him you got it from me that Billy is blackmailing half the chamber using the same girl. If Sami bites at all, we own him—and he'll give up Billy for Spotty John for sure. "

Not for the first time I remarked how little difference there is between the policeman's beat and the newspaperman's. Except, of course, they get to shoot the people they don't like while we have to settle for writing about them. On the plus side, hacks like me tend to get quicker and easier access to the great and the good—they don't feel as threatened. The likes of Cotton, however, wouldn't have had a prayer of negotiating a sit-down with Zucker without a court order—even if he had warm blood on both sleeves.

"Couple of other things might be worth your while to bounce off him," said Jim. "We found a lap-dancing cage in an outhouse at the back of the Oxfordian that we think might be connected to Spotty John's murder."

"What the hell was one of those doing in the Oxfordian?"

"No idea. But the exact same cage was reported stolen from the Lap It Up Emporium on Ormeau Avenue last week. And you'll never guess who owns Lap It Up . . ."

"Sam the Man?"

"You got it. And we've found a couple of thin bruises on John's shoulder which the pathologist reckons could have got there when he tried to bust his way out of it."

"You mean you can lock them?"

"Apparently."

"Wow. Well, at least I know now what I want for my birthday." Cotton laughed appreciatively.

I struck him again while he still found me funny: "You said you'd a couple of things to ask him about. What's the other?"

"Oh yeah. We checked up on that new Merc John got to drive in for two whole days."

"What'd it run him?"

"Twenty grand exactly plus his four-year-old Beamer. But here's the best part: he paid in cash. And the garage still had a batch of the notes."

"They wouldn't happen to match the ones Sami took from his personal account last week?"

"Not quite. But they do match a bunch from a bureau de change that we reckon Billy Hairless has a finger in."

I sighed and shook my head. "The poor dead idiot. I warned him not to get in over his head."

"Poor dead idiot is right," said Jim. "Though of course you're quite wrong. He wasn't in over his head at all."

I was momentarily baffled. "What do you mean?"

"The pool," he said. "It was only four feet deep in the middle. Spotty John was five-four. So whatever else, he was swimming in his own depth."

Zucker's suite at the Berkshire took up the entire second-from-top floor, and his personal office was about as big as my home apartment and the one next door combined.

"Come in," he said warmly, pointing me toward a bar that

looked entirely made of cut glass. "It's just gone one, so we can break open the gin."

I demurred just unenthusiastically enough for him to pour me a treble and invite me to slump into a leather couch, as comfortable as a mother's lap.

Up close, Sami was older and heavier than I would have thought from his TV appearances. His tightly cropped hair was Persil white, and his complexion was very pale, apart from a couple of little brown liver spots on his hands. He'd clearly spent a lot of money on his teeth, though, which were permanently fixed into a shit-eating grin. He sat down on his La-Z-Boy, wiped an imaginary speck of dust off the trouser leg of his five-thousand-dollar suit, and raised his glass. "To happy endings," he announced.

I reached into my jacket pocket and pulled out my tape recorder. But he waved his hand no. "Everything today is off the record." He gestured to a door in the corner. "That's the bathroom in there," he said, still smiling. "Now, go in and take off the wire you've wrapped around your waist, or I'll have four of my men come up here and do it for you."

I toasted him with the glass, got to my feet, and headed for the corner.

"Your editor's a coward with a big mouth," he explained, answering my next question.

Ninety seconds later, I handed him over the wire and bowed respectfully.

"Only the one?" he asked.

I nodded.

"I do hope you're a man of your word."

"I'm too frightened not to be," I answered.

He chuckled. "Good. So, to business. For a start, I imagine you're wondering why the hell I'm talking to you at all."

"Close enough," I said, figuring it was better than my opener.

"Fact is, your people tell me you're a bright man, Rex. And you and I could be useful to one another, not just today, but down the line."

I'd been accused of many things in my time, but bright was a first, so I allowed myself a grin. "I'm flattered."

"Don't be," he said. "You're a natural. You have two great attributes, Rex. The first is that you hear everything, which is very useful for a man like myself in the business world, and the second is you say nothing, which is possibly more useful still. Oh, and you're also exactly smart enough to know your limitations, which means you never try to be too clever. And if there's one thing I have no time for, Rex, it is people who are too clever. Because you have to waste so much damn time watching them—and so much damn energy trying to out-think them—that it's easier in the long run not to have them round you at all."

"Would that include people like Billy Black?"

"Ah, the late lamented Billy Hairless." He sighed, and his face seemed to sadden, though his eyes were still smiling.

"What do you mean *late lamented?*"

He pulled a face like a man at his very first acting class pretending to be astonished. "You mean you haven't heard? The police went to Billy's flat this morning to question him about a horrific incident at the Oxfordian. It seems some poor court clerk was killed up there a few days back. But when the police burst in on Billy, he pulled a gun on them. And I'm afraid, after that, there was only going to be one winner."

"Dead?"

"As an old joke, and it seems the malicious allegations which poor Billy had been making against many pillars of our society have died with him. Coincidentally, it was your chum Inspector Cotton who dispatched him."

I was stunned. "*Jim* Cotton?"

"Oh yes." And all of a sudden Zucker's dancing blue eyes turned cold and grey. "Split John's big bald head open like a watermelon." He paused and stared at me menacingly. "Best ten grand I ever spent."

I had a sudden urge to vomit. Cotton was the nearest thing to straight you'd ever find in the cops. I quickly put my drink on the coffee table and half-staggered to my feet to go. Face flushed and heart pounding.

"Oh settle yourself," said Zucker, the genial host again. "I don't want to harm you. Not when I need you to do me such a big favour."

The new shirt was sticking to my back with sweat. I looked again at the hall door and shook my head. "I'm not for sale."

"I never thought you were," he said. And he flapped his hand at me to sit again.

Slowly, I did as I was bid. Truth is, I didn't know where else to go.

"I don't want you to lie for me," he went on. "I've enough people for that."

"Well, what then?"

"I want you to tell the truth. Not about Cotton and Billy— no, you ever do that and you'll go the same way yourself. But about Spotty John."

"I don't follow."

"It's simple. The cops are 100 percent sure Billy killed John. And there's no one in the press who will doubt it either. Billy was an evil little sewer-dweller. He had the motive—and he had the form. Open and shut. Except . . ."

"Except what?"

"Well, it would be just perfect if Billy's involvement could be, ah, corroborated by an outside source."

"How do you mean?"

"If someone were to come forward and say that they knew how Billy had killed poor Mr. Norway. That would divert attention away from the cops' accidental eradication of Mr. Black—and give the ombudsman enough to say Jim Cotton was damn right to go in with arms held high."

"You mean you want me to frame Billy Hairless, posthumously?"

"Lord no. You won't be framing anyone. Billy sent that man to a horrible end. Don't doubt it. But it'll look better if the story is coming from outside the camp. For example, Rex, you've spoken to Billy many times through your work. You could exclusively reveal that he had once suggested carrying out a carbon-copy murder on an informer he was trying to track down in his ranks."

"And I suppose I alerted Jim Cotton to this just five minutes before he kicked down Billy's door?"

"Precisely. Might even win yourself a press award out of it. Not to mention that news editor's job. Plus, my own undying gratitude and a very decent wedding present. Very, very decent. Certainly as decent as the one Jim Cotton got."

"Only problem is, I've no idea what happened."

"Good point," he said. And he was smiling, mouth and eyes, again. "So listen up carefully . . ."

Four hours later, I finished typing up my copy and e-mailed it through to Mike Mortimer, marked *H.F.C.*—our in-house code for Highly Confidential. In law, you can write what you want about a dead man. And I knew there'd be all manner of fanciful stories about Billy Hairless across the press the following morning, from girls to gambling to a string of gutted corpses.

But I didn't want anyone else from the pack getting a look at what I'd got. Because, not to put too fine a point on it, I, Rex King, had struck gold.

The story began forty years earlier, when Billy was a child. A nasty-tempered brown rat took up residence in the family's outside toilet and refused to leave, or indeed eat Billy's mother's poisoned cheese. Old Pa Hairless, however, was a very resourceful man and built a self-locking cage, which he laced with fresh chocolate. Sure enough, the rat got himself trapped—and it was eight-year-old Billy Junior who got the honour of disposing of the still-live pest. So he took the cage to a nearby ditch and attempted to submerge the rat in the water. The difficulty was that even when he took the cage to the deepest part of the ditch, the rat was just big enough to stand up on his hind legs and get his nose above the Plimsoll line. Then Billy had a brainwave. He went home and boiled up a kettle on the stove. Half an hour later, a drowned rat with a burnt snout was floating toes-up in the ditch.

Enticing Spotty John into the lap-dancing cage had proved just as easy. Billy Hairless knew his mark—all it took was an open door and a fifty-pound note. They'd then taken him from Lap It Up to the Oxfordian in a van, after hours, and used John's key to let themselves into the pool area, before playing four rounds of Boil the Tea Urn. Security, it seems, had been off on the sick.

John, I speculated in my article, took at least forty-five minutes to die. Though off the record, Sami told me it was closer to an hour and a half. At least that's how long it took Billy to ring him to tell him the job had been finished. Not that Sami was too concerned about the delay, mind. He'd had to give Billy two hundred grand of his private stash to pay off the shakedown. John, however, hadn't managed to divulge where he'd stashed the rest of the loot—and took the secret with him to his boiling grave. That's the damn problem with employing help who shoot first and ask questions later, Sami had told me.

Ten minutes after I sent the exclusive through to the news

desk, I got a three-word reply back from Mike Mortimer: *The job's yours.*

I double-punched the air and looked round at the dozen or so others in the room. My subordinates. My staff. My minions. I owned them now.

Not for long though.

My desk phone rang.

It was her. Shit. Shit. Shit. And I knew before she'd the first word out that she'd come home from London a day early.

"I got your note," she said, choking back a scream. "Five years, and it comes to this. You dirty, low-down bastard. You couldn't even tell me to my face."

"I can't talk now," I whispered. "I'm in conference."

"You're scum."

The phone line went dead and I felt a momentary pang of guilt.

Within seconds it rang again.

"Mr. King?"

"Yes."

"Thomas Cook Travel here. Just to confirm we got you on that flight from Belfast International to New York at four thirty tomorrow morning. First class, one way, eight hundred pounds."

"Perfect. Many thanks."

I hung up and waved through the window wall to Mike Mortimer, who was clearly on the line to the higher-ups bumming about his upcoming Pulitzer. He gave me a big thumbs-up, then made a drinking gesture with his free hand. I shook my head no then flicked my eyebrows upward so he'd understand it was woman trouble. I was going to miss him. The gutless prat.

The desk phone rang again. The final call. Long distance this time.

"Mr. King?"

"Yes."

"It's Joanne here from St Kitt's International Finance. We've processed that payment to your account. If you'd like to call into our Manhattan office on Fourth Avenue any day this week and sign the authority, you can make the withdrawal."

"The full amount?"

"Well, we'd prefer you'd leave the account open . . ."

"Naturally—will do."

"But there's no problem with you taking out, say, three hundred and fifty thousand dollars—as long as you leave in the other ten."

"Good to hear."

"Oh, and bring your passport."

"I will indeed."

Three hundred and fifty thousand dollars. Plus the ten grand sterling wedding gift Sami had handed me in an envelope before I left the Berkshire. A lot of bread for a guy who three weeks ago had no ass in his trousers and no needle to sew them.

Three hundred and fifty thousand dollars. Just a few cents shy of one hundred and eighty thousand pounds. And no one knows I have it, and no one's going to miss me when I'm gone.

Three hundred and fifty thousand dollars. By rights, of course, it should have been a straight two hundred grand. But then I had to give Spotty John his ten percent finder's fee. After all, a deal is a deal. The poor dead idiot. I told him not to buy that Merc.

PART IV

BRAVE NEW CITY

CORPSE FLOWERS

BY EOIN MCNAMEE

Ormeau Embankment

UTV News live shot, 5:23 p.m., 23/05/13

Press conference. CID say they are concerned about the whereabouts of Lorna Donnelly, age seventeen, from Lisburn. Last seen leaving her place of work on 13/05/13. The lead detective is DI Jim McCaul. McCaul is early forties, CID, short sandy hair. Lorna's parents sit to either side of McCaul. Lorna's mother is Kay. She keeps her eyes on the floor. As if she keeps some private grief under scrutiny. If she takes her eyes off it, it might get away from her. Lorna's father is Norman. An older man. He is strongly built. There's a steroid mass under his blue shirt. Tattoos on his arms.

McCaul holds up a photograph of Lorna. She is younger in the photograph. Her hair hangs about her face. She looks sullen. A teenage runaway. McCaul thinking about teenage runaways from the films, some backwoods couple on the lam leaving behind a trail of multiple homicides. Bound to each other by a darkness of their own making.

He shows a still taken from CCTV at Belfast Met where Lorna attends a part-time course. She's looking at the camera in black-and-white. McCaul thinks that her face is desolate. He knows that it will haunt him. As though she had seen some horror. Not just seen. He remembers the words they used in chapel in the days when he went to chapel with his wife. *Gazed upon.* She looked as if she had gazed upon horror.

Record this look is what she seems to be saying. *Remember it.*

Traffic cam #1, Shaftsbury Square, 9:48 p.m., 20/05/13
First breakthrough. Lorna standing at the cash machine on the corner of Botanic Avenue. An overexposed night scene, a lens flare from the top right-hand corner, people passing through the frame looking stealthy and achromatic, part of some grisly underclass. There's always the feeling that you're witnessing someone's last moments. Even like now when you are witnessing someone's last moments. The juddery rewind, the uneven tail speed.

CID say do every bar and club on the street. Take the CCTV footage. Spend fourteen-hour shifts watching every frame. Nobody's going home until it is all seen.

Submariner Bar, 11:22 p.m., 20/05/13
Saturday-night CCTV. Security men at bar doors. Girls in heels and beehives. The camera not picking up the detail that gives the place its modish jolt. McCaul observes the '50s look right down to the scratchy film stock from nostalgia shows. The girls are Doris Day–blonde beehive and falsies. Brassy and tottering with Smirnoff naggins in their handbags. Knowing tarts. Security in evening dress and black tie, hair slicked back so you're thinking Kray Twins, Ronnie and Reggie. The night gathering in layers. Somebody's going to get their smile widened with a razor. Somebody's going to end up as motorway road fill.

Security bantering with the beehives. Lorna walks past them. Not belonging in the scene. Not belonging with the '50s look. Lorna wearing a puffa jacket, jeans, and trainers. As soon as he sees it he knows that she is no longer alive. McCaul imagines the clothes scattered across waste ground. You see them in cellophane bags, evidence tagged. A livery for the modern dead.

Submariner barcam, 12:15 a.m., 21/05/13

The anti-pilferage camera's focussed on the bargirl who has her back to the camera. But it picks up the end of the bar in long-shot. Lorna's leaning on the bar talking to someone just out of shot. She's intent. Stabbing the Formica with her finger. A man's hand rests on the bar. That's all you can see. As she talks the hand doesn't move. She keeps talking. You're thinking amphet-amine rush. The bartender's a sallow girl, Latvian, product of some gritty Baltic seaport. Life in the places left behind after history has had its way. CID says bring her in.

Donegall Pass PSNI Station, interview suite intercam,
8:20 a.m., 25/05/13

The bartender is Michaela from Riga. Says she doesn't recognise the screen grab of Lorna. Doesn't remember who she was talking to. She looks bored. McCaul imagines a cheap flat by the docks. A boyfriend with a Saxon T-shirt and a minor criminal record.

CID comes into the room. CID says they've found a body in the river.

Ormeau Embankment, SOC cam, 9:32 a.m., 25/05/13

The water is brackish. The halogen light picking out weed fronds, the frame of a bicycle. McCaul standing at the edge of the water. The weed streams seaward on the ebb, the tidal flux. McCaul thinks of Lorna borne downstream toward the open sea and the channel markers and the Mew Island light.

Sony HVR-Z7U HDV divecam, 11:16 a.m., 25/05/13

The camera on a long exposure. She's snagged on debris. Her hair flares out from her head. The diver's gloved hand comes into shot as he reaches for her. She sways like some mythic Rhinemaiden. Her lips are slightly parted. The tide turns her

face toward the camera. Her eyes are open and the diver is fixed
for a moment by her sombre, violated gaze.

NI Forensic Mortuary, security cam (ext.), 7:10 p.m., 25/05/13
The undertaker backs the Mercedes hearse to the entrance.
The black tin coffin is slid onto the morgue gurney. The footage
is flickering. The speeds are always wrong. Everything's silent-
move era. The undertaker's a gothic villain in a top hat. Death's
attendants coming for you at ten frames per second.

NI Forensic Mortuary, postmortem suite 4, 9:03 a.m., 26/05/13
The camera is high-definition. Nothing is to escape the lens here.
This is not the place for difficult-to-piece-together recollections,
the lyric fragments of the street traffic and retail security cams.
There is to be no room for error. These are the forensics. The
bloodwork. The pathologist and his female assistant make a Y-
shaped incision in Lorna's torso.

They record the organs as healthy. They record no evidence of recent sexual activity. They record several depressed
fractures to the cranium consistent with blows from a heavy
object. Bone fragments are removed from the brain. They record that there is no water in the lungs. They observe that
Lorna was dead before being placed in the water. They record
that her hair colour is black. They record that her eye colour
is green.

Interflora, security cam, Lisburn Road, 3:44 p.m., 20/05/13
Lorna's workplace. The manager says they don't normally keep
the security camera footage but there is some from the previous Saturday. McCaul watches her moving behind the counter.
There was a grace which McCaul had not expected. Good at the
job. The shop manager said she was a natural. Knew the Latin

names of the flowers. This seemed important to her, the manager said. Putting names to the flowers. The night blooms.

Donegall Pass PSNI Station, interview suite intercam,
9:28 a.m., 26/05/13
CID says don't talk to the parents at home. CID says bring them in. Did she drown? Norman says. There will be water in her lungs if she drowned, he says. Then he smiles. You never think you're going to ask if there was water in your daughter's lungs, do you? You never think you're going to put that into a sentence. I know what happens when someone drowns, he says. Kay gets up and walks about the room with a sideways gait as though something is about to fall on her head. Will fall on her head if she doesn't keep moving.

McCaul keeps trying to see Norman's arm. He's trying to make out the tattoo. Two flowers interlaced, he thinks. He can see the petals.

Castlecourt Shopping Centre car park, L2 cam,
11:43 a.m., 26/05/13
Norman and Kay's car is parked on level two. Norman has reversed into the space. Edging the car between the concrete trusses. Blue Renault Megane, Reg. No. BOI 3655. He's attentive to her. Taking her arm as they walk toward the car. Opening the door.

Westlink, traffic cam #7, 3:50 a.m., 21/05/13
Going back over the footage from the night Lorna went missing. Traffic light on the Westlink. Trucks heading south and west off the late ferries. Taxis going west. Focussing on the northbound traffic, running the registrations through number plate recognition. What are you looking for? the traffic controller asks.

I'll know it when I see it, McCaul says. He asks the controller to scroll back on the reg numbers. The controller says that he's been doing this job too long and does McCaul think six years with a joystick between your finger and thumb watching night traffic is long enough. Zoom. Freeze. Rewind. You wouldn't believe what comes off the ferries. Eastern Europeans. Asylum seekers. Prostitutes from countries you couldn't even pronounce. Bartered. Trafficked. This is a haunted road. Sometimes I'm afraid to even look at it. I can't sleep at night.

McCaul sends the night's data to DVLA. Checks the night traffic against the Registered Keeper and Owner database.

There's many a man out there like me, the controller says. Watchers of the night. Legions of us.

Surface car park, security cam, Howard Street,
6:45 p.m., 27/05/13
The Latvian bartender is standing by McCaul's car. Michaela. He crosses the car park. She's wearing knee boots and a coat with a fur collar pulled up round her face. The defence team will later ask to view the tape. CID says that evidence from it will be inadmissible.

She tells him that she remembers seeing the girl now. She thinks she was talking to one of the regulars but she can't remember who it was.

When she leaves McCaul seizes the car park tape. Watches it in the station. He sees himself approaching Michaela. It looks illicit. It looks like some furtive assignation in an occupied city of long ago. You could see tramlines in the car park surface. The grid lines of long-gone streets. Men in belted coats standing at intersections, drab-suited kapos. Cold War phantoms. Letting you know you'd come under their remit. Their ghost authority. He remembers how she'd looked. Her breath in the cold air. Her blue eyes. The harshness of her accent. Her wintry gaze.

DVLA comes back. They've cross-checked. They've found a

blue Renault Megane ROI 3655 registered to Norman Donnelly.

CID says Lorna made two complaints about Norman. Withdrew both complaints. Child protection was consulted. What was involved? McCaul says. Usual, the child protection officer says. Bring Norman in, CID says.

McCaul's mobile rings. Michaela. He had a tattoo, she says. Who had a tattoo? The man she was talking to. Was it a flower? McCaul says. No. It wasn't a flower, she says. Come in tomorrow and draw it for me, he says, thinking that if it isn't a flower then it isn't Norman. He puts the phone down. Her accent stays in his head. A hoarse damaged sound. He remembers the way she put her hand on his sleeve. The earnest way she looked into his face. As if she was saying, We can retrieve something from this. As if she was saying that there was something to be found among the human ruins.

CID says don't get involved. CID says observe the code of conduct.

Donegall Pass PSNI Station, interview suite intercam,
8:20 p.m., 27/05/13
It's a perspective you've seen a thousand times before. The suspect sits on his own at a plain table. It's a camera but you feel as if you're looking through a one-way mirror. You're waiting for the suspect to turn to the mirror glass with a knowing look. But he doesn't. Norman sits at the table with his head down and his hands hanging between his thighs. Slumped. Big man brought to his knees. McCaul asks him if Lorna got her interest in flowers from him. Flowers? Norman says. You've got flowers tattooed on your arm, McCaul says. Norman rolls up his sleeve. It's not flowers, Norman says. It's twin screws. Submarine propellers. Submarine crews get them done like that.

She was jealous, Norman says. What do you mean jealous?

McCaul says. And then the penny drops. Norman looks at him. As though this was a weakness that he might be forgiven.

We sank a ship with torpedoes, Norman says. I dream about it. We were a week out from Ascension Island. We sank the *Belgrano* two hundred and fifty miles south of the Falklands. Tarry corpses floating in the cold water. Gouts of foul air vented from the sinking ship. Bunker oil alight on the surface.

McCaul doesn't know why he's being told this. Norman looks at him as if his dreams give him rights.

I waited until she was asleep, then I hit her with a hammer. I wrapped the body in a sheet and drove it down to the embankment and put it in the water. I threw the hammer into the river. When I put her in the water I thought of corpses afloat in the wake of the *Belgrano*. The screeching of gulls.

Forensic laboratory, Belfast, technician cam, 9:10 a.m., 28/05/13
Forensics work the car from front to back. The white dust suits. Coming right down to the matter of things. The nub of it. Picking through the microfibres. Finding strands of Lorna's hair in the boot. Finding traces of her blood.

Windsor Park Drive, Lisburn, Panasonic HS-DC1,
9:15 p.m., 28/05/13
They fetch Kay at home in Lisburn. A neat estate. A neat house. Diamond-pane windows in PVC. A neighbour comes out with a VHS, starts to record. Follows them up the path. The neighbours' gardens are bare. This one is subtropical. There are moon lilies. There are giant ferns. Pale orchids. Lorna. The man filming the arrest tries to get closer.

The house shows little of Lorna. There is a submarine photograph framed in the hallway. Men in singlets sport on her decks. They put their arms around each other and smile up at the camera.

Kay is sitting at the kitchen table. Kay is ready for them. She is wearing a coat and scarf. She stands up when they come in. It's not right, she says. It's not right. A man and his daughter. It's against nature. McCaul holds her by the arm as he leads her down the path. The crime scene people are parked beside the squad car. They're walking up the path in dust suits. They look like ghosts beside the pale ghostly lilies. A stench of decay in the air. What the fuck is that? one of them says. McCaul tries not to gag. The smell seems to go to the heart of everything, the god-rot at the centre.

Amorphophallus konjac. A tuberous plant of the arum family. At nightfall the sexual parts of the plant expand, emitting a smell of decaying flesh.

Nepalese lilies, Kay says, voodoo lilies. She doesn't break stride or look around. They were Lorna's favourites, she says. She liked filthy things like that. She was drawn to them. The amateur cameraman gets too close. A uniform pushes him away. The camera yaws, falls to the ground. Stays there, lens open to the night as the owner scuffles with the police.

On the way McCaul rings CID. Check what Lorna studied at Belfast Met. They come back. She studied horticulture and botany.

Belfast Harbour Airport Departures, security cam,
10:15 p.m., 29/05/13
Michaela's in the queue for the eleven p.m. departure to Riga. She takes out her phone.

Donegall Pass PSNI Station, evidence room cam,
10:45 p.m., 29/05/13
McCaul can see himself on the monitors writing in the evidence book. He signs out the VHS of home-movie footage that the

evidence team has taken from the Donnelly house. The very fact that you are on camera makes you look furtive, up to something. Other cameras are recording. The rain-lashed station car park. The wildly tossing trees. The Westlink camera records leaves whirling across the empty traffic lanes. The harbourmaster's camera records the passage of ships outward bound into the storm-tossed shipping lanes, the North Channel, and the darkness beyond.

His phone rings. Michaela. He told me stories about being in submarines, she says. He fooled me. I was sleeping with him. He left bruises on my body. Lorna saw us together. She came into the bar that night. She was going to tell Kay about Michaela and him. He told Lorna what would happen to her but she didn't believe him. Michaela says that he is a very violent man and she is afraid of him. McCaul tells her that she has nothing to be afraid of. He asks her where she is. He tells her to come into the barracks in the morning and make a statement. She says she will. She promises.

Belfast Harbour Airport, Stand 2, airbridge cam,
10:45 p.m., 29/05/13
Michaela walks down the airbridge. She steps into the aircraft. She likes McCaul. But then she liked Norman as well. She runs her hand along the dented alloy then steps into the aircraft and the camera loses her. There are weather fronts sweeping down from the north. Soon she will be aloft, storm borne.

HMP Maghaberry, remand wing security cam,
11:10 p.m., 29/05/13
The landing is empty. You see only the cell doors. Norman is locked down. Norman is dreaming of subs moored at Holywell, the streaked plating. Subs under the ice pack. The stressed hull,

veined and streamlined. Ghost wolf packs hunting in the frozen northern seas.

Ravenhill Reach apartment complex, stairwell cam,
12:10 a.m., 30/05/13
McCaul walks up the stairs to his apartment door. He lets himself in and then he's alone. Alone in an empty flat. He looks at his phone. He thinks about ringing his ex-wife. They are on good terms. He can visit any time he likes. He lifts the phone and puts it down. She would smell it off his clothes. He can see her backing away from him. The odour of the night around him. The corpse flowers. He'd heard church bells in the city all day. He doesn't know what they're for. He gets up and goes to the window. The lights of the city glow orange on the underside of low clouds to the east. *Ascencion.* He sees his reflection in the glass, ashen, exhausted. An apostle of bad faith. He goes to the cupboard under the stairs and takes out the VHS and sets it up. He doesn't know what he's going to see.

Memory Lane Photographic Studios, Crumlin Road, 04/08/04
The Memory Lane people have added a fancy intro. *A Day at the Beach,* featuring Kay Donnelly and Lorna Donnelly, directed by Norman Donnelly.

Kay and Lorna come into the shot. Norman working the camera. You'd say Lorna was eight or nine. She's wearing a swimsuit with a short frilled skirt attached to the waist. The film stock degraded, chemicals leaching off. Nothing lasts. She has sand grains stuck to her legs. Kay is sitting on the sand wearing a one-piece swimsuit. Her black hair is cut in a bob. She is wearing dark glasses and a sun hat. You can tell she doesn't like the camera being pointed at her. She hunches her shoulders, gathers herself in, and waves it away. There was a time when she would strike

230 // BELFAST NOIR

poses for him. Do some risky things for him. But not today. She understands the importance of not leaving traces. She senses what's coming down the line. Lorna dances for the camera. It's a trick of the light, maybe, but Norman doesn't seem to be able to get her into sharp focus. She runs into the waves then back up the beach and into the sand dunes. She turns to look down at her mother and father. The sun dazzles. Impossible to get a clear shot of her. Then she ducks down behind a dune. *You can't see me*, she calls out.

You can't see me.

You can't see me.

PURE GAME

BY ARLENE HUNT

Sydenham

E d pulled his Renault to the kerb beneath a tattered Union flag on Island Street and turned off the ignition. He sat listening to the engine cooling, to the rain beating against the roof, the hiss and rumble of traffic from the M3 motorway a quarter of a mile away. He forced himself to inhale slowly and deeply, trying to quell his jangling nerves. The meet had been set up three weeks earlier, and even though he had been assured that his credentials would hold up there was always that fear in the pit of his gut that this time, this one time, someone would throw a spanner in the works, and he'd never see another dawn.

Six p.m. came and went, then six thirty. He cranked the window down a little, felt the winter air against his skin, heard the Bangor train rattle past on the other side of the redbrick industrial buildings. A plane took off from the airport, its lights climbing into the black, probably headed for London Gatwick. Another two circled overhead, ready to land.

Where were they? He wiped the condensation from the glass with his sleeve and glanced at the dash clock. Almost seven: maybe they weren't coming. Maybe something had spooked them? It was more than possible. These men could not have gone under the radar for this length of time without being para-noid and wary. Someone opened the back door, jumped in, and slammed the door shut.

"What about ye?" a voice said in hard-core West Belfast.

Ed's eyes darted to the rearview mirror. He took in the face of the man grinning at him: young, shorthaired, midtwenties, cracked lips, ugly. Sean Lavin. Dangerous territory for him, the east of the city, unless he knew the right people.

"You're late."

"Aye, sorry about that," Lavin said, sounding anything but sorry. "Willie's on his way, we'll take his car."

"What's wrong with mine?"

"We'll take Willie's."

Lavin removed a packet of cigarettes from inside his jacket. He shook one out, placed it to his lips, paused.

"D'ye mind if I smoke?"

"No."

Lavin lit up, inhaled, and sent jets of smoke through his nostrils. Ed licked his lip: he hadn't smoked a cigarette in almost fifteen years, but now, right at that second, he'd have given plenty to accept one and smoke it to the nub.

They sat in companionable silence. Lavin smoking, Ed watching the street. A little after seven, a silver BMW slowly passed the Renault. Ed tracked it with his eyes, thinking: *A great white in urban waters*. A little further on it pulled over to the kerb, and sat there idling menacingly.

"Let's go." Lavin tapped his shoulder. "If you've a phone with ye, leave it here."

Ed removed his mobile from his pocket and placed it in the glove compartment. He and Lavin got out. Ed locked the car and hoped he'd see it again.

Lavin walked toward the BMW with a jaunty lope and opened the back door. "Get in."

Ed did as he was told. Lavin got in after him, forcing him to shift across the seat until he was wedged against the massive shoulder of the other man sharing the backseat. A driver kept his eyes on the road, but the passenger, a man Ed recognised from photos as Willie Lynch, half turned and gave him an appraising once-over.

"Carrying anything on ye I need know about?"

"No."

"Check him, Egg," Willie said, as the car moved off down the street.

The man to his left, Egg, turned. "Lift yer hands."

Ed did as he was asked. Despite the lack of space, Egg patted him down expertly, searching him for guns, phones, and wires: anything that might suggest he was not who he claimed to be.

"Clean."

Ed lowered his hands.

"Sorry about that," Willie said, smiling. "Ye can't be too careful round these parts."

Ed said nothing. He had long ago figured out that a taciturn persona would be easier to sell: nobody likes talkers.

They left Island Street, and Ed expected them to head for the A2, past the airport. They didn't. Instead, the BMW toured the streets of Sydenham, hard lefts and rights, until Ed lost any sense of north, south, east, or west. He tried to note street names as terraced houses gave way to country roads, lampposts to trees, and soon Belfast was retreating in the rearview mirror. But still the flags, hanging like sleeping sentries. B-roads turned to narrow lanes, their signposts lost in hedgerows, white flashes in the dark.

"How long have ye known Craig then?" Willie asked.

"Awhile."

"Aye?"

Ed shrugged, placed his hands on his knees, and held them there. Craig Ellis was somewhere on the continent, Spain they'd heard, shacked up with some barmaid who wasn't fussy about who shared her bed. Intel said he was burning a hole through the money they'd paid him and was a risk to his cover. Ed was not in the least surprised. Men like Craig had no loyalty, they could be bought easily, turned easier. Had it been left up to Ed, Craig would have never seen the light of day again, but cooler heads had prevailed.

Willie was persistent: "Haven't seen Craig in a while, have we?" He addressed this to Lavin though his eye never left Ed's face.

Ed met his gaze. There was nothing to be done about it now. If there was doubt there was doubt.

"Where'd ye know him from?"

"Germany."

"Oh aye?"

"Through Freddie."

"Know Freddie, do ye?"

Ed kept his voice neutral. This was a test, of sorts. Everyone knew Freddie in the business. Small, Dutch, heavily tattooed. He was a pervert, universally disliked, but such an expert facilitator that his predilections were tolerated—to a point.

"I bought a foundation bitch from him."

"Yeah, from Freddie, which bitch?"

"US import, papers carry back to Zebo."

"Don't they all."

Lavin eased back slightly, but Willie's eyes bored right through him. "Red nose, light, and fast."

"That's her."

"Wondered where she'd gone. How'd you meet Freddie?"

"Wennqvist introduced us."

"Wenn did?"

You bloody idiot, stop talking, Ed thought, stop talking: adding a name was a mistake—fuck names—never use names. He'd been told, hadn't he? What the fuck was he doing? Wennqvist: shit, what did he know about him? Born in Finland in 1958, married, divorced, three children, two girls and a boy. None of the kids had anything to do with him. Records for armed robbery, assault, assault again, fraud, handling stolen goods, was shot in the gut in 1988, arrested for—

"When was this, when'd you meet Wenn?"

"Ach, years ago now."

"Yeah?"

"Before the cancer."

"That's right, the poor fuck. Fag?"

This time Ed took the proffered cigarette and accepted a light. It was shocking how sweet and smooth the first drag went, how easily his body accepted that which he had rejected so long ago.

"That bitch was quality," Willie said, settling back in the front seat. He laughed and the mood lightened. "So, you're looking to put new blood in your line?"

"Yes."

"Hard to get quality these days, too many fucking curs, bred by amateurs. Killing the game, killing the fucking game."

"Not us though." Lavin elbowed him sharply in the ribs. "Only thing we got is quality."

"Aye," Willie said. "Pup you're going to see tonight, pure quality. You won't get another like him on either side of the border, I can promise you that. Not even eighteen months old and he's a stone-cold killer."

"Stone-cold," Lavin said triumphantly. "Never backs down, pure game."

"Pure game," Willie agreed.

Ed forced his shoulders to relax.

They took a left, drove along a road for another few miles,

236 // Belfast Noir

hung another left then another, finally turning onto a narrow country road that rose through unfamiliar hills. There were very few signs that Ed could see, and virtually no houses. Up and up the BMW went, the driver changing down through the gears as he navigated the twists and turns. At a set of stone pillars, he swung right and drove over a cattle grid and followed a long rutted lane barely wide enough for the car down to a small stone cottage. Ed had been so intent on not fucking up the conversation that he wasn't sure where he was now.

The BMW stopped and the driver tooted the horn. After a moment the front door opened and a fat man, wearing a T-shirt that was several sizes too small for him, peered out. He waved a hand, went back inside, and shut the door.

They waited. Floodlights went on to the rear of the cottage. Ed saw a number of roofs outlined against the night sky.

"Let's go," Willie said.

Lavin got out, and Ed followed. Willie shut the door and hitched up his jeans. Egg and the driver stayed where they were.

"Are y'not coming, Egg?" Lavin said, bending at the waist and tapping the glass. There was a mocking note to his voice that made Ed glance at the big man, who stared resolutely ahead.

"Leave him be," Willie said, and began to walk toward a side gate.

Lavin laughed, and elbowed Ed again. "Dogs put the shit up him."

"Come on ahead," Willie called.

Ed turned his head: the fat man stood at the gate, waiting.

The fat man, introduced to Ed as Hecky, led them through a small yard to a barn from which a multitude of dogs barked.

He unlocked the door, dragged it open, and hit a light switch. The smell hit Ed hard and he found he had to breathe in shallow sips to keep his gag reflex in check.

On either side of the shed: dogs.

Ed counted at least twenty. Standing there chained to rings embedded in the walls. Each dog wore a heavy-duty chain around its neck, looped twice in some cases. Ed could only imagine the effort required to move, yet the dogs strained toward the men, barking with excitement.

"The lad I'm gonna show ye took out Clancy's Diamond back in September, twenty-four minutes. Never seen anything like it, one latch and that was it, never let go. Near ripped his fucking leg off. Clancy called it before Diamond was killed, but y'could see he was beat from the off. Heard he's gone cold since."

"Not the dog, it's Clancy, the useless fuck, gone soft," Lavin scoffed. "Diamond was game, I'm tellin' ye, Clancy called it too early."

"Diamond was no match for Blue."

"Go on out of that, ever see Clancy's old dog? Diamond's sire, that was his name? I watched him go near two hours with Antrim Jim's Spike, best fucking fight I ever saw. Fuckers couldn't stand up and they were still biting."

"I was there," Willie said. "Game dog all right, even with a broken jaw and a punctured lung, he didn't quit."

Ed said nothing. He watched Hecky move past the leaping dogs and unchain one near the back of the shed. He walked it back toward them and hoisted it up onto a steel table just inside the door.

"Feast yer eyes," he said proudly, "on Blue."

Ed ran his hands over dog: he was a bull cross, heavily muscled, with a broad skull and a wide chest. His coat was short, steel-grey, closer to blue. His ears had been cropped into tight triangular points, scarred along the edges so the skin felt like piecrust. Ed's fingers traced scars all over the dog's body; some were fresh, others old and healed. He cupped the dogs balls, checked both were dropped. At each touch Blue wagged his tail furiously. When Ed prized open his massive jaw to check his teeth were intact, Blue licked his hands and tried to lick his face.

Ed stood back. Willie and Lavin were watching him carefully.

"He looks good."

"Have him on full training. Fucker would swing on a jack line half the day if you let him." Hecky jerked his head behind him to where a well-chewed tyre hung motionless from a rope in the ceiling. This, Ed knew, was where dogs like Blue developed their jaw muscles.

"Well?" Lavin leaned in.

"He's a grand-looking dog," Ed said, putting his hands in his pockets. "I don't know if he's what I'm looking for."

Hecky turned his head and spat, disgusted. "Hold him there, Willie."

Willie did as he was asked. Hecky walked behind the shed and pulled a sheet of tarpaulin from a set of cages on the back wall. He unlocked one, reached in, and pulled a whimpering dog from the shadows.

"You wait and see." Lavin said, grinning wildly. "Wait until you see what this fucker can do."

Ed swallowed. The dog Hecky carried by the scruff was a small beagle, battered and scarred, eyes rolling wildly in its head.

"Let's go."

They left the shed and crossed the yard to another smaller enclosure. Lavin opened the door and hit the lights. Ed stared at a small sand-filled arena, enclosed on all sides by wood pallets nailed together.

Hecky pitched the beagle into the sand pit. The dog ran around in a blind panic, before backing itself into the corner holding one paw up, licking its lips frantically. There was dried blood on the boards, Ed noticed, scratch marks and evidence of worse.

Hecky took Blue from Willie. "Don't even need to face them, this fucker's good to go at a drop." With that he lowered Blue to the floor, threw his leg back over the pallets, and winked at Ed.

It didn't last long. Blue rushed the beagle head-on. The beagle tried to run, but there was nowhere for it to go. Blue, using his superior body strength, flipped him, and before the beagle could rise he had latched onto the side of his neck. The beagle scrabbled his paws against Blue's chest, screaming in agony, teeth slashing and snapping, aiming for any part of Blue he could reach. Blue didn't seem to notice; he shook his head, growling excitedly, patches of the beagle's skin ripped and tore. Blood sprayed across the sand.

"Let him have it," Willie said, when it looked as though Hecky might intervene.

The screaming drove Blue into a frenzied madness. He dragged his opponent round the ring, shaking his massive head from side to side, jerking until the cries went from high to piercing, then stopped.

Lavin laughed like a maniac and slapped Ed on the shoulder. "What did I tell ye?"

Blue dragged the dead dog around the bloodstained sand, whining and growling with delight, his tail whipping back and forth.

"Pure game," Lavin said.

"How much?" Ed asked.

Hecky spat and scratched his belly. He mentioned a price.

Ed slipped his hand into his pocket and took out his wallet. He counted out a large number of bills and passed them over. Hecky licked his thumb and counted them rapidly. He passed one note back to Ed, "For luck," folded the rest, and put them in his back pocket.

Willie held out his hand, and after a moment's hesitation, Ed shook.

The dog was his.

Three Months Later

Ed stared at the coded text message on his mobile screen, pressed delete, and pocketed the phone as behind him, Lavin, whinging and complaining to Willie, approached his car. Lavin had lost a ton on the previous fight when Sadie, a pale gold pit bull bred by Antrim Jim, rallied and defeated her attacker with almost ninety-four minutes on the clock. Both dogs had died in the ring from blood loss and shock, but the bitch had lived long enough to be declared the victor, so Lavin was pissed.

"Can't fucking believe it," Lavin said, lighting a cigarette.

"Shut the fuck up about it, will ye?" Willie said.

Ed ignored them. He wiped Blue down with a special medicated rag, feeling the dog's muscles rippling under his ministrations. Blue's tongue lolled from his mouth, his hazel eyes sparkled with good health.

"Knew I shouldn't bet against Jim, fucker has those dogs of his amped up on some shit, wouldn't be surprised."

Ed wished they would go away and leave him in peace. His nerves were bad enough as it was. Everything they had worked for, all the planning and practice, the subterfuge, everything hinged on this day going smoothly, and Lavin bitching in his ear was not a welcome distraction.

He gave Blue another once-over, lifted him down from the boot, and put him into his cage to rest. He was scheduled to fight a two-year-old UK import, owned by a couple from down Limerick way. Ed had seen the opposition, a square-headed brindle pit. He was a nice-looking dog, but too fat and weak in the hips—Ed knew Blue could take him. So, it seemed, did everyone else: Blue was odds-on favourite, with plenty of money trading hands.

Ed stretched and loosened his limbs.

"Nervous?" Willie leaned against the car, sunburnt, reeking of cheap beer and cigarettes.

"No."

"Good, that other yolk's only a cur. Betting has Blue taking him in twenty minutes."

Ed nodded. He glanced over their heads toward the tree-lined lane. The sun was high above them, the air filled with the scent of honeysuckle.

"You going to bring him out or what?" Lavin asked.

"In a minute."

"You need to let him take a piss."

"Will ye let the man handle his own dog?" Willie said.

Lavin flushed, and stalked off.

By eleven the ring had been raked and men gathered around it. Ed's stomach was in a heap as he let Blue out of his cage and rubbed his head. The dog's body quivered with excitement; he licked Ed's hands and nudged him for a tickle behind the ears, his favourite spot.

People were watching. Blue was impressive, that was for sure, and as Ed led him to the ring, he could not help but feel more than a little bit proud of the conditioning he had put his dog through: hours running on a treadmill to build endurance, best of food; the best of everything. Blue was a champion, a true game dog.

They approached the ring, focussed, confident, Blue out ahead, pulling like a steam train. There was blood in the air and he knew it. Ed spotted the owners of his opponent, standing by the generator just inside the shed. They knew, they *had* to know, their brindle was no match for Blue. Yet they would let him fight to the death.

Ed smiled at them coldly. The last of the bets where made. Hecky, resplendent in a lemon-yellow vest, stained Bermuda shorts, white towelling socks, and brogues, collected fees, cursing and laughing, ever the show man.

Ed waited.

The brindle dog was brought into the pit and unmuzzled. The handler ran his hands over the dog, and tried to jazz him up by talking in his ear and slapping him on the chest.

Lavin leaned over the rim of the pit and shook his head. "Fat fucker, look at him."

Ed stayed where he was; Blue whined.

Hecky gathered the last of the cash and peered at him. "Are ye right?"

Still Ed made no move. A few of the men glanced at him, puzzled.

A shout went up.

"Police!"

The reaction was instant; men scattered and ran for their respective vehicles, but it was no use, two vans pulled across the entrance to the lane and hooded men spilled out carrying baseball bats and clubs

"That's not the fucking peelers!" Hecky roared, lumbering toward the cottage at a pace that was surprising for a man of his size. Lavin and Willie glanced at each other and ran toward the BMW, which was closest to the gate.

Lavin, always a cocky dimwit, tried to talk his way out of it, holding his hands before him. He approached the lead man, yapping high and fast. He took a straight swing that rearranged his jaw and scattered his teeth across the yard. Egg never made it out of the car. Neither did the driver. Willie, assessing the situation and catching on fast, turned and sprinted past where Ed was standing; he was almost to the trees when a sleek shadow raced along the grass, leapt from six feet out, and took him to the ground in a single fluid motion. The German shepherd released Willie, and then clamped his jaws on his upper arm. Willie screamed.

Ed leaned down and scratched behind Blue's ears to reassure him.

"What the fuck's going on?" the guy holding the brindle asked, staring at the mayhem around the yard. "These aren't police."

"Stay where you are if you know what's good for you," Ed replied.

Unlike Lavin, this man was no fool. He stayed exactly where he was as the group rounded up the last of the participants, herded them into the pen shed, and shut the door behind them.

"Gentlemen," Ed said, "my apologies . . . gentlemen and lady." He bowed slightly toward the woman who was staring at him with terror and confusion in her eyes. "We are the DLA, for those of you who might not have heard of us, that's the Dog Liberation Army."

"What the fuck is going on?" Willie was holding his useless arm to his chest. His face was streaked in blood.

One of the masked men jabbed him with the business end of his bat. "Shut your hole."

"What's going on, folks, is that we're here to right a great wrong."

"What wrong? What the fuck are ye on about?"

"And to do this," Ed continued, "we're going to have us a little competition."

Stunned silence. Hecky, who hadn't been able to make it to the cottage for his shotgun, groaned and looked like he was going to be sick. "You're a dead man, Ed."

"We'll see," Ed countered. "So, the rules, we're going to try

to make it as fair as possible. Two go into the ring, the winner . . .
well, the winner might get to go again if he—or she—is lucky."

"You can't do this, you can't—"

"Hecky, you're up," Ed announced.

"I'm not fuckin' fighting no fucker. What is this shite? Do
you know who I am?"

Ed sighed. "You're not going to fight?"

"No."

"No use to me then." Ed inclined his head.

A hooded man stepped up, swung the bat upside Hecky's
head, and that was all she wrote for Hecky.

"Willie? How about it, are you and Lavin good to go?"

Willie stared at Hecky's brain matter and skull pieces on the
bat. He swallowed and looked at Lavin, whose eyes were spinning in his head; his jaw was held onto his face by little more
than muscles and skin.

"I think you could take him," Ed said, smiling.

"If I do this . . . what then?"

"Then," Ed said, shrugged, "then we'll see."

"Don't, please, I'm begging ye, I've got wee kids."

Ed squatted and let Blue lick his face. "Aye, I know you do.
For your sake I hope you've got game."

THE REVELLER

BY ALEX BARCLAY

Shore Road

I don't know which disturbed me more: at night when Paddy Gillen became who he really was or in the morning when he became Publican, beloved.

His forum was the bar that bore his name, its blinkered windows on the Shore Road, its caged door on Dandy Street. Rising up and down from his gaffer-taped stool by the till, Paddy Gillen was like horse and rider: his eyes bulging with the telling of his tales, his smile equine, driving the story and being driven, blooming to fill his form.

But when the punters were gone, the only journey left was up the claustrophobic staircase to bed. As soon as his foot hit the first tread, a narrowing began, until the tall story of Paddy Gillen was pared down into the tiny space of his boyhood room, as though the steps were whetstones.

Once there, he would stand in front of the cloudy mirror above the sink and begin his ritual. He would slide the false teeth from his mouth, then the rippled hairpiece from his head. He would use the face cloth, then slide the grimy towel through the metal ring and pat himself dry. There was a lot of sliding with Paddy Gillen: his tongue across his vacant gums, money across the bar, eyes across a woman's body, chips across a plate until all that was left was a red smear like the one he slid a man through in the public toilets on Shaftesbury Square. He left that man hollow and damaged, turned him into a braced coil of tantrums and

Tourette's on Bawnmore street corners. And only, it seemed, on corners. As if, when nobody was looking, he was whipped up and placed on the next one along.

I believe that Paddy Gillen had a deformity of the mind, a small nub of some kind where thoughts would get caught until, eventually, there was a grotesque knot of slights and grudges that were surely pressing against parts of his brain, impairing their function. For years, this squalid little cockpit had helmed his actions. And he was not a bright man, Paddy Gillen, so these trapped thoughts were rarely new. He was a pickpocket of opinions, and a mark for those who wanted their message to spread. On Paddy Gillen's thick skin, they could brand their burning convictions and he wouldn't even feel it. And he would pass them on, still ablaze, but unnoticed against the ice-cold of a pint glass.

Paddy Gillen's world stank like the balled-up cloth he wiped along the bar, never washed until four in the afternoon whenever Sally-Anne, poor, desperate Sally-Anne, would arrive, her clothes and hair smelling of the next-door café. Next-door Sally with her hopeful air of next-life luck. But time was twisted and unkind to Sally; every day, she looked four days into a spray tan, every night, weeks from decent sleep. And though time should have stolen the skinny jeans from her wardrobe or the black-hole dye from the shelf under her sink, time was too busy being a revelation. Sally finally found time . . . to kiss one of the oul' lads full on. And all she could think of after-hours as she mopped the bar was that it never would have happened if she hadn't been inside the four lawless walls of Gillen's where standards rose no higher than the cracks in the red tiled floor.

Every now and then, Paddy Gillen would lead women across those drying tiles to his private stairs, women whose bodies spoke of multiple children and a gradual letting go; women who turned blind eyes to trips to Liverpool games and what their husbands might do on them. Any of these women were good enough for Paddy Gillen: no age, no shape, no line, no jowl would put him off; he was there just for a little while, for the opening stabs. He felt raped by their tenderness. He was always gone for the words. And they were always gone for the ritual.

He once shot a taxi driver with a hollow-point, the bullet that did its finest work in its later stages, like Paddy Gillen, getting his father's pub and settling a score.

The taxi driver's wife waked him on the sofa bed in the living room, and sat on the arm, greeting the mourners. Her son sat on a chair beside her, numb, pale, best left alone, but watching the miserable parade of faces crumpling as they walked away, their pain reflected in the mirror over the mantelpiece. They came all day and well into the night, some faltering first outside other homes, robbed of the marker of the black taxi in the drive.

"Lift up his head," said his wife to one of her husband's friends in the early hours of the next morning. "Lift it up." She gestured with her empty glass.

"Ach, I don't know, Lisa . . ." But he couldn't deny a widow.

"It's like one of those round plastic things you get at the chemist's for holding cotton wool balls," she said, "only it's the back of his head . . ." She tapped her forehead. "He must have turned. They must have asked him a question at the lights. You know it was only at York Street, there by the Westlink. His dinner was on the table."

Paddy Gillen walked in then.

"Ach, Paddy . . ." said Lisa.

Paddy looked down at her dead husband, his finest work. "He was a good man, Lisa. A good man."

And Paddy Gillen was home not long after, standing in front of his own mirror, no pain to be found.

There was no press conference. They prefer to bring forth those who pardon. One killer versus the victim's loved one who forgives. At the very least, it's a cancelling out. Much more powerful: one killer versus the wife and son who forgive him. It would be less terrifying to hear of a murdered taxi driver on the six o'clock news than it would be to watch his quiet son screaming: "Whoever did this to my father will fucking die, whoever made my father's head like the plastic thing in the chemist's with the cotton wool stuffed in it, is going to die. And maybe your kids are eating beans and chips right now and maybe they ran to the door when they heard you walk in, but if it's you who did this to my father, you will suffer. You will be robbed of all the goodness you've ever known. You will claw through memories and it will be like clawing through a bucket of shells; they used to be full, but now they're empty, some are broken, some are beautiful, others could slice you open. You're alive in the gathering, you're so alive, and then nothing; they always seem to disappear, it's hard to remember where you put them."

How I knew of Paddy Gillen's ritual in his boyhood bedroom is that I had watched it, on and off, for weeks on nights when I knew he was alone. I would stand on a breeze block on the porch over the bar, behind Gillen's, its red lights shining up to my knees, the rest of me in darkness. I wondered why Paddy Gillen never closed his curtains on such a pitiful deconstruction.

That last night, I am watching from inside. I am crouched behind a pink curtain under the dressing table behind him; an embarrassing space, unplanned. I am barely breathing, set to watch his display. Now I am seeing phlegm. It shoots from the back of his throat, but is caught there, a greenish strand suspended over the sink until he hawks again and puckers his lips to break it. He turns on the tap to wash it down, but still he has to poke at the plughole and I wonder, for a moment, if all Paddy Gillen's bodily fluids are thickened with bile.

The tap is running, but he hasn't started yet. The one night I need his routine to consume him, he's in some sweaty holding pattern. The flow from the tap is weak, it's not loud enough.

I can't move.

I have time to think of my father's death. I don't imagine a hollow-point bullet, the movement of which could be beautiful, the expansion of which could be artistic if captured in slow motion. Instead I imagine a rough hand, stinking of stale beer, penetrating my father's chest in one blunt, violent second, and ripping his heart free, the muscles like twitching wires that will never know a power source again. And at that exact moment, with no one laying a finger on us, my mother, on the number ten bus, having her heart burst through her chest, and me, walking home, just the same. Because those wires dangling from my father's ripped-out heart had an external power source. Now, none of us lives.

Paddy Gillen's mistake was made at my father's burial: ending up being there by the grave when my mother collapsed, ending up forced to say soothing words as he took her in his arms, ending up passing her to me as he did, ending up saying something only he could have known from being my father's last fare. Driver and driven, rising up and down, with a gun, though, with a gun, and no tale to tell.

I hear his teeth come out, the sound like the slap of a child's hand. But then I hear them rattle back in. I don't know what gives me away, but he turns to me.

I fire.

I didn't want to kill Paddy the Publican, the cheery figment, but it's too late.

It is my turn, now, to carry out his routine. And I do it. Piece by piece, crouched down beside him, conscious of the soles of my shoes. It was Paddy Gillen's ritual and now it is mine, followed with no deference; the teeth, the wig, the face cloth, the towel.

I am covered in blood, destroyed. I pick up the offscourings of Paddy Gillen's soap and I scrub my face. My hands are weak. I reach for the hardened face cloth, curled at its edges like it was burnt. Despite the fluids that have been released at my feet, despite the stoutness of their odour, my nostrils fill with the stench from the cloth as it collapses under the hot water. I wash the cloth, I wash my neck. I dry myself on his grimy towel. I wonder if my lips are touching the place where his once touched. I gag. I peel everything off until I am standing naked. I imagine someone else with red-lit shins watching me from Paddy Gillen's roof.

I go through Paddy Gillen's wardrobe. I dress in his clothes, with his wig stuffed inside his jacket pocket. I ball my tuxedo into one of his plastic carrier bags.

I was on my way home from my formal. I don't know which disturbed me more: that night, when I became who I really was; or in the morning, when I became reveller, returned, son, beloved.

ABOUT THE CONTRIBUTORS

Sean Breithaupt

ALEX BARCLAY is the author of seven crime novels. She studied journalism in college, and went on to work as a journalist and copywriter before writing her first novel, *Darkhouse*, a *Sunday Times* Top Ten best seller. Barclay won the Irish Book Awards' Ireland AM Crime Fiction Award for her third novel, *Blood Runs Cold*, which launched the ongoing FBI Agent Ren Bryce series.

Mal McCann

GERARD BRENNAN'S short stories have appeared in numerous anthologies, including *The Mammoth Book of Best British Crime*. He coedited *Requiems for the Departed*, a collection of crime fiction based on Irish myths. His novella *The Point* was published by Pulp Press in October 2011 and won the 2012 Spinetingler Award, and his debut novel, *Wee Rockets*, was published by Blasted Heath in 2012. He is currently working on a creative writing PhD at Queen's University Belfast.

Press Eye Photo

LUCY CALDWELL was born in Belfast in 1981. She is the author of three novels, along with several stage plays and radio dramas. Her writing has won numerous awards, including the George Devine Award, the Imison Award, the International Dylan Thomas Prize, the Rooney Prize for Irish Literature, and a Major Individual Artist Award from the Arts Council of Northern Ireland. She is currently working on her fourth novel—her first crime novel—and a debut collection of short stories.

Tracy Mearns

STEVE CAVANAGH was born and raised in Belfast and is a practicing solicitor. Someday he might get the hang of it. He has won a number of high-profile criminal, disability, and racial discrimination cases that have set new laws. His debut novel, *The Defence*, featuring former con artist turned trial lawyer, Eddie Flynn, will be released internationally in 2015.

Sigrid Estrada

LEE CHILD, previously a television director, union organizer, theatre technician, and law student, was fired and on the dole when he hatched a harebrained scheme to write a best-selling novel, thus saving his family from ruin. *Killing Floor* went on to win worldwide acclaim. Lee was born in England of a Belfast-born father, but now lives in New York City and leaves the island of Manhattan only when required to by forces beyond his control.

GARBHAN DOWNEY studied and worked in Belfast—his mother's hometown—before returning to his native city of Derry to ply his trade as a reporter and editor. In his youth, he covered courts, crime, and corpses for media groups such as the *Irish News* and the BBC, before turning his hand to fiction. His work has been described by the *Sunday World* as "a superb blend of comedy, political dirty tricks and grisly murder, and bizarre twists."

RUTH DUDLEY EDWARDS is an Irish-born journalist, historian, and prize-winning biographer. The targets of her twelve satirical crime novels include gentlemen's clubs, academia, literary prizes, conceptual art, and, always, political correctness. Lawyers are next on her list. She won Last Laugh Awards for *Murdering Americans* in 2008 and *Killing the Emperors* in 2013, and in 2010 the CWA Gold Dagger for Non-Fiction for *Aftermath: The Omagh Bombing and the Families' Pursuit of Justice*.

ARLENE HUNT is the author of eight novels, including her most recent, *The Outsider*. When not writing or walking a huge hairy dog, she reviews novels for RTE's *Arena*, and is the co-owner of Portnoy Publishing. She is currently working on a new novel, *Into the Fire*.

IAN MCDONALD lives in Holywood, County Down, and his most recent novel is *Empress of the Sun* (the third book in the Everness Series). He has won the Locus Award, Hugo Award, Theodore Sturgeon Award, Philip K. Dick Award, and John W. Campbell Memorial Award.

BRIAN MCGILLOWAY was born in Derry in 1974. He is a recipient of the University of Ulster's McCrea Literary Award and his novels have been short-listed for a CWA Dagger, Theakston's Old Peculier Crime Novel of the Year, and Irish Book Awards' Crime Novel of the Year. His first Lucy Black novel, *Little Girl Lost*, was a Kindle #1 best seller in 2013. He lives near the Irish borderlands with his wife and their four children.

CLAIRE MCGOWAN was born in 1981 in a small Irish village where the most exciting thing that ever happened was some cows getting loose on the road. After studying at Oxford and living in China and France, she now resides in London, where there aren't any cows but there is the occasional murder in her street. She was previously director of the Crime Writers' Association and now teaches at the first crime-writing MA at City University London.

ADRIAN MCKINTY was born and grew up in the North Belfast suburban town of Carrickfergus. His first crime novel, *Dead I Well May Be*, was short-listed for the CWA Ian Fleming Steel Dagger Award. His novel about a Belfast-based detective in the Royal Ulster Constabulary, *The Cold Cold Ground*, won the 2013 Spinetingler Award. Its sequel, *I Hear the Sirens in the Street*, was short-listed for the Ned Kelly Award.

EOIN MCNAMEE is the author of seventeen novels, including *Resurrection Man*, *The Blue Tango*, *The Ultras*, *12:23*, and *Orchid Blue*. He is the author of a series of thrillers under the pseudonym John Creed. His first book for young adults, the *Navigator*, was a *New York Times* best seller. The last novel of the Blue Trilogy, *Blue Is the Night*, was published in early 2014.

SAM MILLAR is an author and playwright living between Belfast and Dublin. His crime fiction includes the Karl Kane Series and the novels *The Redemption Factory*, *Dark Souls*, *Darkness of Bones*, and *The Bespoke Hitman*. He also writes for the stage (*Brothers In Arms* and *Bloodstorm*) and radio. His memoir, *On the Brinks*, has been optioned by Warner Bros. and was named a Top Twenty thriller by *Le Monde* for 2013. He is the recipient of the Golden Balais d'or, France, for Best Crime Book 2013-14.

STUART NEVILLE'S debut novel, *The Ghosts of Belfast*, won a *Los Angeles Times* Book Prize, and was picked as one of the top crime novels of 2009 by both the *New York Times* and the *Los Angeles Times*. His subsequent three novels have been short-listed for various awards, including the CWA Ian Fleming Steel Dagger. The French edition of *The Ghosts of Belfast*, *Les Fantômes de Belfast*, won Le Prix Mystère de la Critique du Meilleur Roman Étranger and Grand Prix du Roman Noir Étranger.

Andrew Shaylor

GLENN PATTERSON is the author of nine novels, most recently *The Rest Just Follows*. His nonfiction works are *Lapsed Protestant* and *Once Upon a Hill: Love in Troubled Times*. His first film, *Good Vibrations* (cowritten with Colin Carberry), was released in 2013.